HER FEARLESS PURSUIT

MARTINA MONROE BOOK 13

H.K. CHRISTIE

KEEKSTAR MEDIA

For my readers

1

JANE

A SET of eyes glowed through the shrub. They stared, unblinking, watching. What was it? Was it bigger than me? The eyes remained fixed on me. With all the courage I could muster, I propped myself up onto my elbows, blinking against the haze clouding my vision. I glanced back at the shrub where the glowing eyes had been. They were gone now, vanished with the soft rustle of the leaves. Maybe it was just a raccoon, something curious but uninterested in me. The thought brought little comfort. I swallowed, my throat dry, and took in my surroundings. The moon was bright, round and full, casting an eerie glow over the landscape. The air was crisp, and it sent a chill through me.

Where was I? What had happened to me?

I sat up fully, grimacing as a sharp pain shot through my head, throbbing behind my eyes. My side ached with a fire-like intensity. Instinctively, I placed my hand on the back of my head, and my fingers came away wet. It was dark and sticky. Blood. My heart skipped a beat at the thought, but I pushed it aside. There was no time for panic. I needed to focus. I needed to get away.

It was dark, the only light coming from the moon. I felt so small, so insignificant in the vastness of the night. The world around me felt surreal, as if I had been plucked from one life and dropped into another. Slowly, shakily, I crawled onto my knees before managing to stand. My legs wobbled beneath me, weak and unsteady.

I took a deep breath, my lungs burning. I had to figure this out. Should I stay here, wait for someone to find me? But who would even be looking for me? And why was everything such a blur? My memories had been replaced with a blank space. What had happened to me?

I took a step to the left, feeling the ground beneath me. Suddenly, my foot sank into what I could now see was a body of water. A lake. The chill of the water seeped through my shoe. I recoiled, my pulse quickening. I crouched and reached down, feeling the earth beneath my fingers. The ground sloped upward, uneven but steady.

I began to climb, each movement slow and deliberate. My hands grazed branches, and my skin stung from the scratches they left behind. Rocks jutted out from the ground, pressing painfully into my palms as I crawled forward. I tried not to think about what other eyes could be watching me.

Finally, my fingertips brushed something smooth and cold—pavement. Asphalt. I was on a trail. It didn't tell me where I was, but it meant civilization was nearby.

I stumbled to my feet and followed the path, one foot in front of the other. My steps were slow, deliberate, and each one felt like an enormous effort. In the distance, a faint light flickered—what looked like a streetlight.

I headed toward it, my slow movements making the trek seem to stretch on forever. The sound of my breathing mixed with the noises of the night—the chirping of crickets, the rustling of leaves. None of it was familiar. It was like waking up in a dream, the kind where everything is strange, and no matter how much you try to make sense of it, you never seem to.

Finally, I reached a fence. The streetlight loomed above, casting its pale glow onto the area. Beyond the fence, I could see a parking lot with a few cars, their outlines blurred in the early morning light. I didn't recognize the area. My heart thudded in my chest, each beat loud and disorienting.

Someone would surely help me if I could reach them. Feeling hopeful, I froze at the sound of footsteps. Someone was near. My body tensed, and fear crawled up my spine. I spun around, my breath catching in my throat.

A man, and the light from a flashlight, appeared from the trail across the parking lot. Relief washed over me when I saw the small, fluffy dog trotting beside him. The dog was white, its tail wiggling with each step. Surely, a man walking a cute little dog wouldn't hurt me. Right?

I waved hesitantly, my hand shaking. The man stopped, startled, as if he hadn't expected to see anyone. He was older, his face lined with age, his hair almost completely silver. His eyes, however, were sharp and alert, taking me in with concern. The dog pulled on its leash, eager to greet me. It wagged its tail furiously, its friendly energy a small comfort.

I reached out my hand, and the dog sniffed it before giving a contented wag of approval. I couldn't help but smile, just a little.

"Are you all right?" the man asked, his voice gentle.

"I... I don't know," I stammered. "Where am I? What time is it? Do you know what day it is?"

The man blinked, then glanced at his watch. "You're in Fremont, California. It's about 5:30 in the morning. Saturday, August 23." He paused, then asked, "What's your name?"

I opened my mouth to answer, but the words wouldn't

come. I searched my mind, but there was nothing. Just a hazy spot where my name should have been.

"I'm... I'm not sure."

2

MARTINA

THE SIGHT before me nearly brought me to my knees. Standing on a pedestal in a fitted white gown was my baby girl. Obviously, she wasn't an actual baby anymore. She was a grown-up and stunning. Engaged to be married, wearing a wedding dress. *My girl.* Eight months earlier Zoey came home and introduced me to her fiancé, Henry, someone I'd never even met before, and then told me she was engaged. I'd nearly had a heart attack. I thought she was too young, but I kept that opinion to myself. Selena and I had immediately decided to perform a full background check on the man who would be her husband. Since that moment, we'd learned Henry had no criminal record and we hadn't found anything alarming. But even now I couldn't believe Zoey was getting married and I wasn't sure I was ready for her to be a full-blown adult. *Married.*

How had the years flown by so quickly? I remembered when Zoey was born, those big blue eyes looking up at us—her father and me. My eyes welled up with tears as I stood in the bridal salon. Trying to keep my composure, I feared I would fail.

She was so beautiful, so smart, so kind. Jared would have

been so proud. I covered my mouth with my fingertips, trying to calm the storm of emotions.

She had been so excited to go dress shopping, but I now realized I was still in a bit of shock over the whole thing. My daughter was brilliant, with a good head on her shoulders, and she was ready to make a lifelong commitment to the man she loved. I had to trust and support her decision. "Mom, what do you think?" Zoey's voice pulled me back to the moment.

It was rare that I found myself at a loss for words, but there I was, speechless. As gorgeous as she looked...I hesitated. "It's pretty, sweetheart. I just wonder if..."

Zoey's grin widened, her bright blue eyes shining. "Not enough sparkle, right?"

I nodded, a huge grin spreading across my face. She'd always loved sparkles and glitter for as long as I could remember. The dress was beautiful, but it wasn't Zoey. It didn't have her pizazz.

She turned to the attendant. "Let's try on the next one. I need more sparkles. I want to be bedazzled!"

Selena laughed beside me. "Basically, it can't be too blinged out."

The saleswoman in charge of helping Zoey with the dresses nodded with understanding.

Looking at Zoey and then at Selena, my stepdaughter, with her dark flowing hair, and tough yet petite exterior, my heart warmed.

My two daughters.

For so long, I believed Zoey would be my only child—my only biological child—but when I married Charlie four years earlier, I gained a bonus daughter. A sister for Zoey, something she'd always wanted.

Zoey and Selena were different in so many ways, but in others, they were alike. Selena was smart, just like Zoey, but a bit more reserved, with a love for black clothing and a personality more like mine. But Zoey... Zoey was sparkly, like a string of stars in the sky. When the two met five years earlier, they had hit it off immediately. If their last names weren't different, you would assume they were born and raised by the same parents their whole lives.

Zoey lifted the skirt and carefully stepped down from the platform. "I'll be right back with another one. You're right, I can't be plain on my big day," she said as she hurried off to the fitting room.

Selena walked over and stood next to me. "Well, it looks like she's really doing it, Martina."

"She is."

I was so proud of Zoey. She was such a fine young woman—independent and in her second year of veterinary school. Soon she'd be a wife. Oh my gosh, would I be a grandparent one day too? Was I too young for that?

Selena turned to me, her voice soft. "Does this remind you of your wedding to my dad?"

"Yeah, a little." This was the very bridal shop Zoey had insisted I visit to get my own dress. If it had been just up to Charlie and me, we would've kept things simple. I would've picked a nice dress off the rack. It was a second wedding, after all. But Zoey, my maid of honor, had other ideas. She planned an entire event to pick out my dress as well as the dresses for my bridal party that included Zoey, Kim, Selena, and Audrey. It was a fun day filled with laughter and friendship.

I'd picked a simple-fitted, floor-length dress. My hair had been pinned back with a crystal encrusted barrette, insisted upon by Zoey, of course. Charlie and I had stood in our back yard on our wedding day, surrounded by friends and family under the beautiful arch Zoey and Selena had decorated for us. It had been a perfect day.

Zoey's wedding would be on a much grander scale. Her fiancé, Henry, came from a big family, and he was the first to get married. The guest list had already ballooned to 200 people. I had told her that whatever she wanted was what I wanted, too. And Jared—her father—would have said the same.

"Has it been tough on Zoey without her dad?" Selena asked, breaking my thoughts.

Selena was a very intuitive young woman. And considering Selena lost her mother when she was seventeen, I wondered if she was imagining her own wedding and not having her mom there. "She hasn't said too much, but she did mention wanting a seat reserved for him at the ceremony," I said, my heart swelling at the thought. Zoey was so young when she lost her father, I worried she didn't remember him at all. But clearly, he was in her thoughts.

Selena said, "I like that idea. It's sweet."

That was Zoey—always thinking of others. I worried sometimes that she didn't express her feelings enough, always bubbly and smiling, but maybe holding back what scared her. Maybe I needed to have a heartfelt talk with her.

Just then, Zoey emerged once again, wearing a dress that sparkled as the light hit it. The bodice was tastefully beaded, and the skirt flowed with delicate sparkles woven throughout. The attendant placed a veil carefully in her hair, and Zoey turned to face us.

My hand flew to my chest as she smiled at me with tears in her eyes. "This is the one."

Selena nudged me toward her, and I wrapped my arms around Zoey. "I'm so proud of you," I said, my voice catching in my throat.

Zoey pulled back, wiping her own tears. "Mom, don't start!" She laughed, a smile brightening her face again.

Selena chimed in. "This is just the dress fitting. How are you going to handle the actual day?"

I wiped the corners of my eyes. "I'm not sure."

The three of us hugged, my heart so full it could burst.

After we stepped back, Zoey said, "It's perfect, right?" as she twirled around like she had when she was a little girl.

"It is."

"Gorgeous," Selena added.

After a few more poses in front of the mirror, she stopped. "Okay, I'm going to change so we can get lunch," she announced, heading back to the fitting room.

The saleswoman smiled. "If it's the one, let's get your measurements and get the order started. It'll take several months to arrive."

Zoey eyed me.

I said, "Let's do it."

She grinned, hurrying off to get measured.

Just then, my phone buzzed in my pocket. Surprised at the caller, I turned to Selena. "Give me a minute." I answered. "Hey, Hirsch."

It wasn't surprising to hear from him, but we had just talked the day before about a BBQ. Why was he calling again so soon?

Gone were the days when he would call me for help with a case, since he'd retired from the sheriff's department two years earlier. Finally, he'd put in his paperwork, eager to spend more time with Kim and Audrey. I was happy for him. It was time for him to leave behind the dark life of a homicide detective.

"Hi, is this a bad time?" Hirsch asked.

"I have a minute while Zoey gets measured. Selena, Zoey, and I are at the bridal shop—Zoey just picked out her dress."

"My gosh, Zoey's getting married. I can't believe it."

"You and me both."

"Maybe this isn't the time to talk, but..."

"What is it?" I asked, curiosity piqued.

"Well, I just got a call from a friend of mine over at the Alameda County Sheriff's Department. They're working a tough case. I told them you might be able to help."

"Oh?"

Hirsch explained the details. I listened intently, my interest growing.

"I can help, for sure," I said. "Zoey goes back to school Sunday night. I'll call them first thing Monday morning. Does that work?"

"Absolutely. Tell Zoey and Selena I said hi."

"Will do."

I ended the call and looked over at Selena, who raised an eyebrow. "What is it?" she asked.

"A case."

Selena gave me a knowing smile.

Just then, Zoey emerged from the dressing room, back in her jeans and pink striped sweater. "I'm ready."

"What do you want for lunch?" I asked.

"Pizza?"

I laughed. Oh, how my girl still loved her pizza. "Sounds perfect."

As I left the bridal shop with my two daughters, my heart was full of joy for the future, but also a small part of me couldn't help but feel excited about the case that awaited me too.

3

JANE

LISTENING TO THE PSYCHIATRIST, I wondered if I would ever know who I really was. The words *dissociative amnesia* hung in the air, clinical and devoid of emotion. It was strange how something so sterile could describe the depths of my confusion, my fear. It made me feel like a case study, just another file in a drawer filled with people whose lives had unraveled. The truth was, I didn't need a medical term to tell me I was lost. I could feel it every time I closed my eyes and tried to pull up something —anything—from the dark void that had become my mind.

They said there was no physical reason I couldn't remember my past. My body was battered—bruises, cuts, a cracked rib, a head wound—but none of that explained why my memories were gone.

My mind had shut down, they said, because it couldn't handle what had happened. They believed the trauma had caused me to forget everything.

They ran tests—so many tests. Each one made me feel less human and more like a puzzle they were trying to solve. My brain scanned, blood drawn, questions asked over and over. But all the tests in the world couldn't give me back the one thing I needed: my identity. I had no idea who I was, and the more time passed, the more I feared I never would.

My body was healing. That was something. The bruises were fading, the cuts too, but what good was it if my mind stayed broken? I couldn't stay in the hospital much longer. Physically, I was no longer in need of care. So, they were planning to send me to a shelter—a place for people who had nowhere else to go. It filled me with a deep sense of sadness. By going to a shelter, I was accepting that I had no family and no life to return to.

I clutched the necklace around my neck, my fingers tracing its smooth surface, desperate to feel something familiar. It was the only thing that connected me to a past I couldn't remember. Was it a gift from someone I loved? Someone who loved me? I didn't know, but it was all I had.

As the psychiatrist explained the treatment options—cognitive behavioral therapy, working through trauma—it all sounded so... terrifying. The idea of unlocking memories, of diving back into whatever had caused me to forget in the first place, was scary. What if I wasn't ready to remember? What if the truth was worse than having lost my memories?

But I couldn't stay like this forever, wandering through life as a blank slate.

It was disturbing enough not knowing my name, my age, or where I came from. But worse than that was the loneliness.

They had run my fingerprints through every database, searched for any trace of my existence, and found nothing. They explained DNA testing to me as they took my sample and checked it against the missing persons database. All the searching came up with the same answer.

I didn't exist, and no one was looking for me.

I was a woman with no identity, no past, no family or friends. The idea that I had been forgotten, that no one in the world was missing me, weighed heavily on me. How could I have lived an entire life and left behind so little? Was I really that unimportant?

And then, there was the child.

The doctors were fairly certain that I had given birth at some point. I was a mother. But I couldn't remember my child. I couldn't picture their face or recall their name. The thought twisted in my gut. How could I have forgotten something so important?

It was one thing to forget where I grew up or what job I had, but my child? That felt like a betrayal, not just of myself, but of them. Were they out there somewhere, waiting for me to come back? Did they need me? Had I given them up for adoption, or worse, had they been taken from me or were they dead? The uncertainty gnawed at me, and with each passing day, I felt more and more like a failure—like I had abandoned someone who depended on me.

The psychiatrist assured me she would continue to meet with me, even after I was placed in a shelter. It was meant to be reassuring, but it only reminded me of how little I had left.

At the hospital, I was at least in the care of people who I had become familiar with, even if they only knew me as Jane Doe. The nurses smiled at me, brought me food, and chatted with me as if I were a person, not just a mystery to be solved.

Detective Cromwell, the man in charge of my case, seemed genuinely invested in figuring out what had happened to me. He visited once a day, determined to piece together how I had ended up beaten and abandoned in that park.

They believed I hadn't been there long—less than a day. My injuries were fresh when they found me. If it hadn't been for Edward, the man with the fluffy dog, I'm not sure where I would have ended up. Edward and his dog, Snowman, had been my saving grace. But now, I was left wondering what happened before that, how I had gotten there in the first place. Who had left me there to die?

Now, as I sat alone, the weight of everything pressed down on me. My past was a void, and the future felt just as uncertain. I had to have parents, didn't I? I had to have grown up somewhere.

There was a knock on the door, soft but firm, pulling me from my swirling thoughts. I glanced up, already feeling the tightness in my chest, that ever-present tension that never really left me these days.

Detective Cromwell stood in the doorway. He was with another man, older, with graying blond hair. Standing next to him was a woman—dark-haired, tall, and lean. Her presence was strong, almost commanding, yet there was a softness in the way her eyes met mine.

"Hi, Jane, how are you feeling?" Detective Cromwell's voice was calm, steady.

"A little sore still, but doing fine," I replied, my voice quieter than I intended. "I'll be transferred to a shelter soon."

The word *shelter* hung in the air, and I saw a flicker of sadness in the woman's amber eyes. There was no judgment in her gaze, but the pity was unmistakable. It was as if she knew what it meant.

The reality of it hadn't fully settled in for me yet either—that I was going to live in a shelter, and I didn't even have a name. Just "Jane Doe." A placeholder. An anonymous existence. They told me I was free to pick another name while they were trying to figure out my true identity, but I figured Jane was as good a name as any.

Detective Cromwell cleared his throat gently, breaking the silence. "I have a couple of friends I'd like to introduce you to." He patted the older man on the shoulder, a gesture that seemed both casual and full of respect. "This is retired Sergeant August

Hirsch, and this is his friend and former associate, Martina Monroe. She's a private investigator. I'm going to let them explain why they're here."

Martina stepped forward slightly, her expression soft but focused. There was something in her presence that immediately set her apart from the others. She wasn't here out of duty or obligation—there was something personal in the way she looked at me.

"Jane," she began, her voice steady and warm. "Detective Cromwell explained to me what happened to you and that you're unable to remember your life. I specialize in finding missing persons, and they reached out to me to help you find your family and discover what happened to you."

Her words washed over me, and for a moment, I didn't know how to respond. There was a flicker of hope, a spark. Could she really help me? Could she find out who I was when I couldn't even remember my own name?

"You've done this before?" I asked.

Martina stepped closer and sat down in the chair next to me, closing the physical space between us in a way that felt comforting. "Not exactly like this," she admitted. "But I found a missing person who had been gone for thirty years. I used to work on cold cases with Sergeant Hirsch." She glanced up at him, and the exchange between them spoke of shared experience. "So, in a way, this is kind of like that. I want to help you," she said, her eyes locking onto mine. "Is it all right if we work together to find out who you are and where you're from?"

I hesitated. "I don't have any money," I confessed, my voice barely more than a whisper. "I can't pay you."

Martina shook her head immediately, her dark hair swaying slightly with the movement. "No need," she said. "My firm handles some cases pro bono. We won't charge you a thing. We just want to help."

There it was again—kindness. First, there was Edward, with his dog, Snowman, who had found me in that park. Then the nurses, always bringing me extra blankets or offering a smile when they didn't need to. Detective Cromwell, showing up day after day, refusing to give up on my case. And now Martina and Sergeant Hirsch, people who didn't know me, who owed me nothing, offering to help without any strings attached.

Everyone had been so nice, and yet, for some reason, it didn't feel right. It didn't match what I felt about most people—or at least what I thought I felt.

Was I the kind of person who didn't trust easily? Had life taught me to be wary, to expect the worst? But since I ended up in this hospital, I had been treated with nothing but kindness, and it left me wondering—did I deserve it?

I didn't know the answer. I wasn't sure I wanted to. But looking at Martina, at her calm, unwavering gaze, I felt the tiniest glimmer of something I hadn't let myself feel before she arrived—hope.

4

MARTINA

LOOKING into the eyes of this woman—this Jane Doe—I couldn't help but feel sympathy. I couldn't imagine waking up one day, battered, bruised, and bleeding from a head wound, with no memory of who I was, where I had been, or what had happened. She seemed apprehensive to talk to us, uncertain about trusting us or letting me help her.

Hirsch had agreed to assist on the law enforcement side of things since I wasn't officially contracted through any police or sheriff's department. He said he'd take it on as a little side project in his retirement. He said he had extra hours in his day considering Audrey, his daughter, and Kim, a teacher, were at school during the day. I could see the excitement of the new challenge in his eyes, but there was also empathy for the woman in front of us, whose future was now dependent on the system. Not a fate I'd want.

I wondered which shelter she'd end up at. If her attacker had known her, he could be looking for her. She needed a secure location until we could determine she was safe. Whoever had done this to her had likely left her for dead, and that thought gnawed at me.

But looking at her now, I could tell she was strong. The fact that she had crawled up from that dark hill, fighting for her own life, showed a resilience not everyone had.

Finally, Jane spoke, her voice barely audible. "Okay."

"That's great. Is it all right if I ask you a few questions?" I asked softly. I'd been given a briefing of the case but had yet to review the police and medical reports.

"Sure," she said, her voice tentative. "Will you be able to find out what happened to my child, too?"

The doctors must have informed her that she'd given birth. "Of course."

That elicited the tiniest hint of a smile.

"Before we go into the details of what happened, how are you doing?"

Her face scrunched as though she might tear up. "I'm tired, but all right."

That was to be expected. "That's good to hear. Do you know which shelter they're going to place you in?"

"I'm not sure. The social worker will tell me when she gets here."

"Well, if you'd like, I could speak with your social worker for you and discuss the different shelter options," I continued. "As I mentioned, my firm, Drakos Monroe Security & Investigations, is taking your case pro bono. We'll be acting as the conduit to law enforcement as we unravel things. Hirsch is going to help us with the law enforcement side, but as part of our service, we offer specialized housing for people in situations like yours. It would be a private apartment with security cameras—that are constantly monitored—until we can ensure that you're safe and that whoever did this to you can never hurt you again." There were shelters that provided security, but there weren't a lot of them and usually had a waiting list.

"Oh," she said hesitantly. "I'll have to ask the social worker. She's supposed to be here soon."

"It's up to you," I ensured her. "If you decide you prefer one of our secure apartments, consider it done, and I'll make arrangements immediately."

I could sense her internal struggle, but I had a feeling I already knew her answer. Who wouldn't want the comfort of a private apartment with round-the-clock security?

"A private apartment sounds nice," she admitted softly. "You'd really do that for a stranger?"

Hirsch and I exchanged glances, and I noticed a small smile tugging at his lips.

"It's one of Martina's specialties," he said. "Trust her when she says you'll be well taken care of. Any resources you need will be provided. We'll make sure you get through this."

"Why do you do this?" she asked suddenly.

"What do you mean?" I asked.

"You just help strangers. Everyone's been so kind... and I don't remember my past. But it seems surprising so many people are willing to help a stranger."

Even though Jane didn't remember her past, her instincts were telling her kindness wasn't normal—that made me believe she wasn't a stranger to cruelty and could definitely still be in danger. "I've seen a lot in my career, and I know how important a helping hand can be—how it can change someone's life. I always hope that when I help someone, that not only are they able to make progress but the next time they're in a position to help someone, they will. It's kind of like a 'pay it forward' thing."

For the first time, I saw a glimmer of joy on her face. She said, "I like that."

"We can definitely set up that apartment for you," I said.

"And we can speak with your social worker with you, if you prefer."

She nodded.

"Now, can I ask you about the last two weeks?"

"Sure," she replied.

As she told her story—crawling through the darkness on that small hill, the path leading to the man who found her, all the tests and endless prodding at the hospital—her voice wavered. "The strangest part," she continued, "was when the doctor said it sounded like somebody tried to kill me. They just left me there. Who would do that?"

Too many people, I thought. Fortunately, it wasn't the majority, but there were those who did such things for their own twisted pleasure. Or perhaps it was related to her past. Most victims of violent crime are hurt by people they know.

"We're going to help you figure that out," I reassured her. "Hirsch and Detective Cromwell are on the case too." Looking at her in slacks and T-shirt, I said, "Was this what you were wearing when they found you?"

"No. They took those for evidence," she said, glancing down. Her fingers moved to the necklace around her neck, a little gold medallion with an interesting design on it. "The only thing I still have is this necklace."

I noticed a small tattoo on her wrist—three hearts intertwined. "Do you remember anything about the necklace?"

"No. All I know is that it makes me feel... I don't know... soothed, like maybe it was something good, you know?"

I made a note of that. "How about your tattoo? Do you have any more?"

"Just the one on my wrist."

Hirsch and Cromwell had promised to share the police reports, but I would also need her consent to look at her medical records. "And you have absolutely no memory of the area? Being in California? Being at that park in Fremont?"

She shook her head again. "It's all blank. It's so strange because I know how to walk and talk, and I can read and write. It seems weird I can't remember anything about my life."

From what I had read about her condition, dissociative amnesia is a psychological condition where individuals are unable to recall important personal information, usually following trauma or extreme stress. This kind of amnesia primarily affects autobiographical memory, which includes personal experiences and knowledge about one's life events.

People with dissociative amnesia retain their ability to read, write, and perform other learned skills because these abilities are part of procedural memory or semantic memory, which are stored differently from personal experiences. Procedural memory involves the learning of skills and tasks like riding a bike or typing, while semantic memory includes general knowledge such as facts, language, and other learned information. In contrast, autobiographical memories, which tend to be lost in dissociative amnesia, are part of episodic memory—a memory system that stores details of personal life experiences.

"From what I understand, the mind stores different types of information differently. Your dissociative amnesia only affected your personal life experiences. Your brain is protecting you from memories that are just too traumatic to recall. Did your psychiatrist not explain this?"

"Her explanation was more complicated. What you say makes more sense."

We may need to find her a new therapist. I knew quite a few good ones I'd refer her to. "One last thing," I said. "Before we set up your new housing, would you let me look at your medical records? It could help us with the investigation into what happened to you."

"That's fine," she agreed.

"We'll have some paperwork for you to sign to give us access. Are you sure you're comfortable with that?"

"I am," she said. "Do I need to do anything else?"

"Not right now," I assured her.

We continued talking for a little while, trying to ease her discomfort and help her feel more comfortable with us.

We excused ourselves after a brief conversation with her social worker. Out in the hallway with Hirsch, I said, "What are you thinking?"

"The fact the police couldn't identify her and nobody has reported her missing is puzzling. In normal circumstances, fingerprints or facial recognition would pull up a driver's license or ID. She seems to be in her early twenties. Someone must be missing her."

"That's what I was thinking." Because none of the usual routes for identification brought back any results, we'd have to think outside the box to find her identity.

"How do you want to tackle the investigation?" he asked.

"After I review all of the records, I'm going to have a few people help out on this," I said. "One of them being Selena. She has great instincts, even though she's young. She's seen some horrific things herself. I think having her act as a sort of buddy for Jane—someone who checks in regularly, takes her to lunch, helps her socialize—will be good for both of them."

"Good idea. She likely could use a friend. How about research? Are you going to have Vincent on the team?"

Hirsch's interest in the case made me wonder how much he missed the job. "Vincent for sure. Maybe a few others too, if needed. I'm sure everyone will want to pitch in."

"And you'll let me know if there's anything you need from me," Hirsch said. "You've got my full support."

We had known each other for over fifteen years, and I knew

that was true in any situation I found myself in. It made me feel good that even though Hirsch was retired, and I was getting older too, here we were, still together fighting for victims and survivors alike. And that's exactly what I was going to do for Jane Doe. She may have been given a generic name, but she was somebody. I was going to find out exactly who she was, and almost as importantly, I was going to find out who had hurt her —and make sure they never hurt her or anyone else ever again.

5

MARTINA

Stepping into the conference room, I saw my two favorite investigators sitting around the table. Vincent was busy texting, likely to his wife Amanda, who had recently taken a year off from her job. She had decided to take the sabbatical to spend more time with their six-year-old son, Caden. Amanda wanted to do some "mom things" like volunteer in his first-grade classroom and chaperone field trips to the zoo. At the last barbecue, she had told us that while she wanted to return to work, for now, she was really enjoying being a full-time mom.

And there was Selena. She was, of course, also preoccupied with her laptop. She was always working. She had a tumultuous past and some seriously bad luck with boyfriends, which left her with a barely existent social life outside of her best friend, Dee, and Zoey, when she was in town, which wasn't very often. I wished there was more joy outside of work for Selena. She was such a wonderful young woman with so much to offer—but for now, she had chosen to devote herself to investigations. And she had solved quite a few cases this year. She was my daughter, but she was also an investigator at Drakos Monroe Security & Investigations full-time for the last eight months and a part-time helper during her college years.

Vincent set his phone onto the conference table, and I smiled before sitting down. Seeming to take the cue, Selena closed her laptop and grinned up at me.

"Martina, take it away!" Vincent cheered, his usual joyous demeanor breaking the silence.

"Thanks, Vincent. First of all"—I looked at the two of them —"I want to thank you for being here. In my email I mentioned this was a pro bono case, so any time you spend on it is in addition to your existing work."

"You know I'm always down for helping out someone who needs us," Selena said.

Vincent said, "You couldn't keep me away."

I smiled, knowing that each one of their sentiments was true. I had worked with them long enough to know that this was the team to ask, and this was the team that wouldn't hesitate to agree to help.

"I got a call from Hirsch over the weekend about a young woman who was found nearly beaten to death. Miraculously, she managed to climb her way to safety, where a man helped her and called the police. She has dissociative amnesia. Basically, she doesn't remember anything about her past—her name, her family, or where she lived."

I paused to see if anyone had any questions. Selena spoke up. "And we're sure she's not making it up? I mean, I've read that some people fake amnesia because they're running from something. Criminals do that sometimes."

The thought had crossed my mind, but I didn't think that was the case—or at least, I hoped not. "There's always that possibility," I admitted, "but I met her earlier today, and I believe she genuinely doesn't remember. She's scared, and she's obviously disoriented by the fact that she has no idea who she is or who tried to kill her."

"And you want us to figure out who she is?" Vincent asked.

"And where she came from," I answered. "We're also going to help the police figure out who did this to her, why they did it, and we're going to bring the perpetrators to justice."

"Who is investigating the crime?"

"Alameda County Sheriff's Department. Hirsch is going to be our liaison with law enforcement. He's coming out of retirement to help on this one, too."

"Woot! Just like the old days of the Cold Case Squad. We're going to solve this one, no problem," Vincent said, eyes gleaming with excitement.

Selena smirked. I didn't know her back in the Cold Case Squad days, and if I had she would've been too young to join us anyhow. But she'd heard enough way-back-when stories to understand Vincent's enthusiasm.

Selena and I met five years earlier after her father, my then fiancé, was looking for her when she hadn't returned his phone calls. Turned out, her mother had died and Selena had been kidnapped by an abusive boyfriend. The police and I had gotten to her just in time before he'd killed her. We'd been through a lot since then.

"What have you learned about her so far?" Selena asked, leaning forward ready for the answers.

"Well," I began, "two weeks ago, she—we're calling her Jane Doe—was found at a park called Quarry Lakes in Fremont. She had contusions to her head, bruises, scrapes, a cracked rib, and she was bleeding from a head wound. She was unconscious until she woke in the early hours of the morning. The medical exam shows that she hadn't been sexually assaulted, but based on her appearance when they brought her in, they think the assailant assumed she was dead and left her there." I paused, taking a breath. "Another thing is, during the medical exams, they discovered she had given birth at some point, but they don't know how long ago. They're not sure how old the child would be today, or if the child is alive. Jane is most likely in her early-to-mid twenties."

"What did the police do to try to determine her identity?" Selena asked, all business as usual.

"They've taken her fingerprints and DNA. Her DNA isn't in CODIS. No hits on any criminal databases or missing persons reports fitting her description." CODIS, the Combined DNA Identification System, included DNA profiles from convicted criminals, missing persons, and unidentified human remains.

"Just because there's no DNA match doesn't mean she's not in NamUs. Did they look for her photo?" Vincent asked, being quite familiar with NamUs, the National Missing and Unidentified Persons System.

"They ran facial recognition against NamUs and government issued document databases. They didn't find any matches."

"That's bizarre," Vincent said.

It really was. "Exactly. It means she's never had a driver's license or ID or passport issued in the United States."

"Maybe she's from outside the US?" Selena theorized.

"Maybe. But she speaks perfect English."

Vincent smirked and stroked his chin. "This is going to be a *very* interesting case."

"Indeed."

With a mischievous grin, Vincent popped out of his chair. "We should put together a board."

Vincent was our resident visual artist. He usually led the teams to visualize all the evidence, open questions, and next steps for the team to take. He kept us organized. And he loved doing it.

"I've made copies of all the reports. Review them and then let's meet to come up with a comprehensive plan. This afternoon, if possible."

Vincent said, "Sure thing, boss."

After I gave each of them a copy of the reports, the room filled with a sense of urgency. As Vincent rushed off, promising to work quickly, I stopped Selena. "Can you stay back?"

She turned back, raising an eyebrow. "Sure. What's up, Martina?"

"I was hoping you could take on some additional responsibilities with Jane. You're close in age, and I think she could use a friend, someone to make her feel less isolated. I'm not asking you to spend every moment with her, but maybe you could check in with her, help her feel more comfortable. She's in a secure apartment, but I'm sure right about now, she's feeling a little like a prisoner too."

"Absolutely," Selena agreed without hesitation. "She's getting all the help she needs, right? She has a psychiatrist?"

"She has one through the county, but I think she could use a new one."

Selena frowned. "Can we get her one of our preferred psychiatrists? On the house?"

She was right. Jane needed more than just the basics. "Yes. Let's see if we can get her someone who can meet with her frequently—maybe three days a week. We'll feel it out, talk to Jane, and see what she's comfortable with."

"Got it," Selena said with a nod.

"I'll give you Jane's number, and you can make arrangements with her. I'll let her know to expect your call."

"Cool," she said. "Is the call you took at the bridal shop on Saturday about this case?"

"It is," I confirmed.

Selena smirked playfully. "I could tell by the look on your face it was a big case. You love a challenge."

It was true. "You know me too well. Are you coming over for dinner tonight?"

"If I'm not working."

All work and no play was not a way to live. "Your dad would love to see you."

"Okay, I'll come by," she agreed, reluctantly.

"Great," I said, feeling lighter. Having Selena and Vincent on the case, I knew we'd learn the truth and help Jane through this turbulent time in her life.

6

SELENA

After a brief knock on the door, it opened. Jane knew I was coming over, but I still thought she should've asked who it was—or at least had me hold up my ID to the peephole. Although, considering the surveillance cameras pointed at the front door were being monitored and the personnel watching them knew me, the risk was low. But based on what happened to her, she needed to be careful and to learn some basic self-defense and maybe even some weapons training. She likely had plenty of time on her hands, so I hoped she'd agree to be trained.

As she stood before me, I noticed the yellow and green bruises still visible on her heart-shaped face. A bandage covered part of her forehead, though she tried to hide as much as she could with her long, dark hair.

"You're Selena?" she asked nervously.

"Yes, would you like to see my ID?"

Jane looked surprised but then nodded.

I pulled out my driver's license, and she looked at it, as if really studying it. Maybe she was trying to remember if she ever had one. Had the police told her she hadn't?

Reluctantly, she said, "C'mon in."

With a nod, I walked in and sat down at the small dining table as she awkwardly stood by.

"Can I get you anything? I think I have water... and cups," Jane offered, gesturing to the cupboards.

"I'm fine," I said, trying to put her at ease.

"So... you're a private investigator?" she asked, hesitantly sitting down across from me.

"I am. It's been about a year and a half since I've been licensed."

"Oh. Martina told me you're one of her best," Jane said, her voice soft.

"Well, I've been doing investigations longer than I was probably supposed to. And when I say probably, I don't mean probably—I mean, I wasn't supposed to." I laughed lightly. "Truth be told, Martina is my stepmother, and I basically asked for forgiveness instead of permission."

She nodded as if she understood.

"Martina asked me to spend some time with you and help you get out of the house. I'm fully trained in combat and weapons, so you're safe with me."

Jane gave me a once-over, like most people did. I wasn't exactly physically imposing. I was only five feet three inches, and my appearance lacked the typical marks of strength. But I had other skills.

"I work out six days a week—if you don't count the seventh day when I like to hike," I said with a small grin. "I always carry a firearm and sometimes a baton for good measure. I'm also trained in hand-to-hand combat. Trust me, I've taken down some pretty messed-up people. You're safe with me."

"Cool."

"I could teach you self-defense, if you want. I personally think all women should learn."

Her eyes lit up. "I'd like that. If you have time."

"We'll fit it in, when you're ready. Once the doctors clear you and your ribs are healed." The medical records indicated she needed to take it easy for the next six weeks. Combat and weapons training would have to wait.

"I'd like that. So, what's the plan for today?" she asked, rubbing the necklace that Martina had mentioned in our planning session. It was a unique design, and the team would be checking with jewelers online and around the Bay Area to see if anyone recognized it. If they did, we could learn who had purchased the item, and it could lead us to Jane's identity or to her family.

"Well, I don't know if you're ready for this, but one of the things I've been assigned to do is check out your tattoo. Take a photo. See if any local parlors recognize it, or maybe someone out of state. As you can see—" I pulled up my sleeve to show her my own ink. "I've got experience in that area."

Jane gave the Celtic tattoo on my wrist a quick glance, though she seemed a little distracted.

"But that's not all," I continued, my tone softening. "There's another thing I'd like to do, but I'm not sure you're ready for it."

"What is it?"

"I'd like to take you to the park. Have you walk me through what you remember. See if anything feels familiar now that you're feeling a little better. Maybe something will jog your memory."

Jane's expression changed. "You want me to go back there?"

I had a feeling she'd be hesitant. If she really didn't want to, I'd go on my own. I wanted to walk the scene to have a feel for what had happened. "You're safe," I reassured her.

"Can we get lunch first?"

"Of course." I smiled. "What do you like?"

She hesitated, her fingers still rubbing the necklace. "Honestly... I don't know."

I could see why Martina was fairly convinced this woman had no memory of her past.

She was scared, and there was a haunted look in her eyes that made me wonder if it went deeper than just being left at the park, bleeding and alone. Not that an event like that wasn't traumatic enough, but I had a hunch it was more than that one event.

AFTER LUNCH, we parked in the lot and headed down the trail at Quarry Lakes. I read the sign aloud, explaining that there were five different lakes, with trails and trees, and it looked like there were a lot of little paths where someone could easily hide a body. Hopefully, returning to the scene didn't scare her more than she already seemed to be.

As we walked along the path in silence, I admired the beauty of the place. Sparkling blue lakes lined by evergreen trees with a golden hill backdrop.

"It's really pretty here," I said, glancing at her.

"It is," she said quietly as she studied the park.

"Do you remember being here?"

"It was dark when I was here. It seems like a different place during the day. Quiet. Peaceful. Not a place where you'd expect to be attacked."

"True," I agreed, leading her farther down the path to where she was found, recalling the description from the report. "How are you doing?"

"I'm all right," she said, though her voice wavered. "It feels different now."

I had read the police report, and I knew they had scoured the area for clues and evidence. But police officers make mistakes—things get missed or moved by animals or the elements. Maybe something had washed up in the water. I was looking for anything—anything that might tell me more or connect her to the scene.

As I walked, I glanced down and noticed a cigarette butt. I stopped, pulled a plastic bag from my backpack, and with a gloved hand, picked it up and placed it inside.

"Evidence?" Jane asked, watching me.

"You never know," I said with a shrug. "Do you remember someone smoking?"

She shook her head and I continued down the path. She walked silently beside me, her eyes scanning the trees and bushes.

The trail was rough—brambles, gopher holes, gravel, dirt, trees, and plenty of bushes. There were so many hiding places. Standing at the water's edge, I turned to the left, where she'd been attacked.

We continued on, the crunch of my sneakers on the gravel filling the silence. I glanced at Jane, who was walking next to me, wearing khaki pants and a plain T-shirt. She was dressed like a soccer mom or someone's grandmother.

"Was that what you were wearing when they found you?" I asked.

She looked down. "No. The hospital gave them to me."

"They're nice."

"They're fine," she replied with a shrug.

I looked at her, considering. "Do you want to go shopping for maybe some clothes that are more... youthful?"

She blinked, surprised. "I don't have any money."

"I've got you," I said with a smile. "Let's go shopping—see if there's anything you like. It'll be fun."

She gave me a small smile. "Everyone's so nice."

Martina had given me full control on how I'd keep her company, and I figured taking her shopping might help—maybe seeing clothes she liked would trigger something. Fashion trends varied from region to region. People in the Bay Area tended to dress differently than those in the Midwest or who were living off the grid. Considering she had no digital footprint, my bet was she had been living outside of the city. Maybe a rural or remote area. If we shopped, maybe something would feel familiar to her.

The water's edge was right next to us, and I turned back toward her. "Are you okay?" I asked again.

She took a deep breath.

"We can go back if you need to."

"I'm fine," she said, though there was an edge to her tone. "It's just... weird being here."

"I can imagine."

She glanced at me, then hesitated before asking, "Have you ever had anything like this happen to you? You said you've gone up against some really bad guys."

"I've been beaten, and I've almost been killed." I started to list all the scrapes I'd found myself in over the years but cut myself off. She didn't need to hear that right now.

"Oh."

Hopefully knowing she was around someone who knew what she'd been through would make her more comfortable.

I continued scanning the area, looking under branches, wondering how thoroughly the police had searched for evidence. There was so much ground to cover, and a lot could've been missed. I knelt down, opened the flashlight app on my phone, and began crawling around in the bushes.

"Should you be doing that?"

"It's fine," I reassured her. "Just keep an eye out—let me know if you see anyone coming."

I scoured the ground for anything—anything that could be connected to Jane's case. As I was moving through the brush, something furry brushed against my arm. I jumped, scraping my face on the bushes. A squirrel darted away.

I exhaled, laughing at my own nerves. I'd be fine. But then I stopped, blinking in disbelief. There, half-buried under the leaves and debris, was the blade of a small knife.

I picked it up, carefully holding it in my gloved hand. Crawling out of the bushes, I went back to my backpack, pulled out an evidence bag, and placed the knife inside.

"Is that a knife?" Jane asked, her eyes wide.

"I found it a few yards under the brush. Do you recognize it?" I asked, holding it up for her to see.

She stood there, staring at the knife. Dumbfounded.

For a moment, I could almost swear there was a flicker of recognition in her eyes. When I had pointed out other items, like the cigarette butt, and asked if it jogged any memories, her response had been an immediate "no." But with the knife... her reaction was different. Did she remember something?

7

JANE

THE SUNLIGHT off the blade sent a shiver down my spine. I didn't know why. All I knew was that it had caused me to be afraid. Of what? Could Selena tell it had scared me? An uneasy feeling washed over me. I didn't want to be at the park anymore. I wanted to run, to flee. Was it connected to my attack? Was that knife used to lure me to the scene? Selena's voice broke through my spiraling thoughts. "Do you recognize it?"

I stared at her, distracted by the scratches on her arms, neck, and face from crawling through the bushes. The sight of her injuries made me feel a twisted sort of encouragement. It made me believe she would go to all lengths to figure out what happened to me. Not just her, but Martina too.

But what if the truth was something so awful, I wished I hadn't known?

My therapist told me the dissociative amnesia was due to trauma. It must have been pretty terrible to have lost all memory. Maybe I should have rejected their help. Maybe I was better off not knowing. "No. I've never seen it."

"Okay, well, we'll have it tested to see if it's related to your case."

Looking at Selena, I nodded, though a gnawing feeling remained. Who was Selena? She was young, dressed all in black, with tattoos and piercings that ran all the way up her ears. There was a deep, dark sadness in her eyes. I couldn't help but wonder what caused *her* trauma. She had said she'd been face-to-face with danger on more than one occasion. Maybe it changed her, just like whatever happened to me had surely changed me.

"Can we go?" I asked, my voice trembling slightly.

"Is something wrong?" Selena's concern was evident, but I wasn't sure I could explain the fear creeping up on me.

"I don't know. Something about seeing that knife... I just... I don't feel safe. I'm sorry, I just—can we please go?"

"Of course." Selena looked down at her hands, lines of red where thorns and branches had cut into her skin. A few cuts had bled. "How about we head back to your place? I'll meet you a little later to go shopping. I probably should get cleaned up and drop this off at the office."

"All right," I muttered, feeling a sense of relief at the prospect of leaving. We headed back up toward the hill.

As we walked in silence, I felt as if the dread was following me, sticking to my skin like sweat. I kept glancing over my shoulder, half-expecting someone—or something—to be there. But no one followed us.

What if the memory came back, sharp and vivid, and I couldn't bear it? Did something happen to my child?

Maybe it was better not to remember. Maybe forgetting was a gift, and here I was, trying to tear open a wound that might never heal.

Selena's footsteps were steady beside me, grounding me in the present, but my mind was already running down dark paths. The same thought kept swirling over and over. *What if the truth was worse than not knowing?*

I shivered as a gust of wind blew through the trees, rustling the leaves like a warning. My heart thudded in my chest, heavy and uneven.

We reached the top of the hill, and something inside me was screaming at me that uncovering the truth might be worse than never knowing at all.

8

MARTINA

Selena charged into my office, her clothes streaked with dirt and her face marked by angry, pink scratches. She looked like she had been in a fight with a feral cat. "What happened to you?" I asked, studying her from head to toe.

"We went down to the park where Jane was attacked," she said, breathless. "I crawled around in the bushes, looking for evidence. I found something."

She handed me a couple of evidence bags. Her hands were shaking slightly as she explained what she'd found and Jane's reaction to it. One bag contained a small knife, with a four-inch blade and flecks of brown near the hilt, and the other a cigarette butt. The police had either missed them or they weren't there two weeks earlier and had nothing to do with Jane's case.

"We should hand these over to the police," I said, holding up the bags.

Fists on her hips, she said, "But we don't know that they have anything to do with the case." She paused and eyed me. I remained silent, so she continued, "I looked at the police report. They didn't find any evidence at the scene other than Jane's blood. So I was thinking that after we test them, if they turn out to be related, we can hand them over."

I could hear the determination in her voice, but I knew better than to test and then hand it over. If it was critical evidence, the police needed it ASAP and in their custody, tested by their lab. "If you think it could be evidence, we have to give it to the Alameda County Sheriff's Department."

She shrugged, a hint of defiance in her body language. Selena had come a long way since I first met her, but she still often played by her own rules, putting herself and others in dangerous situations. I thought she'd learned her lesson by now, but I suppose she still needed a few more before she fully understood.

"We're helping out the sheriff's department here," I reminded her, trying to keep my voice calm. "We're not working on a freelance investigation. Jane's depending on us to not only learn who she is but solve the case and put the bad guy in jail. There are rules we have to follow—even if we don't like them."

Selena gave a slight nod, but I could tell she wasn't fully convinced. She had never worked on an investigation alongside law enforcement before. It was up to me to show her how it was done. Following protocol wasn't just a formality; it was how we ensured justice was served. "I'm meeting with Detective Cromwell and Hirsch later," I continued. "I'll bring the evidence to them and let them know what we found."

"Okay," she said reluctantly, her tone revealing she still wasn't thrilled with the idea of giving up control. "Are there any updates on the familial DNA or the necklace?" she asked, likely trying to steer the conversation in another direction.

We had decided to look for a familial connection on Jane's DNA. Perhaps a mother or father or other relative was in CODIS. "Not yet," I replied, glancing at the clock. "But it's only been a day. It could take some time. We'll get there, Selena. We just have to be patient."

There were no smiles from Selena. At twenty-two years old, she was still working on her patience. Not that I was one to talk. "How is she doing?" I asked.

"She's hanging in there. She was really spooked when I found the knife. She has kind of an intensity about her too. I told her I knew what she was going through and that I'd encountered my share of bad guys and sticky situations."

Sticky situations. That was putting it lightly. "I bet that will help her feel less alone, knowing she's not the only one to have been through trauma."

"I think so."

"Do you have plans to see her again today?"

"I'm going to take her out shopping for some more modern clothes, see if that helps her—maybe she'll find her old style or see something familiar."

That was smart. "Great."

"Have we thought about putting her face on the news? Or starting a Facebook page to draw attention to her? See if anyone knows who she is."

"That's a good idea. But maybe not quite yet," I said, though cautiously. "I want to talk to Detective Cromwell first. I'd also like to explore some additional medical procedures for Jane. So far, they've only done a head CT scan and chest X-rays but they didn't check for broken bones or previous fractures on other parts of her body. And they didn't do dental X-rays. All we really know is that at one point she had a child. I'd like to know if she suffered any kind of abuse before—it can help us better understand her life. But we need her to agree to more medical tests."

"I can talk to her," Selena offered.

Selena was like me and preferred being in charge. "I'd like to have a tag-team approach. I want your perspective, especially since you're willing to do things like crawl in the bushes and get all cut up looking for clues, which I appreciate. But let me talk to her. I'll get her consent for the medical exams. If we can get dental records from her, it could be a relatively quick way to determine her identity." It wouldn't tell us who had attacked her, but it was an important first step.

Selena said, "Okay."

"What time are you going to shop?"

"I told her I'd take her to dinner and then hit the mall. I said I'd be back to pick her up around six."

"I'll call her and see if I can stop by after I meet with Cromwell and Hirsch. I'll let you know how it goes. As of right now, I'd prefer we don't put her face out there yet."

"Why?" Selena asked, raising an eyebrow.

"If somebody tried to kill her, maybe it wasn't the first time she's been attacked," I explained. "It's possible the trauma that caused her amnesia may have happened before the attack. Maybe it wasn't just this attack but an accumulation of violence over time. Or violence toward her child."

"Domestic violence?" Selena suggested, her tone softening.

"It's possible. She was likely in a relationship since she had a baby at some point."

"It makes sense."

With a reassuring nod, I said, "That's what I think. I'll talk to the guys and then get her consent for the test. We'll talk soon."

Selena agreed and walked out of my office. I could see she was less enthusiastic than when she'd charged in. I was sorry for that, but this would be her first lesson in understanding that following procedure was non-negotiable when working with the police department. I didn't like the bureaucracy any more than she did, but I knew it was necessary. Protocol led to solid convictions and ensured the bad guys didn't go free. Still, I knew it didn't make it any easier.

9

MARTINA

AFTER A QUICK MEETING with Detective Cromwell and Hirsch, I dropped off the evidence—the knife and cigarette butt that Selena had obtained at the scene of Jane's attack. I explained my approach and what I wanted to do. They were all for it and agreed it was a good idea to hold off on putting Jane's face in the press.

If Jane's attacker thought she died in the spot they left her, we didn't need to alert them to the fact she hadn't. We didn't want them coming after her again. Our first priority was to protect her until we understood more and could ensure her safety.

Later, I arrived at the safe house where Jane was staying. The building itself was nondescript, just like any other apartment complex in the area. It was clean but impersonal, with pale gray walls and sterile hallways. But unlike similar units in the area, it had special features like strategically placed surveillance cameras that were monitored by our firm 24/7. Overall, it was kind of a depressing-looking place, and I thought that dinner and shopping with Selena would lift her spirits. I knew firsthand, having stayed in a very similar safe house before, that being stuck inside all day could drive a person mad.

When Jane opened the door, her face lit up, despite the tiredness in her eyes.

"It's good to see you, Martina."

"You look like you're doing well," I said, though I could sense the strain the situation had put on her. There was a fragility to her that made me feel a deep ache inside.

"As well as I can, I suppose," she said, her tone uncertain, as if she were trying to convince herself.

She led me inside.

The apartment was almost like a model home—generic and forgettable. The walls were a neutral beige, the kind of color that blended into the background. A plain, beige sofa sat in the middle of the room, facing a small TV mounted on the wall. It was a space meant to hold someone for a short time, not a place to call home.

I followed her to the sofa and sat down beside her. I offered her a reassuring smile, though I felt the weight of everything we didn't know pressing on my chest. How long would she have to stay here, in this limbo? Hopefully not for too long.

After a breath, I said, "I talked to Selena earlier. She told me what she found at the park, and the team is working to determine if the items are related to your case. In addition, we're all working to figure out your identity and what happened to you, with what we currently know. There's another angle I'd like to pursue, but I'll need your help."

"What is it?"

Sitting there in that sterile, uninviting space, I felt a pang of sadness for her. She didn't remember who she was, and this apartment wasn't going to give her any clues. It was just a holding place, a reminder that her life was still in pieces, waiting to be put back together.

"Well, one thing we often do when we have an unidentified person, like yourself, is put your picture on the news to find out who you are," I began, choosing my words carefully. "But in the event that someone intended to end your life and assumed they'd been successful, we don't want them to realize you're still out there. We don't want them to come after you again. So, before we do something like that, it might be useful to find out if this was the first time you were attacked or one of many."

Jane frowned slightly. "I'm sorry, I'm not following."

"By getting dental X-rays and a full-body scan, we could see if you had any previous injuries—maybe you've been attacked before, possibly by the same person or by someone else entirely. We might also be able to find a match for your dental records if DNA isn't able to help us."

Understanding began to dawn in her eyes. "Okay."

"Are you willing to do that?" I asked gently. "My firm is willing to cover all costs. We just need your consent, and I can be with you every step of the way—or Selena, whichever you prefer."

"Oh," Jane said quietly. "I like Selena. She seems determined."

She wasn't wrong. Selena had decent instincts, but she was also stubborn to a fault. The young woman was relentless, often putting herself in harm's way. I could easily picture her crawling through the bushes until she found something—even if it hurt her physically. The scratches on her arms looked bad, and I was certain she'd end up with bruises too.

"That she is." I agreed with her assessment of Selena, but was she avoiding my request? Did she not want to do additional testing? Why?

Jane's voice softened, taking on a more vulnerable tone. "I didn't tell Selena this, but when I saw that knife... I didn't recognize it. But there was a fear inside of me. And I wanted to leave right away. Maybe you're right. Maybe this wasn't the first time."

That was her instincts telling her to be afraid. Her mind was locked but not her muscle memory. "Most people are attacked by someone they know."

Jane's eyes darkened, the implication sinking in. "So, it could be someone I know. Someone who knows my identity?"

"It's possible," I said. "That's why it's so important we proceed carefully."

Jane took a deep breath, then looked me in the eye. "That's why you wanted me to be in this safe house."

"Yes. And it's important for you not to leave the apartment without Selena or me or a member of my staff."

"I get it."

"Are you comfortable with having the X-rays done?" I asked again.

She looked away, staring at the beige carpet. Avoiding the question.

"Jane. You don't have to, if you don't want to."

She met my gaze with tears in her eyes. "Can I tell you something?"

Did she remember something? "Of course."

"I'm scared of learning about what happened. What if it's so bad I'll never recover—mentally I mean."

A valid fear. "That's completely understandable. If you need time to think about it, that's fine too. But don't you want to at least know your name? And where you're from?"

"I guess."

She guessed? That was surprising. "Have you spoken with the new therapist yet?"

"She called me earlier and explained how it works. I'm meeting with her tomorrow."

That was good. "Why don't you take some time to think

about it? Talk to the therapist and we can revisit the topic. How does that sound?" Her reservation about learning her identity had me a bit concerned, but I couldn't force her to do anything she didn't want to.

We sat in silence for a moment, the weight of her decision hanging between us. Finally, she said, "Thanks. I'll call you after my appointment."

"Sounds good."

I would be sure to tell Selena about the conversation. Perhaps she could get Jane to confide in her about why she wouldn't want to learn her identity. Jane must be going through all kinds of feelings that were leading her to resist knowing the truth. I was confident she'd change her mind, but I didn't want to push and cause her more anguish than she was already feeling. I only hoped she decided, and soon.

10

JANE

I BOLTED UPRIGHT, heart pounding in my chest, sweat trickling down my forehead. I glanced around my room. It was dark, and the red numbers on the clock by my nightstand glowed 4:00 AM.

"It was just a dream," I said to myself, trying to calm my racing thoughts. A nightmare. A terrifying one. But... it was just a dream, right?

I rubbed my eyes, trying to shake off the vivid images still swirling in my mind. It seemed so real—the blood, the woman, the anger, the man. I couldn't just see it, I could feel it.

Was it... a memory?

This wasn't the first nightmare since my attack, but it was the first time I saw a face—blurry, but a woman's face.

Who was she? Did I know her? Was she real? Or was she just a manifestation of myself?

I started to doubt my own thoughts. Maybe the woman was symbolic, an image of me in my mind. What happened to the woman—it felt like it was supposed to happen to me. And yet somehow, in the dream, I wasn't just witnessing it. I was... involved.

If it was supposed to be me, then how, in the nightmare, had I glanced down at my hands and saw blood on them? In that weird way we know things in dreams without knowing, I knew it wasn't my blood.

I had blood on my hands.

But whose?

And more importantly, what had I done?

Unable to stay in bed any longer, I climbed out, my legs trembling beneath me, and walked into the kitchen. The apartment was unnervingly quiet. I almost wanted some noise—anything—a distant bang, a bird chirping outside. Instead, there was nothing. Just the heavy silence.

I stood there, alone with my thoughts, still trying to piece together the fragments of the nightmare. Was any of it real? A part of me knew the dream was a clue, a glimpse of something I couldn't quite figure out.

But what?

I pulled a glass from the cupboard and filled it with water from the faucet. I gulped it down until the entire glass was empty, hoping the cool liquid would calm the knot in my stomach.

Do I tell Martina and Selena about the dream? I wondered as I stared at the empty glass in my hand. The police wouldn't do anything with the information since it was literally a dream. For some reason, I believed Martina and Selena might see it differently. But I still hadn't given Martina an answer about whether I'd undergo medical tests to try to determine my identity. Would she be upset if I didn't consent?

What would happen to me if I didn't? Martina's firm was paying for the apartment, trying to uncover my past, my identity. Without her help, I'd be in a shelter. For some reason, that seemed like the worst place I could go. I couldn't explain why. It wasn't like I had a bad memory of shelters or been to one before.

Whatever I'd done, whoever I was, perhaps I couldn't keep running from it anymore. After Selena found the knife, I knew she was getting suspicious of me. It was like she didn't believe me I didn't recognize it—I could see it in her eyes.

I sat down at the dining table and let my mind wander to the last 24 hours: the knife at the lake, Martina's compassionate, motherly demeanor, and Selena, always observing. We'd gone to dinner, then shopping. Selena was probably around my age— young, dark-haired, serious. She wasn't chipper or bubbly; she was direct, unapologetically opinionated. Martina, on the other hand, was much more reserved.

When we went shopping for clothes, I could tell Selena was trying to figure me out, trying to see what I liked, maybe even what I used to wear before all this happened. But none of it felt right, and I didn't understand why.

In both situations, neither Selena nor Martina had pushed me. They were patient, but I couldn't help wondering: for how long? Certainly not forever.

I rested my head in my hands, staring down at the table. Should I run? Running seemed like the easy option. Had I been running when I was attacked and left for dead?

Despite my nerves, despite my fears, I realized what I had to do. Because even if I didn't help them, Martina and Selena were going to learn the truth. Martina had told me I was brave, and I hadn't believed her. But maybe... maybe I just had to fake it until I made it.

"I'll be brave," I said to myself. Whatever it was, whatever they learned, I had to face it. I just wished I knew who that woman in my dreams was—or if she was even real.

11

MARTINA

With the phone pressed against my ear, I said, "That's great to hear." I knew she'd come around eventually. Perhaps the visit with her new therapist had helped her come to the decision. There was something in her voice, though—cautious, but maybe a bit more certain than before.

"So... what's next?" Jane asked, her voice tinged with curiosity, yet still guarded.

"Let me set up some appointments," I said, keeping my tone light. "I can go with you to the dental office as well as the medical center for X-rays. I might be able to get us in as early as tomorrow. Does that work for you?"

She laughed, but it was the kind of laugh that didn't quite seem genuine. A bit hollow, as if she didn't quite know how to engage fully yet. "I don't have anything else going on," she said, a trace of resignation lingering in her words.

"I'll make the appointments and let you know the time," I said, hoping to infuse some reassurance into my voice. I didn't want her to feel overwhelmed by appointment making or worrying about anything else.

"Okay," she said quietly.

"Did you meet with your therapist today?" I wanted to know if she was really starting to open up and if the new therapist was helping her feel more grounded.

"I did," she said, her voice neutral, almost as if she was testing the waters, seeing if she should share more.

"Was it a good fit? Did you like her?" I pressed, carefully. I knew how important this was for her healing process.

"She's nice. I think it will help," Jane said, but there was a slight hesitation, like she was unsure whether she should trust me with more information.

"That's good to hear," I said. "But if you don't think she's the right one for you, I have others I can refer to you." I wanted her to know she wasn't trapped, that she had options and control over who she spoke to.

"She's fine," Jane said. "I'll let you know if anything changes."

"Great," I said, offering a small nod even though she couldn't see me. "Is there anything else you need?"

"No." She paused. "I think I have everything I need right now."

"Good," I said. "I'd like to invite you to our house for dinner. If you don't have other plans?" I glanced out the window, watching the sun lower in the sky. "Selena offered to pick you up. It'll be my husband, Selena, and our dog Barney. All friendly, I promise."

"That's so kind," Jane said, her voice softening. I could tell she was trying to decide if she should accept.

"So, will you join us?" I encouraged. "My husband's a great cook."

"Yes, sure. Thanks, Martina," she said, quietly. "That sounds great. You're so, so nice. It's just... it's a little overwhelming sometimes."

"I understand," I said. "But I don't want you to feel alone. I told you I would help you get through this, and I meant it."

"You've done this before?" Jane asked suddenly, her tone laced with curiosity. "Taken in strangers like this?"

"A few times," I admitted. I could hear the sound of footsteps from the hall, but I stayed focused on our conversation. "I've always protected my clients. Sometimes I've even had them stay at my house if I thought it would help."

"I know I've already said it, but really, thank you."

"You're very welcome," I said, feeling trust growing between us. "I'll let Selena know to pick you up around five. Does that work?"

"Perfect, thanks."

I ended the call and placed the phone on the table, feeling a quiet satisfaction settle over me. As I lifted my gaze, I was startled to see Selena standing in the doorway, watching me silently. She had a knowing look on her face, her arms folded casually across her chest, as if she'd been listening to the whole conversation.

"Was that Jane?" Her dark eyes glinted with curiosity as she leaned against the doorframe. She brushed a strand of her sleek, dark hair behind her ear and glanced at me expectantly. The scratches on her face were not as angry looking as before.

"It was," I said, smiling. "She's agreed to the medical tests, and I told her you'd pick her up at five for dinner."

"What's Dad making for dinner?" Selena said, her usual seriousness giving way to a playful spark.

"He promised lasagna with garlic bread," I said, raising an eyebrow knowingly.

"Yes!" Selena exclaimed, her eyes lighting up. She didn't often show excitement, but food—especially lasagna—was a surefire way to bring out a little joy in her.

"Any luck with the tattoo?" I asked, steering the conversation back to business, though I couldn't help but smile at Selena's enthusiasm. She was in charge of trying to find the tattoo parlor where Jane had her heart tattoo inked. We were hoping to find the artist and see if they remembered Jane and maybe had a record of the transaction or any other details that could lead us to answers about her identity.

"I've been working with Vincent," Selena said, standing a little straighter now. "He's been showing me a couple of tricks on how to find a match online. It's common for tattoo artists to take pictures of their work and post them on social media. He's helping me see if we can find anything online before we start pounding the pavement at every tattoo parlor. But... so far, no matches."

"It's a good start."

"Vincent also said he hasn't had any matches on the necklace yet. He's doing the basics—searching online for jewelers who post photos of their stock to try and match it up."

"Vincent is resourceful and can find almost anything on the internet," I said. "But there's something unique about her necklace. It seemed custom-made, which means it might not be on a website or social media. We might need a different approach."

Selena said, "You're probably right. If it's a custom piece, we won't find it online."

Just then, Selena turned her head, her face lighting up as she waved at someone approaching the doorway. Vincent appeared. With a grin, he raked his fingers through his dirty blond hair that always seemed to be charmingly unkempt.

"Hey, Selena. Hey, boss."

"Hi, Vincent," I said. "We were just talking about the necklace."

"No hits yet," he said. "But I've got an algorithm running to see if we can find any matches from the photograph of Jane's necklace and any photos online. It's kind of like facial recognition but for jewelry. So far, no luck, though."

"Have you thought about talking to a jeweler?" I suggested, watching Vincent with calm patience. "Getting an expert's opinion on the materials or craftsmanship? If it's a custom piece, it may not be online at all."

"That's a good idea," he said decisively, as though adding it to a mental checklist. "If we don't get any hits today, I'll definitely make some calls tomorrow."

"Great."

"Any word back from the sheriff's department about the testing on the cigarette butt or the knife I found at the park?" Selena asked, her voice serious again, but there was an eagerness in her posture. She was sharp, always on top of things. And likely curious to see if her find near the lake bore any fruit.

"Not yet. But I'll let you know as soon as we hear something. I'm meeting with Hirsch and Cromwell tomorrow morning."

"Cool," Selena said, nodding, though a hint of impatience flickered in her eyes.

We chatted about next steps for a few more minutes, exchanging ideas and theories, before Vincent and Selena left to continue their search for the tattoo and necklace.

Meanwhile, I lingered for a moment, glancing down at my notes in preparation for my meeting with Cromwell and Hirsch to discuss the evidence. What Selena and Vincent didn't know yet—what we hadn't told anyone—was that the knife had tested positive for human blood. The lab techs believed there was possibly some material on the hilt of the knife that might give them DNA too. The DNA analysis wasn't complete, but it would be soon.

12

SELENA

Driving down the highway, the tunes were turned up loud, and Jane sat quietly in the passenger seat. I realized I wasn't being much of a conversationalist. With a quick motion, I turned the volume down and glanced over at her.

"How are you holding up?" I asked.

"I'm hanging in there. The therapist is helpful, I think."

"How often will you see her?"

"Three times a week. Is that a lot? I guess I need all the help I can get," she said with a bit of amusement in her voice.

"Trust me, it's not a lot," I reassured her. "It's probably just what you need. When I first started therapy after I was nearly killed and my mom had been murdered, I went three days a week."

Jane's eyes widened slightly. "How did you find a therapist?"

I smirked, remembering the series of events. "Martina. Believe it or not, the first time I ever met her was the day I almost died. My dad had been looking for me, along with some detectives. One of the detectives killed my boyfriend—when he was trying to kill me. Martina was there, at the scene, and that's when we met. I didn't know she was engaged to my dad, who I hadn't seen in years. It's kind of a long story, but anyway, therapy definitely helps. In the beginning, three days a week sometimes felt like a lot, but sometimes it didn't feel like enough."

"Are you still in therapy? Is that too personal to ask?"

Glancing briefly at her before focusing back on the road, I said, "Yeah, I'm still in therapy. I've gone through a lot of trauma. Not only was I nearly killed, but I'm also the one who found my mom's body after she was murdered. I've worked with victims and seen horrific things." I left out the details about how I got my boyfriend Brendon killed. Everyone, including Martina, kept telling me it wasn't my fault he died, but I didn't believe them. I kept pushing and pushing until some dangerous people sent me threats, telling me to stop or else. If I had stopped, Brendon would still be alive, and his parents wouldn't think I was a monster.

Jane was quiet for a moment before asking, "You really think therapy helps?"

"Trust me," I said, the words coming out softly. "I'm not sure I'd be a functioning adult without therapy. I had support from Martina, my dad, and my sister, Zoey. She's back at school now —she was just home for the weekend to get fitted for a wedding dress."

"Oh, you have a sister too?"

"Yeah, she's my stepsister. She's Martina's daughter."

"Martina seems really motherly, very protective."

I chuckled at that. "You don't know the half of it."

"She's very kind," Jane said softly.

"She is."

"What if I told you I'm a little afraid to learn about who I am?" Jane's voice trembled slightly.

"Why do you say that?" I asked, sensing she was starting to open up to me. I hoped she would feel safe enough to continue.

"I've been having these nightmares... and they seem so real, you know? But then, they're the kind that don't really make sense. But somehow, they feel like they do, if that makes any sense."

"Oh, I know exactly what you mean."

Jane continued, "My therapist told me I have PTSD in addition to the dissociative amnesia and that nightmares are pretty common. Even if I can't remember things when I'm awake, my subconscious might. Sometimes, they could be real memories." She hesitated for a moment and then said, "What if I did something bad?"

I looked over at her, offering a reassuring smile. "Trust me when I say this: whoever you are, whoever you were, and whatever you've done, Martina will find out. Trust me on that. But it's never too late to make amends, to start over, or to reevaluate your priorities. What you did in the past doesn't necessarily define your future."

She smiled, though it seemed faint. "How did you get so wise? What are you, twenty-one?"

"Twenty-two, thank you very much," I said with a grin. "I guess trauma ages you."

Jane tittered.

"So, do you ever dream about your child?" I wondered if it was too intrusive.

"No. It's strange, though. How can a mother not remember her own child?"

"I don't know how that happens," I said. "But I'm sure, in time, the answers will come."

Before I could say anything more, we had arrived. "We're here," I said, pulling into the driveway.

Jane stared out the window at the house, her gaze lingering. "Did you grow up here?"

"Nope," I said, shaking my head. "I grew up in apartments. I didn't move in here until after I met Martina. Dad had already moved in with her. This was her house, where Zoey grew up. Zoey's in veterinary school now, and she's getting married next year."

"Oh, wow," Jane said, clearly impressed. "Martina says your dad cooks. Is that normal?"

"Ever since he got sober and met Martina, yeah, it's normal," I explained. "It's a little weird, but hey, people change."

We exited the car, and I noticed Jane trailing behind me, a bit apprehensive. She wasn't afraid, exactly, but there was an eagerness in her steps, like she was anticipating what it would be like to be in someone else's home. Her nightmares, the bad things she hinted at—maybe she had been running from something, and now that something had finally caught up with her. She didn't seem like a bad person, though. I thought that if she'd hurt someone, it was probably in self-defense, and her dreams and memories just hadn't synched up yet.

I put the key in the door and opened it, greeted immediately by Barney, our magnificent, wiggly dog. I knelt down to give him a good scratch behind the ears, but he quickly wriggled away from me and trotted over to sniff Jane.

"That's Barney," I said with a smile. "He was Martina and Zoey's dog, but he's all of ours now. He's getting older, but he's still got plenty of energy left."

Jane smiled, her eyes lighting up as she reached down to pet Barney, who was more than happy to accept the attention. Seeing her like that, genuinely enjoying herself, made me think Barney could be her therapy dog—at least for a little while. He seemed to have a calming effect on her.

I shut the door and led her into the kitchen where Dad and

Martina were standing. Dad leaned casually against the counter while Martina was setting out dinner.

"Hi, Selena," Martina said with a warm smile. Dad waved and gave a little nod.

"This is Jane," I introduced. "Jane, this is my dad, Charlie, and of course, you already know Martina."

They shook hands, and Dad chimed in, "We've got lasagna, garlic bread, iced tea, and bubbly water. Does that sound good?"

"That sounds great," Jane replied.

Martina added, "Can I get you a drink, Jane?"

"I'll just have some water," Jane said.

"Of course," Dad said, before turning around and filling a glass and handing it to Jane.

Our house was a dry one. Not that I drank much, but Zoey liked to have a glass of wine or two when she was home from school. We never kept alcohol in the house. When Zoey was home, we usually went out or met up at my apartment for alcoholic libations.

"Why don't you two hang out in the living room with Barney while we get dinner ready," Martina suggested.

I nodded and led Jane into the living room, where I plopped down on the sofa. Barney hopped right up beside me, then made his way over to Jane, resting his paw on her leg.

"He likes you," I said with a grin.

"He's so cute," Jane replied, scratching Barney behind the ears as he wagged his tail.

"He is, and trust me, it's easy to fall for him. Before you know it, you'll be making homemade dog treats and playing fetch endlessly."

Jane chuckled, clearly taken with the dog. It was the happiest I'd seen her since we met, even though it had only been a few days. I made a mental note to talk to Martina about Jane maybe taking Barney on walks. It could really lift her spirits.

She stopped petting Barney for a moment and looked toward the kitchen, watching Dad and Martina together. "For some reason, it seems unusual to see your dad, a man, in the kitchen," she said thoughtfully.

"Maybe you grew up with a dad who didn't cook," I suggested.

"Maybe," she said softly. "It seems so nice here. Do you still live here?" she asked, looking around the cozy room.

"Not anymore. I have my own apartment now."

"That's really cool. Everyone here seems so educated, smart, and kind. It just feels so... different from what I know."

"If your past doesn't include loving people, once we discover who they are, we'll get rid of them," I said firmly. "Then you can start fresh."

Jane's voice was quiet but hopeful. "I think I'd like that."

The vibe I was getting from her was that she came from a bad place and had probably seen some terrible things. The amnesia, the nightmares, the fact she had no idea where her child was—there was more to her story, and I was certain we were going to find out what it was. And when we did, whoever had hurt her would pay for it, *dearly*.

13

MARTINA

Hirsch was already in the waiting area of the Alameda County Sheriff's Station, standing tall with his sandy gray hair slightly tousled from the breeze outside. His blue eyes, sharp but carrying the weight of years in law enforcement, looked up as I approached. His broad shoulders and solid frame carried the authority of someone who had spent decades solving crimes.

"How's it going?" he asked.

"Okay," I said, sensing that Hirsch, despite his calm demeanor, was already calculating several steps ahead, as usual.

"How's Jane? How's she holding up?" Hirsch leaned forward slightly, with concern in his eyes.

"She's doing all right. Selena is keeping her busy, and we had her over for dinner last night. She seems... guarded," I said, my own voice dropping as I thought about how withdrawn Jane had been.

"Understandable, considering what she's been through," Hirsch said, his expression softening.

"Yeah," I continued. "I've been thinking... I might have a theory about where she's from."

"Really?" Hirsch's eyes narrowed thoughtfully. "You know,

I have a few theories of my own. I have a lot of time to think these days," he said with a hint of self-deprecation in his voice.

"You're not getting bored in your retirement, are you?" I asked with a half-smile, teasing him just a bit.

"Well, I'm not bored yet. But Kim has lovingly suggested I pick up a hobby," he said with a soft laugh, though I caught a trace of wistfulness in his words.

"What are you thinking about doing?" I asked, genuinely curious as I folded my arms and leaned back against the wall.

"I don't know," Hirsch said, rubbing the back of his neck in thought. "I like the idea of solving cases... but, you know, without the paperwork or managing people. Just the case."

Something sparked inside me. I almost couldn't believe it—almost didn't want to say it out loud. "You know," I began carefully, "we do have some freelancers who just take a case every now and then. We get some tough cases."

Hirsch gave me a lopsided grin, one that made him look ten years younger, reminding me of the old days. It was a look I hadn't seen in a long time, and it made me smile wide in return.

"Are you serious? Are you seriously willing to come work with us at Drakos Monroe?" I asked, my excitement bubbling to the surface, barely contained.

"I was thinking about talking to Kim about it," he said. "Not full-time, of course. Just maybe a case here and there. Something interesting—maybe a cold case or a missing person."

"I got you, Hirsch. We *always* have room for you," I said, unable to hide the enthusiasm in my voice. The thought of working with him again after so long was exciting.

"Well, it's not official yet," Hirsch said, his calm demeanor returning as he gave me a small, amused smile. "Let's just focus on the task at hand for now."

That was Hirsch—always the calm, collected one. Even

now, with a hint of something new in the air, he remained grounded, careful, methodical.

But I couldn't help feeling a surge of excitement at the idea of continuing to work with him on a regular basis. It had been so long. I'd always told him that anytime he wanted to work at Drakos Monroe, there was a spot waiting for him. He'd put it off, saying he was law enforcement through and through. But perhaps retirement had changed his mind. And I couldn't be more delighted.

Cromwell approached with a wave. He was a solid, no-nonsense man in his mid-forties, with a square jaw and a perpetual five o'clock shadow that hinted at long shifts and little sleep.

"Hey, how's it going?"

With his deep, gravelly voice, he said, "Pretty good. How about you two?"

"Not too shabby," I said. Hirsch gave a similar sentiment.

"Need anything before we head into the conference room?" He gestured toward the door, his large hand motioning us forward.

"I'm fine, thanks." I shook my head.

"All right then, let's get to it."

I hadn't known Detective Cromwell personally, even though I had worked with the Alameda County Sheriff's Department before. He was an old pal of Hirsch's, someone Hirsch had worked with back when he was at the SFPD. Cromwell had that hardened look that seasoned detectives develop—a kind of quiet, unshakable composure that comes from dealing with too many tragedies.

"So," Cromwell started as we settled into the small, sterile conference room. He sat and said, "Have we made any progress on the identity of Jane Doe?" He leaned back in his chair, folding his arms over his chest.

"No," I said, glancing at Hirsch. "One of my team members, Selena—she's young but sharp—I've had her spend some time with Jane. Jane's also in therapy three days a week, and she's in a safe house. Overall, she's hanging in there, but she's a bit guarded and seems afraid to learn who she is. Jane's been having nightmares and she told Selena she's worried she might have done something bad."

Cromwell's dark eyes narrowed slightly. "I can see why she might think that."

"Oh?" I asked, intrigued by his insight.

"I was told the DNA results from the knife and cigarette would be in any minute now," Cromwell said, sitting up straighter in his chair.

"Yeah?" I asked, my interest piqued.

A knock on the door interrupted us. Cromwell stood up quickly, his wide frame moving with surprising agility. "That might be them now," he said, heading over to the door and opening it with a quick turn of the knob.

A man entered, holding a file under his arm. He was younger, maybe late thirties, with wire-rimmed glasses perched on the bridge of his nose. His dark hair was neatly combed, and he had a serious expression that seemed to suggest he wasn't one for small talk.

"Do you have the results for us?" Cromwell asked.

"Yes," the man replied, his voice confident, like he was already mentally sifting through the data in his head.

Cromwell said, "Well, then let's get started," and introduced us. "Martina, Hirsch, this is Jenson. He's one of our best in the forensics department."

Jenson nodded, then opened the file, his eyes scanning the pages quickly.

He got right to it. "There was DNA recovered from the cigarette. We ran it through CODIS—no hits. However, from my experience—given how many cigarette butts I've processed —the one you brought in didn't seem older than two weeks. I'd actually guess it was fresher, maybe only a couple of days old. It was in pretty good condition." Jenson's voice was calm, analytical, the kind of tone that came from someone used to delivering cold facts. He looked up from the file briefly to gauge our reactions.

"So, probably not related to our victim or the crime scene?" I asked.

"I wouldn't think so," Jenson replied, glancing between us. "But we'll definitely keep it on file just in case. Sometimes, creeps like to go back to the scene of the crime, have a cigarette, and relish what they've done."

"And the knife?" Hirsch asked, his voice calm, though I could tell from his posture that he was just as eager for the results as I was.

We exchanged glances, bracing ourselves for what was coming next.

"There were two contributors on the knife," Jenson explained, his tone steady. "One from the handle—touch DNA from skin cells—and the second contributor was found from blood samples taken from the blade. There wasn't much blood, so it likely wasn't plunged deeply into someone, more of a cut or scrape, but it was definitely in contact with a person."

"Did you run the DNA through the system?" I asked, impatience creeping into my voice, though I knew Jenson was about to get to that.

"Yes, I ran the DNA," Jenson continued, flipping a page in the file. "The DNA from the handle of the knife is a match to your Jane Doe."

Jane had handled the knife. Was she the attacker or simply defending herself?

"And the blood on the blade?" Hirsch asked.

Jenson looked up from the file and said, "We ran it through CODIS. No match, but it was from a female."

Hirsch's blue eyes narrowed as he processed the information. "So, it's possible Jane was fighting off a female attacker?"

Cromwell shrugged, his wide shoulders rising and falling. "Or Jane was attacking a female and they got the better of her. Or someone came along and protected whomever Jane was attacking."

The room fell silent for a moment. Could we have gotten it all wrong? Was it possible that Jane wasn't the victim after all?

14

MARTINA

THE REVELATION about the knife was startling. My mind raced with possibilities, but one thing was clear: I wasn't the only one caught off guard. I could tell by the look on Cromwell's and Hirsch's faces that they were just as surprised as I was. The question was, why? Why hadn't the victim come forward if Jane was the attacker? The more I thought about it, the less it made sense.

I broke the silence. "Is there any evidence pointing to Jane as the attacker? Or perhaps she used the knife in self-defense?" I asked, trying to piece together the puzzle that felt more like scattered fragments than a clear picture.

Cromwell shifted his weight, adjusting his belt—a telltale sign that he was uncomfortable with the direction of the conversation. "Self-defense? Sure, that's why you'd use a knife. But she was in a park—who carries a knife to a park?"

It was a valid question, but my gut told me there was more to this story. Jane didn't strike me as a vicious criminal. She wasn't the type. "What if somebody chased her there? The scene of the crime isn't far from the parking lot. Maybe she was in her car, and when they went after her, she ran. She pulled the knife to protect herself."

Cromwell raised an eyebrow, skeptical. "Why would she have a knife in the car?"

I felt frustration bubbling up inside me. It was the kind of frustration you get when your instincts scream one thing, but you lack the hard evidence to back it up. "I don't know," I admitted, a slight edge to my voice. "Have you ever tried being a woman at night? Maybe it's just something she carried with her, something she thought she might need to protect herself from an attacker. You don't have to be a criminal to feel like you need protection."

Cromwell said nothing, but I could tell he was thinking it over. Still, his skepticism lingered in the air.

Hirsch, who had been quiet the whole time, finally spoke up. He didn't seem entirely convinced either. I could sense that, like me, he didn't believe Jane was some kind of cold-blooded criminal. "Has she agreed to the X-rays?"

"She has," I said. "I plan to take her to the hospital later today for full-body X-rays as well as dental X-rays."

Cromwell said, "So, you're thinking this wasn't the first attack on her? Looking for previous injuries, maybe a pattern?"

"Exactly," I said, nodding. "If those X-rays show she's been a victim before and survived, that could explain why she'd carry a weapon. Maybe this isn't the first time she's had to defend herself. Or maybe the struggle started somewhere else—near the park, or even at a house nearby. Did you canvas the area? Go door-to-door? Ask if anyone heard or saw anything suspicious?"

Cromwell let out a heavy sigh, as if I had asked him to do something unreasonable. "There are a lot of houses surrounding that park. And the park is huge. It would take a lot of time..."

I thought to myself, *That's a no.* I looked him squarely in the eye. "What about the witness? The one who called the police—

did he mention hearing or seeing anything before he found her? Did he ask his neighbors?"

"He said he hadn't heard anything," Cromwell said, the defensiveness creeping back into his tone. "And he lives in the neighborhood across the street from the parking lot."

I wanted to believe Cromwell was on the up and up. He seemed trustworthy enough, and Hirsch had vouched for him. But canvassing the neighborhood should've been standard procedure. I couldn't shake the feeling that something was off here. But, then again, maybe asking the neighbors if they'd seen anything was a bit of a long shot. From what Selena had explained, the park was surrounded by housing, but the homes were far enough away that it was possible no one had seen anything—if the incident had occurred inside the park.

But what if it didn't happen in the park? What if it started elsewhere, closer to those homes? Someone might have seen something—maybe caught a glimpse of Jane or her attacker before she entered the park. And what about doorbell cameras? Nowadays, every other house had one. Why hadn't they checked? Lazy or not enough resources?

"I'll question the man who called it in," I said firmly.

"Be my guest," Cromwell said.

"Martina, you said you had a theory. What is it?" Hirsch asked, his tone calm, ever the diplomat trying to defuse the tension in the room.

I glanced at him, appreciating his measured approach. He was good at this—at getting me to focus when I felt the weight of the case pressing down on my shoulders.

Memories of my time with the CoCo County Sheriff's Department flashed through my mind. We had a solid team back then, one that could be trusted to do their jobs thoroughly. But I knew not every department operated the same way. Crime was everywhere, and some teams simply couldn't keep up with the pace. Corners got cut. Maybe that's what had happened here. Maybe this case was just another file on a pile they had to get through.

I considered letting it go. After all, Jane was alive and stable, and for now, that was what mattered. But I couldn't shake the nagging feeling that there were still too many unanswered questions about the crime itself. I'd need to question the witness, and we'd have to canvas the surrounding neighborhoods. There was no way around it.

"Well," I said, trying to gather my thoughts, "I guess we'll know more after we get dental records for Jane. But considering she has no government-issued ID and nobody's reported her missing—at least not around here—maybe she was living off the grid. Could be she's homeless or far from home. Or maybe she grew up without the means to get a driver's license. It's not a given that everyone has one, despite what we usually assume. Or she could be from somewhere else entirely—someone who slipped through the cracks."

Hirsch said, "We could start by talking to local shelters, see if anyone there has seen her. Are you comfortable sending her picture and story to the media?"

The thought of broadcasting Jane's face, even for the sake of finding out more about her, made me uneasy. It was a delicate balance—protecting her while trying to figure out who she really was. "Not yet," I said. "But if we can't find anyone who recognizes her at the shelters or reports her missing, we'll have to put out a photo eventually."

Hirsch said, "Agreed."

From the corner of the room, Cromwell, who had been listening intently, said, "If you find anything else that could help the case, let me know."

"I will," I said, trying to gauge his level of engagement. "You let us know if you get any hits on the DNA or get any new information about Jane?"

"Of course," he said with a curt nod, his professionalism holding steady, though I wondered how deep his commitment ran. Initially he had visited Jane every day in the hospital, maybe he did care but had a full case load preventing him from investigating more.

Hirsch and I wrapped things up and said our goodbyes. As we walked away, leaving Cromwell behind, I couldn't help but voice my frustration. "They didn't do much investigating, did they?"

Hirsch sighed, rubbing the back of his neck. "Cromwell is good police, but they're drowning in cases, Martina. You know how it is. According to the reports, it's not likely that any of the surrounding homes or apartments witnessed a struggle. And since Jane is fine, physically anyhow, newer crimes that are more likely to be solved take priority."

Maybe, but I wasn't ready to let it go. "The neighbors could've heard something, and if Jane's attack was random, there is a violent predator running around and there will be more victims," I pressed. "If there had been an argument, footsteps, someone running through the neighborhood, it may have been caught on home surveillance—doorbell cameras, security systems—something that might've caught her and her attacker before she entered the park."

Hirsch stopped walking. "You're right, you're right," he said. "We've got to cover every angle. Let's come up with a plan. We'll canvas the neighborhood, talk to local homeless shelters and encampments—the whole nine yards. If someone's missing her in the Bay Area, we'll find out."

"Yes, we will."

As we walked in step, a flicker of something familiar passed between us, a reminder of why we worked so well together. And for the moment, it felt like I had my old partner back.

15

JANE

I TRIED NOT to act nervous as I smiled at Martina, who stood at my door. She had come to pick me up to take me to the hospital for X-rays, and from there, we would go to the dentist's office. The idea of going to the hospital and meetings with investigators felt so foreign, as if I were living someone else's life. And my mind felt foggy, disconnected from the present. Everything was a blur except for one thing: Martina. I could see it in her eyes—determination, compassion, and that unspoken promise that she wouldn't stop until she learned who I was and what had happened that night at the park. She seemed so relentless and that gave me a sense of comfort. Someone was looking for the truth, and maybe, just maybe, that truth would set me free.

But the idea of the truth terrified me.

I'd had another nightmare—vivid, with blood on my hands. A baby. A woman's scream. And a horrible, suffocating sense of dread that left me gasping for breath in the dark. The images were so sharp they could have been memories. Could they be? Should I tell Martina what I saw? Would it help with the investigation, or would it only make things worse? I wanted to help, right? Yes, of course, I did.

It was time.

I had come to terms with it, at least on some level. If I had done something bad, I had to face it. I had to admit it. No more running, no more hiding. It was time.

"Hi, Martina." I said quietly.

"Hi, Jane. Are you ready to go?" she asked with a gentle smile.

"Yes," I said, tugging at the hem of my jeans. I hadn't realized how tight my grip had been on the fabric, twisting it nervously in my fingers.

"Did you get those when you went shopping with Selena?" Martina asked, her eyes flicking to my outfit.

I grabbed my bag from the hook near the door, trying to ignore the lump forming in my throat. "Yeah," I said, managing a small smile. "She said I needed something other than slacks. Something about old people wearing them." I tried to laugh, but it came out awkwardly.

Martina smirked, a sparkle in her eye that I hadn't noticed before. She was fond of her stepdaughter; it was obvious. In some ways, they were similar—both strong, both quick-witted. But in others, they were as different as night and day. Martina was steady, calm, and confident. Selena? She had a fire in her, a wildness that I admired.

"Okay, I'm ready now," I said, pulling the bag over my shoulder and stepping outside, shutting the door behind me.

The cool air hit me, grounding me for a moment. For a fleeting second, I thought about what it would be like if this were a normal day—just another routine appointment, just another errand. But nothing about my life felt routine or normal. We walked down the path in silence, the sound of our footsteps echoing. The apartment complex was quiet, almost eerily so.

Martina moved with the same quiet efficiency she always

did. Once we reached the parking lot, she opened the passenger door of her car for me like it was second nature. I hesitated for a moment, looking at her. She made me feel as though she was my own private bodyguard, always watching, always ready to protect.

I climbed into the car, sinking into the seat. Even though I had only known Martina and her family for a few days, I couldn't help but think of them as something close to family. They were pretty much all I had at this point. The thought was bittersweet, filling me with both comfort and a sharp sense of loneliness.

Martina slid into the driver's seat and glanced at me as she started the engine. "How's your day been so far?" she asked, her tone casual, but I could sense the underlying concern.

"It's all right. I had breakfast and watched a little TV." I forced a smile, hoping it would be enough to convince her. But who was I kidding? Martina had become an expert at reading me in the short time we had known each other. She always knew when something was off.

She gave me a quick side glance, her eyes sharp. "More nightmares?"

Unable to meet her gaze, I mumbled, "Yeah."

"Anything you want to talk about?"

I shook my head. It didn't feel like the right time to tell her what I saw in my dreams—not yet. I would when I was ready, not anxious about the doctor's visits. And how could I put those horrible images into words? The baby's cry, the blood, the suffocating feeling of guilt. "Any new developments with the case?" I asked instead, eager to shift the conversation away from myself. I needed to focus on something else—anything else.

Martina drove quietly for a few moments, her hands steady on the wheel. I could hear the faint hum of the engine, the rhythmic sound of the tires rolling along the road. Finally, she spoke. "Yes, there has been a development."

I tensed, bracing myself. What now?

"They tested the knife Selena found at the park," she said, glancing at me again. "There was blood on it, but it didn't belong to you. But your DNA was on the handle. They think you stabbed, or tried to stab, someone."

Her words sent a wave of nausea rolling through me, my stomach twisting painfully. The images from my nightmares flashed before my eyes—the blood on my hands, the sickening feeling of dread, the fear that I had done something unforgivable. *The knife.*

As she continued and tried to reassure me that this development didn't mean I was guilty of anything, I couldn't help but interrupt her, my voice trembling. "If I did do something... you'll find out, right?"

Martina's expression was neutral and difficult to decipher. "We will find the truth. Who you are, what happened to you, and how you ended up in the park that day."

I swallowed hard, my mouth dry. In my nightmares, I felt responsible for something terrible, but I was also filled with a deep, gnawing fear. "If I hurt someone... will I go to jail?" The words came out hesitantly. My mind rapid-fired questions at me. *Is that what happened? Did I try to hurt someone, and they attacked me to protect themselves? Am I... am I a terrible person?*

Martina's eyes softened as she looked at me. "Let's not worry about that today," she said. "For now, we're still going to assume that you're potentially in danger. We'll keep you in the safe house. We're not putting your picture on the news just yet. We'll keep looking for people who might know you or what happened to you. Don't worry."

She placed her hand on top of mine, a small gesture, but it

felt like an anchor in the storm of uncertainty I was drowning in.

For that moment, I believed her. I believed that Martina would find the truth, and I believed she would do her best to protect me—from whoever had hurt me. But deep down, the fear lingered. What if the truth wasn't something I wanted to face? What if the person I had been wasn't worth saving?

16

MARTINA

INSIDE A LOCAL COFFEE shop in Fremont, near the park where Jane was attacked, I spotted Hirsch sitting at a table with a big mug of coffee. I waved as I approached.

"Hey. What do you have there?" I asked, sliding into the seat across from him.

"Vanilla latte," he said, taking a sip.

"Is it good?"

"It is." Above Hirsch hung a display wall filled with mugs for sale—various kinds. Some featured cartoon characters, others nostalgic floral patterns, birds, and animals. There were some really interesting ones; if I were a mug collector, I might have been tempted to buy one.

I stood and headed toward the register, passing a display of decadent dessert options alongside breakfast treats. After a quick scan of the menu, I ordered my usual—black coffee—which they promptly provided with a smile. Coffee in hand, I returned to the table with Hirsch.

"How's it going?" I asked, feeling a small surge of excitement. I couldn't help it—meeting with Hirsch and working on a case together felt like old times. When I told Charlie the night before that Hirsch was considering working part-time at Drakos Monroe, he said he hadn't seen me look so elated since our wedding day.

But my happiness wasn't all about working with Hirsch. I think it had to do with how much in my life was changing too. With Zoey, my girl, getting married, the future was bright with possibilities. I'd *sort of* accepted she was a grown up and not likely to ever live at home with us again since she and her fiancé wanted to buy a home once she finished veterinary school. And maybe soon after, grandchildren? There were so many things to look forward to. I was truly blessed.

"Kim said she's glad to have me out of the house," Hirsch commented, pulling me out of my thoughts.

I smiled. "What does Audrey think about you working again?"

"She says it's about time I get a hobby," he said with a dry laugh.

"Pre-teens," I said, shaking my head knowingly. "She's at a fun age."

"Twelve going on twenty-five," he muttered, running a hand through his hair and pointing to a thick patch of silver. "This is just from this year. I call it the 'preteen gray.'"

I laughed. "You'll get through it."

"I will. She's still sweet most of the time," he said.

My thoughts drifted to Zoey at that age, with all her sass and sparkle. She hadn't changed much, not really. Even with all the changes in her life, she'd always be my girl. She had even told me she wasn't changing her name after the wedding. She'd always dreamed of becoming Dr. Zoey Monroe and told me she would fulfill that dream.

"Are you familiar with Fremont?" I asked, steering the conversation back to the case.

"I don't usually come out here, but I did a quick drive

around Quarry Lakes and the surrounding neighborhoods. There's a lot of ground to cover."

Setting my coffee down, I said, "I spoke with the witness on the phone. He says he doesn't have anything new to add from his original statement, but I think we can try to jog his memory. I told him we'd stop by before we go door-to-door in his neighborhood."

"I've got my comfortable shoes on," Hirsch said with a grin.

"Good," I said, teasing.

We chatted for a while longer about the area we planned to cover today. We both wondered whether we should bring in some more team members to help us out. We had mapped the area beforehand, and there were quite a few homes to check. Given it was a weekday, there might not be many people home, but we could at least try to see if any houses near the park had external surveillance cameras.

We finished our coffee and drove in our separate cars to the first parking lot, the one close to where Jane had been attacked and was later found by the witness and his dog.

Parked, I stepped out and surveyed the area. I couldn't help but think how unexpected it was for something so awful to happen in such a beautiful place. The tranquility of the park didn't match the violent scene that had played out here.

Jogging up next to me, Hirsch said, "You wanna walk the scene first?"

I nodded in agreement, and we headed toward the path that led into the park. I had studied the map beforehand, so I knew where we were headed. We carefully made our way down a small hill that sloped toward the first lake. The path was narrow and shaded, with tall trees casting cool shadows on the ground.

I glanced up the hill as we walked. If someone was passing by on the path, you'd see them, but from there, you wouldn't be able to see the shore of the lake—it was tucked away, private.

We approached a thick cluster of bushes, and I stopped, pointing toward them.

"That's where she was found," I said, my voice low, "and where Selena crawled under to find the knife."

We both stood there for a moment, staring at the quiet lake. It was hard to imagine such violence happening in a place like that. The water shimmered peacefully.

"I can see how it happened," I said, thinking aloud. "She could've been running through the parking lot, trying to get away from her attacker. Maybe they chased her down here. She was secluded, and he overpowered her and then just left her there. But I don't think this is where the fight started."

Hirsch's face was serious as he surveyed the area. "That was my thought exactly," he said, pulling out his phone to take a few pictures of the scene.

I took a few photos as well, documenting the path and the layout of the bushes. The quiet of the park felt heavy now, the weight of what had happened lingering in the air. After a few moments, I turned and made my way back up the hill, Hirsch following close behind.

Once we reached the top, we headed down the street toward where the witness lived, ready to see if he could recall any more details that might help us piece together what had really happened that day.

We crossed the two lanes of traffic and walked into the first housing development. The homes were decent-sized, most with two-car garages, well-kept yards, and an air of affluence. From what I had read about Fremont, the city was home to many tech workers—high-tech industry professionals commuting to Silicon Valley. That certainly explained the wealth on display there.

We knocked on the door of the witness, and I heard barking from the other side, a yap that reminded me of my own dog, Barney. According to the police report, the witness had a small white fluffy dog, and sure enough, when the door opened, a large man stood there holding exactly that—a fluffy little dog.

"Hello," he greeted us warmly.

I introduced myself and Hirsch. "We're with the investigation team looking into the attack on Jane Doe. We spoke on the phone."

"Oh yes, please come in," the man said, stepping aside to let us in.

The house was nice but slightly outdated, and the man himself was older, likely retired. He offered us coffee or tea, but we declined. He set the little dog down, and instinctively, I put out my hand to pet the pup.

"That's Snowman," the man said with a smile.

I grinned at him. "I've got a little black fluffy one at home. His name is Barney. They look pretty similar except the color."

"Does Barney yap like Snowman?" he asked, grinning.

"A lot of the time, he does," I admitted, sharing a smile.

The old man sat down, looking a little more serious now. "So, what can I help you with? Any luck finding out what happened to that poor girl?"

"No, actually, we haven't been able to identify her or her attacker," I said, leaning forward. "We were hoping to talk to you, to see if you'd heard or seen anything unusual in the days before or after the attack. Maybe something suspicious, something that could be connected?"

He shook his head. "Not really, no. It's a pretty quiet area, to be honest. But if you head down the road to Union City, about a mile away, well, that's a different story. There's a lot more crime down there. It's almost literally on the other side of the tracks, if you know what I mean."

"Maybe we should check down there next."

"I'm guessing a lot of your neighbors have security cameras," Hirsch added. "Do you?"

The old man said, "I don't have any cameras. But you're right that quite a few neighbors do. I've been here a long time, and we don't get much crime in this area. Break-ins every now and then, sure, but violent crime? Hardly ever."

"Did you mention to your neighbors that you found the woman?" I asked.

"I talked to a few, but nobody saw anything either," he said. "It was early in the morning, and most people around here are on their way to work, not paying attention. Folks aren't out for leisurely walks at that hour. Mostly just Snowman and me."

"We're planning on going door-to-door, seeing if anyone would share surveillance footage or might've seen something," I said, hoping for a lead.

He said, "It couldn't hurt. I wish I could help more, but I didn't notice anything unusual that day or the night before."

"We appreciate your time," Hirsch said, standing up to leave.

"Is the girl doing all right?" the man asked.

"We have her safe for now," I said, "but she doesn't remember anything about her past. She's a bit out of sorts."

The man sighed. "Well, I hope you find out what happened to her. I'll be praying for her."

We thanked him and said our goodbyes, heading to the next-door neighbor. After a brief questioning there, we moved on to more houses in the development. Unfortunately, many people weren't home, and the ones who were didn't have any cameras or useful information. A few shared camera footage, but all we viewed was darkened streets and no activity.

We left notes on the doors of houses with visible surveillance systems, hoping someone might reach out and let us view their footage from the night before or the morning of the attack.

After two hours of canvassing, it became clear that the

police's assessment was right—there wasn't much to find here. We had only gone through about a quarter of the homes, but I could tell we weren't going to get much more.

As we stood at the edge of the development, Hirsch looked down the road and said, "Maybe it's not the street we need to focus on. The witness said there's more criminal activity in Union City, it might be worth checking out. It's only a mile or two down the road."

"That's what I was thinking. Let's hop in the car and start asking questions down there."

"Are you armed?"

With a smile, I said, "Always."

17

SELENA

AFTER AN EXHAUSTIVE ONLINE SEARCH, I didn't find a picture of Jane's tattoo on any of the local tattoo artists' websites, nor on the ones from surrounding states or on social media. Each new page or profile I scoured only added to the sense of futility. The deeper I dove, the more I realized just how many places someone could go for a tattoo. They could go to a small, out-of-the-way shop that didn't bother with flashy websites or an Instagram page. It was beginning to seem like I was looking for a needle in a haystack.

I decided to investigate in the real world and go to one of my favorite tattoo shops, hoping the artists there could give me a lead. Maybe they could assess how old Jane's tattoo was or knew the artist who had done it. Tattoo artists have distinct styles, signatures in their work—some even use specific shading techniques or tools. It was a long shot, but I was hoping today would bring me closer to something useful.

As I pushed open the door to the parlor, a wave of familiarity washed over me. The smell of antiseptic mingled with incense, a mix I'd always found oddly comforting. I passed by the glass cases filled with smoking accessories and knick-knacks that seemed to change every time I visited. The buzz of tattoo guns hummed softly in the background, punctuated by occasional laughter from the back rooms. The air was thick with the kind of laid-back energy you'd expect from a place where art and lifestyle blended seamlessly.

A man with large gauged earrings and tattoo sleeves covering both arms waved at me from behind the counter. He was bald and heavyset, and his smile was familiar. "Hey, Selena! How's it going? I didn't see you on the appointment log."

"Hey, Dwayne. Actually, I'm not here about me," I said, offering a small smile. "I was hoping maybe you could help me with something."

"Oh?" His eyes lit up with curiosity, his interest immediately piqued. Dwayne Keller was the artist who had given me my first tattoo, and we'd hit it off immediately. Despite his tough looking exterior, Dwayne was a sweetheart.

I pulled out the photo of Jane's tattoo from my bag and laid it on the counter. "This is a tattoo from an unidentified person we're hoping to identify," I explained, watching him closely as he picked up the photograph.

Dwayne shook his head. "Haven't seen it before. But it's not particularly unusual either. Hey, Christian, come here for a sec."

Christian, one of the other artists, joined Dwayne behind the counter, and I explained the situation. Christian leaned in to take a look at the photo. He studied the picture with the same intensity he probably applied to his own designs, holding it up to the light as if it would reveal hidden details under the right angle. His face scrunched in concentration.

"Not particularly detailed. It's a simple design," he murmured after a moment, his voice thoughtful as he continued to examine the tattoo.

Maybe I should have brought Jane in. Seeing the parlor,

hearing the hum of the machines, smelling the ink—any of it might have triggered a memory for her.

"Can you tell me anything about the tattoo, other than that it's not very unusual or detailed?" I asked, hoping for any new scrap of insight.

Christian glanced up from the photo and met my eyes. "Well, it'd be better if I could see the person who has the tattoo," he said, his tone cautious. "But if you say she's an unidentified person, does that mean she's... dead?"

"I can't get into that," I said, trying to keep my voice even, professional. "What can you tell me from the photo alone?"

After a puzzled look, he said, "Hmm." Christian scrutinized the image once more, squinting at the edges of the lines. "Three interlocking hearts. Pretty simple design. It's not the most precise. I wouldn't be surprised if this wasn't done in a regular tattoo parlor—probably someone who bought a kit online and did it themselves. An amateur."

Great, that would get us absolutely nowhere. A homemade tattoo? It was like chasing a shadow, no trail to follow.

"Did you check online to see if there's any photos from local tattoo parlors?" Christian asked.

"I did," I said, feeling the frustration starting to bubble beneath the surface again.

"Honestly, my bet is you're not gonna find it online either," he said with a shrug, his words adding to the sinking feeling in my stomach. "The more I look at it, the more I think it was from an amateur—homemade. Not by someone with a lot of skill."

"Thanks," I muttered, trying to mask the disappointment that was crawling up my throat. A homemade tattoo—just one more obstacle in an already impossible case. As if identifying someone with no memory and no past wasn't hard enough, now we had a DIY tattoo to contend with.

"Sounds like that's not very helpful?" Christian asked as if he could sense the frustration radiating off me.

"It's not unhelpful," I said, trying to sound upbeat. "At least it tells me I can stop searching online." It wasn't a complete loss, I reasoned with myself. It was one less blind alley to wander down, even if I felt no closer to the truth.

"I appreciate it," I added.

"Since you're here, you need any work done?" Dwayne offered, his smile returning.

"Not today, but thanks, Dwayne. Thanks, Christian."

"You take it easy, Selena," Dwayne called after me as I walked toward the door.

I pushed open the door and stepped out into the late afternoon sun, the light almost too bright after the dim interior of the parlor. I sighed deeply, the sound loud in the relative quiet of the street. Another dead end. Another lead that evaporated the moment I tried to hold onto it. *Frustrating.*

Maybe Martina would have better luck with the medical records for learning more about Jane's past or finding a witness who had seen Jane the morning she was attacked. I pulled out my phone and called her to let her know what I'd found, though the update wasn't exactly promising. She didn't answer, and I wondered if she was busy. She'd mentioned earlier that she was going to question people in the area near the park where Jane had been found. Maybe she and Hirsch were talking to someone who might have seen something. I left her a voicemail with the details and let her know she didn't need to call back right away.

Now what? I thought to myself, staring at the screen as I slipped my phone back into my pocket.

I decided to go see Jane. Maybe take her out driving in the area surrounding where she was found, to see if anything looked familiar that could jog her memories. After we could grab dinner.

If the tattoo wasn't going to lead us anywhere, maybe the answers were buried in her memory, locked behind the nightmares she'd been having. Maybe she'd remember something— anything that could point us in the right direction. Perhaps we could solve this mystery the old-fashioned way—by getting her to remember who she was.

18

—————

MARTINA

WE THANKED THE MAN, and he shut the door with a soft click. The air outside was cooler now, a subtle breeze tugging at the edge of my jacket as we made our way down the narrow path toward the sidewalk. Hirsch walked beside me, his eyes darting from one house to the next, as if searching for something out of place, the only sound a buzzing, a notification that I'd received a voicemail.

"Who was that?" Hirsch finally asked, breaking the stillness and glancing at me out of the corner of his eye.

I'd received a call while we were talking to the last witness but let it go to voicemail. "It was Selena," I said, reaching into my pocket for my phone. "She left a message. Let me listen."

I tapped play, and Selena's voice crackled through the small speaker. "Hi, Martina, it's Selena. Not an emergency. I just talked to the tattoo parlor. They think it's probably a homemade tattoo, so kind of a dead end for us. Anyhow, I'm going to stop by Jane's, take her for dinner. Good luck."

I let out a quiet sigh as I slipped my phone back into my pocket. Another lead turned cold. I turned to Hirsch, trying not to let the frustration show. "Looks like the tattoo lead didn't go anywhere. Likely homemade."

Hirsch furrowed his brow, his face unreadable as usual. "Interesting," he muttered.

I agreed as I glanced down the street at the rows of houses, each one a little more run-down than the last. Union City had a rough edge to it, the kind of place where you had to keep your guard up. The witness, Edward, had been right—this neighborhood was definitely on the sketchy side. The houses were in need of repairs, and yards were mostly filled with weeds and broken-down vehicles. There weren't many doorbell or other surveillance cameras that I could see. And my guess was that it wasn't the type of neighborhood where people liked to talk to the police or those who worked with them.

Even though we weren't official law enforcement, the way Hirsch carried himself left no room for doubt. His posture, the way he surveyed every inch of the street like a hawk scanning for prey—it all screamed cop.

"So," I began, trying to shift the conversation away from the dead ends we were running into, "are you really serious about working part-time with us?"

"I am," Hirsch said, his voice steady, though his eyes were still busy taking in the neighborhood. "Why? Did you talk to Stavros?"

"Not yet. But I know he won't have an issue with it." Stavros had been stepping back from management of the firm lately, spending more time with his family, especially his grandkids. He liked to joke that he was getting too old for the job, ready to pass the baton to the younger generation. But beneath the humor, I knew there was truth—he wasn't the same energetic guy he'd once been, and the years had started to show.

"I appreciate that," Hirsch said. "I'll talk it over with Kim after this is all over."

"Okay," I said, nodding as we continued down the street. As we approached the next house, I noticed something at the corner of the roof. My eyes immediately locked onto the small, boxy shape of a security camera mounted just above the door. The faint red light blinked steadily, and I felt a flicker of hope. Maybe, just maybe, this could be the break we needed.

"They've got surveillance," I pointed out, tilting my head toward the camera.

Hirsch followed my gaze, his expression focused. "Let's see if they're willing to help," he said, his voice low as we made our way up the path.

I knocked three times, the sound dull against the wooden door, and instinctively took a step back. It was an old habit—giving space, letting whoever was inside feel less threatened by the unexpected visitors on their doorstep—and keeping myself safe.

A few moments later, the door creaked open, and a woman in her late twenties appeared in the doorway. She had dark hair that fell loosely around her shoulders, framing a pair of deep brown eyes that flicked between Hirsch and me, as if sizing us up. She wore a black sweatshirt and matching joggers.

"Can I help you?" she asked, her voice cautious, the tone of someone used to keeping strangers at arm's length.

I gave her a small, reassuring smile, hoping to ease some of the tension. "I'm Martina Monroe, and this is August Hirsch. We're here investigating an assault, and we're hoping to see if anyone saw or heard anything on the night of Saturday, August 23—maybe early into Sunday morning. It would've involved a woman. Did you notice anything unusual during that time?" I kept my voice casual.

The woman's expression shifted slightly. She hesitated, her eyes lingering on us, clearly uncomfortable. "I don't remember anything from that night. I was probably asleep," she said, the words clipped, as if she wanted to end the conversation before it even began.

I could feel Hirsch watching her closely, picking up on the same unease I was. Something wasn't adding up. I glanced upward at the security camera mounted just above the door. "I noticed you have cameras," I said, gesturing toward them. "Would you mind if we took a look at the footage from that night? It might have picked up something relevant."

She followed my gaze, almost as if she hadn't realized the cameras were there. "You're not cops?"

"No. Just a couple of private investigators."

She eyed me. "Those are just for show. The don't work anymore," she said quickly. A little too quickly. Her hand moved to tug at the hem of her sweatshirt, and she shifted her weight awkwardly. The avoidance in her eyes was hard to miss now, and a prick of suspicion crawled up my spine.

The red light on one of the cameras blinked steadily, and while it could have been fake, something about the way she reacted didn't sit right with me.

Before I could press her further, footsteps echoed from inside the house, and I glanced over her shoulder. A man appeared at the top of the stairs, making his way toward us with slow, deliberate steps. He was fit, with dark hair and sharp features, probably in his early thirties. He had a large snake tattoo on the tan skin of his forearm. His eyes, much like hers, were dark and calculating. "What's going on?" he asked, his tone flat.

"These are investigators," the woman said quickly, her body shifting slightly in the doorway, almost as if she was trying to block him from stepping too close to us. "They're just asking if we saw anything unusual two weeks ago, on Saturday night or Sunday morning."

The man barely blinked. "Sorry, no. We were probably

asleep," he said with certainty. Too certain for my taste. He didn't even take a moment to think about it. No hesitation, no curiosity about what we were asking. Just a swift dismissal.

I tried again, hoping something might stir their memory—or their conscience. "It would've been two weeks ago. A young woman, maybe running away from someone. Or perhaps you heard an argument?"

His expression didn't change. "Like I said, we were probably sleeping," he repeated, the tone just a bit firmer now, as if he wanted to close the door on the entire conversation.

Hirsch's eyes flickered toward the security cameras again, and he was about to speak when the man said, "We already erased the footage. We only keep it for twenty-four hours."

I raised my brows. The woman said, "No, don't you remember they're not working anymore? They broke last month."

Their stories conflicted.

"Oh, right," the man said, his face tightening for a brief moment before relaxing into a casual expression again. "They're not working. I forgot. She usually manages that stuff."

It was clear we weren't going to get any useful information out of them. Whether it was fear, distrust, or something else, they weren't going to cooperate, and pressing further would probably only make them shut down completely. The man said, "We really have things to do. If you have no other questions."

Not wanting to push our luck, I said, "Well, if you remember anything, let me leave you my card." I pulled out a business card and handed it to him.

He took it without saying anything, and closed the door rather quickly, with a metal clink following after. Likely the sound of the lock clicking. Message received: *Go away.*

As we walked away, I couldn't shake the feeling that they were hiding something. But for now, we had no way to prove it.

I made a note to look up who owned the home and see if they had a reason to be withholding information. It was possible they were involved in something criminal completely unrelated to Jane's case.

Hirsch and I walked back down the sidewalk in silence, the faint sounds of the city around us—cars in the distance, the occasional bark of a dog.

"Not very friendly, huh?" Hirsch said.

"Nope," I agreed. "But we haven't had much luck around here." My voice trailed off as I thought back to the countless doors we had knocked on, the hesitant eyes that peered out at us, the excuses and blank stares. It was as if no one wanted to remember, or worse, no one cared. I shoved my hands into my pockets, feeling exhaustion settling in.

"All right, let's keep going for a bit longer, see if we can find anything," I said, though I wasn't sure if I believed my own words. We had been at this for hours, but hope was a stubborn thing, and it hadn't left me completely. Not yet.

"You got it," Hirsch said, though the edge of weariness in his voice matched mine. "After this, though, we need to grab something to eat. We've been going for quite a while."

I managed a small smile, the hint of humor lightening the tension just a little. "I've got protein bars," I offered, knowing there was no way he'd want one.

Hirsch shot me a look, one eyebrow raised in mock disdain. "Yeah, no thanks."

"One more hour," I negotiated, glancing at my watch. Time was slipping away, and I wasn't ready to call it quits just yet.

"We could always split up," Hirsch suggested, his tone suddenly more serious.

"Good thinking. We can cover more ground. We'll stay close. Buddy system."

"Let's do it."

An hour later, we stood next to our cars, both of us empty-handed, though a few people had promised to email us surveillance footage—promises that rarely amounted to anything. Most folks were pretty sure they hadn't seen anything, anyway. It was possible Jane had never been in the area.

Just then, my phone buzzed, the sudden noise startling me out of my thoughts. I fumbled for it and glanced at the screen. My heart skipped a beat—it was the Medical Examiner's office.

A knot tightened in my chest. They had promised to call after reviewing Jane's X-rays and dental records from the day before.

What had they found?

19

MARTINA

WITH A SENSE OF ANTICIPATION, I picked up the phone, a tightness forming in my chest. "This is Martina Monroe," I said, my voice calm but my mind already racing.

"Hi, Martina, it's Dr. Ellison, the Medical Examiner in Alameda County," came the voice on the other end.

I straightened my posture, gripping the phone a little tighter. "Yes, hello, Dr. Ellison. It's nice to hear from you. I'm assuming this is about Jane Doe?"

"Yes," Dr. Ellison said. "My team ran a search for matching dental records, but there were no matches. Looking at the X-rays and the fact that we can't find a match in the system, it's likely she's never had much dental work done—and likely never had X-rays done."

I felt a knot form in my stomach. No dental records? That's unusual. My mind began to churn, trying to make sense of it. What could that mean for who she was—or who she wasn't? I said, "In your experience, what does it usually indicate when someone's never had dental work or X-rays done?"

"Well," Dr. Ellison said after a pause, "it could mean she grew up without dental insurance, and her parents never took her to the dentist. Or it could also mean if she's had any dental work done it was in another country, outside of our system. Or" —she hesitated for a moment—"she may be from a community that didn't believe in modern medicine."

Her words hung in the air, wrapping around my growing suspicion that seemed to align with what I was already beginning to suspect—that Jane Doe wasn't part of the usual system. She might have lived off the grid, or maybe she came from a family that couldn't afford regular dental care. Both possibilities painted a picture of a life lived in the margins, where even something as basic as dental visits could have been out of reach.

Going to the dentist wasn't cheap, even with insurance. It was another clue, pointing to a life where the routine things so many people took for granted—healthcare, identification, a paper trail—just weren't part of her world.

"How about the full-body X-rays?" I asked, feeling my pulse quicken. "Anything noteworthy there?"

"Yes," Dr. Ellison replied, her voice shifting, taking on a more somber tone. "She's had a few broken bones, some of which didn't set properly. They likely weren't treated the way they should have been. One, in particular, was a spiral fracture —usually caused by a twisting force, like someone forcibly twisting an arm. It's the kind of injury we often associate with abuse."

"What else can you tell us about these injuries?" I asked. "Based on your experience?"

"Usually," she began, seeming to choose her words carefully, "these kinds of injuries suggest sustained physical abuse over a period of years. And from what I can see, she wasn't taken to a doctor to have them treated properly. It's as if whoever was responsible didn't want anyone asking questions. Or, again, didn't believe in modern medicine."

I let that sink in, feeling the bitter taste of anger rise in my throat. Sustained abuse. Years of it. Jane Doe had been trapped in someone's control, isolated, and denied even the most basic care. It was what I had feared from the beginning. Jane Doe hadn't just been a victim of one horrific act of violence. Her body told the story of repeated trauma, of someone who had endured far more than anyone ever should.

"Can you tell how old the injuries are?" I asked.

"I would say some of them are more than five or ten years old," Dr. Ellison said. "But I'd estimate that the majority of them happened over the last three years."

Three years. That detail hit me hard. It pointed to something more recent, possibly tied to her adult life. Maybe the father of her baby. I couldn't shake the gnawing feeling that whoever had done this to her was still out there—a continued threat to her and likely to others too.

"Is there anything else the X-rays can tell us?" The details might be bleak, but they might just help us find the person behind them.

"No, I'm afraid not. I wish I could have been of more help," Dr. Ellison said.

"You've been very helpful," I said, grateful for what she had shared. "Thank you, Dr. Ellison."

"Any time. Let me know if you need anything else."

"Thanks," I said, before hanging up the phone. The silence that followed felt heavy, but I didn't let it linger. I turned to Hirsch, the tension still buzzing beneath my skin.

I explained everything Dr. Ellison had told me—the broken bones and the years of abuse. Hirsch listened, his expression unreadable, but I knew he understood the gravity of what we were dealing with. Jane Doe wasn't just a victim of circumstance. She had been someone's target for far too long.

And now, we had to find out who that someone was.

"What are you thinking, Martina?" Hirsch asked, clearly sensing the wheels turning in my head.

I exhaled slowly, organizing the fragments of information swirling around. "Well, here's what we know so far," I began, mentally stacking the facts into some semblance of order. "Nobody's reported her missing. She's never had any dental care or X-rays. Likely no professional medical care. No government-issued driver's license or ID. And that tattoo—it's homemade."

The more I pieced it together, the more this woman's life seemed to slip further from any framework I could relate to. How did someone exist in modern society without leaving a trace? "Considering the injuries were never treated at a hospital, I'm guessing Jane wasn't living amongst general society."

"No?"

"At first, I thought it was possible she came from a family without a lot of money—maybe they couldn't afford medical care, which could still be true. But even in child abuse situations, when injuries get bad enough, someone usually rushes the kids to the hospital. They still have to go to school, and that's when people—teachers, neighbors—start asking questions." I paused before continuing my train of thought. "But nobody's come forward. Not before and not now." I felt my throat tighten. "Maybe nobody reported her missing because her family or friends or partner doesn't trust law enforcement."

"That would make sense."

As I thought it over, a realization hit me like a cold splash of water. "The typical high-tech methods we're using to try to identify her—dental records, X-rays, a driver's license—it's not going to work in this case, is it?" I looked at Hirsch, hoping against hope for a different answer.

"I think you're right."

"How do you find someone who has no digital footprint, no

medical records, no state-issued ID, and no one looking for them?" I asked, more to myself than to him. It was like trying to chase a ghost—someone who, by all modern standards, didn't exist.

Hirsch leaned back against his car, arms crossed. "I guess we have to do it the old-fashioned way."

He was right. There would be no shortcuts here. No quick digital traces to follow, no instant hits in a database. This was going to take legwork—grit, persistence, and a heck of a lot of digging through layers of anonymity. Jane Doe hadn't just fallen off the grid; it was possible she had never even been on it.

20

SELENA

AFTER DRIVING around the Bay Area to see if Jane recognized any buildings or the area, we stopped off at a small cafe in Hayward. She had said nothing looked familiar, but I sensed there was something different about Jane, like something was off. Had she remembered something new and hadn't told me? She'd been pretty quiet most of the day. Maybe the memories resurfaced during her therapy session, or perhaps it was another nightmare. I grabbed a piece of sourdough bread from the basket and asked, "How are you sleeping?"

Jane frowned. "Nightmares. Lots of waking up in a cold sweat."

That sucked. At least she was comfortable telling me. "I'm sorry to hear that."

She shrugged, as if resigned to being tortured by her dreams.

"Are you seeing anything different in your dreams? You said before that you had seen a woman and a baby. Anything new?"

She was quiet for a moment, then said, "I saw the knife."

I dropped the bread onto the plate, startled. "The knife? Like the one we found at the lake?"

Jane nodded slowly.

"What was the knife doing in your nightmare?" It was a knife, so it couldn't do anything without a person using it.

"I was holding it," she whispered, her hands fidgeting in her lap.

"Holding it?" I repeated.

"It was blurry, but... I think they were trying to get me," she said, her expression troubled. "I've been so concerned, thinking maybe I did something wrong. But I think they were trying to get me, and that's why I had the knife."

"Self-defense," I stated matter-of-factly, trying to reassure her.

"I think so," she murmured, as though unsure.

That was at least some good news. Maybe she was the victim. Martina had suspected as much, and she was rarely wrong. *If ever.* "Did you see who it was?"

She shook her head. "But I saw the baby again. It was in a crib. Just lying there."

Even if the images didn't make sense on their own, perhaps we could piece her life together by the images her subconscious was showing her. "How old is the baby in your dreams?"

"I don't know," Jane said with a frown. "Not quite an infant, but not much older. Not big enough to walk."

I wasn't exactly versed in how babies grow and change, but I tried to make sense of it. "So, maybe less than a year old, but not fresh out of the oven?"

"Yeah, something like that," she agreed, with the hint of a smile.

I hesitated before asking, "Was it your baby? Do you get the feeling that it was yours?"

Without a pause, she said, "I think it was."

My heart skipped a beat. "Maybe somebody took your baby, and you were trying to fight them off."

Jane's eyes met mine, filled with worry. "That's what it felt like. There were two of them. I had the feeling it was a man and a woman."

It made sense to me. She was trying to stop them from taking her child, so she grabbed the knife to protect herself and her baby. That would explain why there was a woman there in her dreams and how a second person was able to wrestle the knife away from her so quickly.

The details were coming together, piece by piece, but we still didn't know the whole story. Not yet. "Can you see the man's face?" I asked.

"No, everyone's faces are kind of blurry. You know how dreams are—it's like they're not real, but in the dream, they feel real."

"Is anything else coming back to you? Like, while you're awake, do your dreams help you piece any of it together?"

"Not really. It's just this feeling... I don't know how to describe it. It's like I'm on guard all the time. I know I'm not safe."

That was interesting. Before I could say anything, my phone buzzed on the table. I glanced at it. "That's Martina. Do you mind if I get it?"

"No, please."

I answered quickly. "Martina, what's up?"

Martina's voice was somber as she recounted all of Jane's injuries, stretching from childhood to adulthood. It told the story of someone who had been through more than her share of suffering. My instincts were telling me that there was a man out there—someone she had trusted and then he betrayed her.

"Thanks for the update, Martina."

"No problem. Let's meet at the office later. Tell Jane I said hello."

"Okay."

With my phone away, I returned my attention to Jane.

She scrunched up her face. "Was it bad news?"

How to explain there was no trace of Jane anywhere? "Martina says hello," I said. "Not necessarily bad news. But they weren't able to match up any dental records for you. You likely never had any dental work. And it appears you sustained other injuries throughout your life that didn't heal properly making it likely you weren't seen by a doctor."

"That seems right."

"How so?" I asked, thinking her response was a bit unexpected.

"Well, being in the hospital or going to the dentist... it all seemed really foreign. Like I shouldn't be there. It was very new. And I had this idea that I couldn't trust the staff, but since I had no memories, I didn't have a choice or reason to not trust them."

Interesting. Had she been unable to afford medical care? But if that were the reason for not visiting a hospital, why wouldn't she trust medical professionals? *Puzzling.*

As I considered this, I watched Jane absentmindedly rubbing the necklace around her neck. I wondered if Vincent had made any progress in tracking down the jeweler who made it or finding out where it had come from.

After I paid the check, Jane and I stood up to leave. As we headed toward the door, a woman walked past us and suddenly stopped. She placed her hand on Jane's arm. "Angie! How are you doing? It's so good to see you."

Jane looked completely dumbfounded. "I'm sorry... do I know you?"

"It's me, Jolie," the woman said confidently.

My heart nearly jumped out of my chest. This woman knew Jane—or rather, she knew her as Angie. What else did she know? Did she know where Jane was from and what had happened to her child?

21

JANE

STARING into the eyes of the woman, Jolie, I saw she was older, dressed in a pair of jeans and a simple cotton T-shirt with little butterflies embroidered on it. There was a familiarity in her expression that tugged at something deep inside me, but I couldn't place it. "How do I know you?"

The woman looked shocked, as though she couldn't believe what I was saying. We must have known each other—maybe we had been friends or something.

Selena, who had been watching closely, stepped forward. "Ma'am, my name is Selena Bailey, and I'm a private investigator working with the sheriff's department. This woman has been in an accident and doesn't have her memory. But you seem to know who she is?"

Jolie placed her hand on her chest, concern evident in her eyes. "Oh dear, are you all right?" she asked, turning to me.

"I am," I said, though I wasn't sure of much at that moment. "But I'm not sure I'm Angie. I'm sorry, I have dissociative amnesia. I was attacked."

Jolie stared at me, as if she couldn't believe what she was hearing.

Selena spoke again, her tone reassuring. "It's true."

"Oh my goodness," Jolie said, clearly taken aback.

"Ma'am," Selena continued, "how do you know her? Do you know her last name or where she lived?"

Jolie shook her head slowly. "Oh, I may not be much help there. I work at a shelter here in Hayward. Angie would come in to sleep, to get a good meal." She paused, her brow wrinkled in thought. "But I'm sorry, I didn't know her last name or where she lived. I assumed she didn't live anywhere."

Selena kept at the woman. "Ma'am, can I get your information? Like I said, we're working with the police to figure out who she is and who attacked her. Do you mind if I take your contact details, so we can follow up?"

Jolie glanced at her female companion, perhaps a friend or relative, before she said, "Of course."

Selena pulled out a notepad, and I watched as Jolie carefully wrote down her information. As she wrote, Selena asked, "How often did you see her... I mean, Jane... how long had she been visiting the shelter?"

Jolie handed Selena back the notepad. "She'd started visiting the shelter a few months ago. Maybe three months. She stopped coming around a few weeks ago," Jolie said. "We assumed she'd found somewhere to live or was staying in one of the encampments."

"Did she ever say where she was from?" Selena asked.

"No, but I always assumed she wasn't from around here, or at least not from the cities."

"Why do you say that?" Selena asked.

It was strange to be talked about, like I wasn't there.

Jolie said, "Well, she wasn't familiar with cell phones or computers. I thought maybe she came from a religious community, maybe a Mennonite, or another group who doesn't prescribe to modern technology."

Was that true? Had I been part of a secluded community? Did that feel right?

"How did she arrive at the shelter? Did she take the bus? Did she have a car?" Selena asked.

I watched as Selena continued to grill the woman—this woman who knew me as Angie. It didn't feel right, like I was watching from a distance. Why didn't I remember Jolie?

Selena asked another question, her voice sharp. "Did she come in with a child?"

The woman shook her head quickly. "No, no child."

"Did she have any friends, or did you see her hanging around with anyone? Did she ever speak of any family or friends?"

The woman's companion said, "Jolie, should I get a table, or do you want me to wait?"

I said, "I'm so sorry to hold you up. We can follow up later, right, Selena?"

Jolie smiled. "It's no problem. Linda, give me a few minutes, all right?"

Her friend, Linda said, "No problem."

She turned back to Selena and me. "Where were we?"

"Did she ever hang around anyone? Have any friends? Speak of family back home?"

"She was always alone and never spoke of her past." She looked at me with sad eyes. "I'm so sorry to speak as if you're not here. If you need anything, please reach out."

"I appreciate that. I'm being well taken care of. Thank you though."

Selena kept probing, asking more questions, each one making me feel more disconnected from the person this woman claimed to know. Finally, Selena said she would arrange a time to talk to the woman and the other staff at the shelter to learn more about me. Jolie gave me one last look of pity as she walked away, saying softly, "Be well."

Her words echoed in my mind as she disappeared into the crowd. Why didn't I remember her? Why was I at a shelter in the first place? Was something bad happening at the shelter? Maybe that's why the idea of going to one when I was in the hospital seemed so terrifying. I had been to one before—maybe that's how I ended up battered and left alone at the park.

22

MARTINA

BACK IN THE office bright and early Monday morning, Hirsch set his coffee down on the conference table. "How's Charlie doing?"

"Charlie's pretty focused on his new book," I said, folding my hands on the table. "He spends a lot of time in front of the computer. He only takes breaks to make breakfast, lunch, dinner, and to walk Barney."

"Sounds intense."

"It is." Charlie was up to his eyeballs with his latest manuscript, and when he got that way—hyper-focused—it was hard to pull him out. The longer I lived with Charlie, the more I could see where Selena got her work ethic from.

Zoey was supposed to come home for the weekend, but she couldn't get away because she needed to study for a big exam. Since she'd gotten engaged, she'd come home more often—not just to talk about the wedding, but, I think, to be closer to the family too. I worried she was more nervous about all the impending changes in her life—a husband, in-laws, and a career —than she let on. I was thrilled to see her as much as I could.

With Zoey at school and my husband working around the

clock, I had a bit of time to myself. And I knew at least one or two people—maybe even three—who wouldn't mind taking the opportunity to check out some local shelters, see if anybody knew Jane Doe or Angie, as she'd been known at the Hayward shelter. What we found was a little surprising, and I wasn't exactly sure what it meant yet.

"Did Audrey and Kim get back from the Girl Scout trip?" I asked.

"They did," Hirsch said. "I received the whole download of all the talk about cookies, glitter, and giggling girls." Hirsch grinned at that, his smile warm.

"Did you get a chance to talk to Kim about maybe working part-time at Drakos Monroe?"

"She's all for it," he said.

I wasn't too surprised, but I was excited all the same. "That's great," I said. "We can get the paperwork started soon if you like."

"Let's do it once the case is over," he said. "This one's proving to be pretty challenging."

"I agree. It seems like we're hitting a lot of dead ends—or at least ends that aren't leading to anything that makes sense."

Selena waved and walked in, with Vincent right behind her.

"Good morning, boss and previous boss!" Vincent said with a huge grin before sitting down.

When we worked at the CoCo County Sheriff's Department together, Hirsch was everyone's boss, and Vincent preferred to call him that. But since Vincent joined Drakos Monroe, I'd earned the nickname. Selena gave Vincent a look. I think she was still getting used to him, even though they'd been working together for a while now. Selena was more reserved at work, intense—like her father. Vincent, on the other hand, was all about the flair.

Hirsch said, "Good morning, Vincent. Good morning, Selena."

I repeated the greeting.

"Morning," they both responded in unison.

"Everyone sufficiently caffeinated?" I asked.

Both Vincent and Selena nodded, holding their cups up as confirmation.

"All right then, let's go over what we found this weekend and figure out what the heck we're gonna do next," I said, getting down to business.

Hirsch said, "As you know, Martina and I hit about twelve shelters in the Bay Area, showing Jane Doe's photo to each of them—trying to be discreet, not saying whether she was still alive or not. Two of the shelters outside of Hayward recognized her."

"That's great," Selena said, her voice perking up.

"It's good, but it's also strange," Hirsch continued.

"What's strange?" Selena asked.

"Well, as the woman you bumped into at the restaurant—Jolie—said, she was at two other shelters that recognized her, but they knew her by different names: Stephanie and Emily."

Selena's eyes narrowed. "She used different names at the shelters? Are we sure it's the same person?"

"We're fairly certain," I said. "The staff at both shelters said the same thing. She stayed at each place for a few months before moving on. We assume she found another place to live, but maybe she was running."

"She's running from someone," Selena said, leaning forward. "Not staying in one place too long, changing her name."

I said, "That's what it sounds like to me."

"And based on the injuries we saw on the X-rays," Hirsch

said, "I would say she might've been caught by whoever she was running from."

"I think it's the boyfriend," Selena said with a slight edge to her voice. "Or the husband, or whoever got her pregnant."

"It's a strong possibility," I agreed. "But we won't know for sure until we figure this out."

Vincent shifted in his seat. "Still no luck on the necklace. I couldn't tie it to any specific jeweler. It certainly stands out, though. I took it to a small jeweler for an evaluation, and from what I was told, it's not mass-produced. It's likely one-of-a-kind, hand-forged by someone with a lot of skill—but not something you'd typically find in a jewelry store at the mall."

We all exchanged glances, likely the same thought crossing our minds.

"It's consistent," Selena said quietly.

"Yep," Vincent agreed. "She must've been living in a community that didn't visit hospitals, dentists, or schools—maybe an anti-government group or preppers waiting for doomsday."

"That would explain the homemade tattoo," Selena added. "And maybe a local jeweler or metalsmith made the necklace for her. Possibly someone in her family. Maybe that's why she feels protected by it. Have you noticed how she touches it whenever she feels anxious?"

"I have," I said, recalling the moments when Jane Doe would reach for the necklace. "It seems to soothe her when she touches it. That's a good point."

Selena said, "It might be more important than we think."

Hirsch leaned forward, his fingers drumming softly on the table. "If our theory is correct—that Jane grew up outside of typical society, anti-government, maybe even no school or doctors—how do we find her family? Do we just start hitting the road, visiting local areas we know have these communities?"

"That's one way," I said. "And it may be what we end up having to do. But I'm starting to think it might be time to put her picture on the news."

Hirsch raised an eyebrow. "Would those kinds of communities even watch television or go online?"

"I did some research," I said. "And some definitely do. They may be isolated, but some go into town to use computers or even have them at home. The problem is, the more we ask around the Bay Area, the more likely we'll get different identities."

Hirsch stared at me, his eyes thoughtful. We had worked together long enough to know each other's thought processes, almost as if we could read each other's minds.

"True," he said slowly, "but we may not want to say she's alive just yet. If our theory holds up, and she was living off the grid, the necklace might have come from someone she saw as a protector. Maybe a parent. Or maybe the person she's been running from was a romantic partner who took her out of that community and into a world where she was abused—where she eventually ended up at the park." He paused. "It could be the person who attacked her is living in the Bay Area, not part of a fringe community."

The pieces started to fit. "True."

Hirsch turned to Vincent. "Let's talk to Jane and see how she feels about having her picture on the news. If she agrees, you've got your media outlets. You can talk to them."

"You bet," Vincent said. He'd helped on more than one occasion with his media contacts—some sanctioned, some not. It had gotten us both into a bit of trouble back when we were with the sheriff's department, but now, we weren't bound by the same rules.

Selena said, "I can ask Jane about it and tell Vincent her decision."

Hirsch rose from his seat. "All right. You talk to Jane, and I'll call Cromwell to let him know we want to distribute her photo to the media, but we'll keep it quiet that she's alive."

"Got it, boss," Vincent said with a quick nod.

The picture of who Jane was—and what she was running from—was beginning to come into focus, but there were still too many unknowns. We didn't know her real identity, who had attacked her, or what had happened to her child. But we were getting close. *I could feel it.*

23

JANE

I PACED the living room as I tried to make sense of my latest dream. The fragments of images swirled in my mind, but I couldn't piece together what it all meant. Maybe Selena and Martina could help me figure it out when they came over. They were coming to talk to me about something, something that needed a face-to-face conversation. Had they finally figured out who I was or at least where I came from? How did I feel about that? Scared. Worried. Excited.

The images of tractors and fields lingering from my dream were vivid and persistent, as if they were trying to tell me something. They weren't frightening—just strange, unsettling in their simplicity. The rustle of tall grass swayed in my memory, the sounds of machinery in the distance. It was peaceful, yet unnerving, like I was remembering a place I should know but didn't. I touched my necklace, the metal grounding me as I ran my fingers over its familiar surface. Somehow, those fields felt like home. Could this new dream help with Selena and Martina's investigation? Fields and tractors didn't fit into the world I found myself in now—no bustling cities, no speeding cars. It didn't explain who I was or how I ended up here, did it?

What was puzzling was the who and the how. Someone had wanted to hurt me. Or had I wanted to hurt them? Self defense? Martina had told me my attacker was likely someone who had been hurting me for a long time and keeping me from getting the help I needed. If that were true, why? Why would someone do that to me?

My thoughts spiraled, dark and muddled. Since coming to this safe house, I'd filled my days with an endless loop of Lifetime movies and true crime documentaries. People did such horrible things to each other—sometimes for reasons that didn't make sense to me. Sometimes they were angry, sometimes they wanted money, and sometimes it was just the twisted need to control another person. An abusive partner who couldn't let go when the other person wanted to break free. Was that what happened to me? Had someone tried to control me, trap me? And what about my baby?

I needed to know the truth. If I never knew who I was, I didn't see how I could move forward. I was stuck.

A sudden knock on the door jolted me, stopping my pacing mid-step. My heart pounded in my chest, adrenaline spiking through me. I hurried over to the door, every sound magnified in the stillness of the room. My fingers hesitated on the handle. Selena had strongly advised that I always look through the peephole before opening the door, even if I was expecting someone.

I peeked through the peephole, holding my breath.

Sure enough, there stood Selena and Martina. My body relaxed a smidgeon as I opened the door. I said, "Hi. C'mon in."

With smiles and nods, I ushered them in and quickly shut the door behind them. "Can I get you anything?"

"We're fine, thanks. How are you?" Selena asked.

I led them into the living room, gesturing toward the sofa. "I'm fine," I said as we all sat down. There was silence for a moment before I spoke again. "I've been having dreams—not nightmares—but I'm not sure if it'll help the case. It's strange... fields, tractors, and I think a barn." I paused, trying to find the right words. "It felt... like home."

Martina's expression grew serious, and Selena's eyes widened. They exchanged a look before I asked, my voice shaking a little, "Is that something? Have you found out who I am and where I'm from?"

Martina hesitated for a moment, then spoke. "We have our suspicions," she said. "We've talked to people who remember you from different shelters where you used different names. We believe you might've been running from someone—someone who had been hurting you. And we think you may have come from a community that doesn't participate in typical government activities or use modern medical practices. More... isolated."

"So, I could be from a farm or something like that?" I asked, my heart pounding.

Martina said, "Yes. That could explain a lot of the things you've been remembering."

"That means we're getting closer?" I asked, feeling a surge of hope.

"We do think we're getting closer," Selena said. "But we wanted to talk to you about something important today. Given the situation and what we're learning, we'd like to show your photo to the media—put it on social media, traditional news, and TV—to see if anyone recognizes you, maybe someone from your home or your community."

"But... I thought you said I could be in danger?" And I felt it. I wasn't safe. Not yet.

"We won't reveal your health status," Martina assured me. "We won't say you're alive. We still believe whoever you were running from—or whoever attacked you—could come after you again if they found out. We're being careful."

"Oh," I whispered.

Selena said, "We want to make sure you're comfortable with this. Are you all right with us putting your picture out there?"

I thought about it, the decision pressing down on me. It seemed like the only way forward. If I was ever going to get answers, this was how. And I needed answers. "I'm okay with it."

"Great," Selena said, visibly relieved. "We'll talk to Detective Cromwell and let him know we're moving forward with this. Our goal is to keep you safe and figure out who attacked you. Once we know that, we can put him—or her, or them—in jail so they can't hurt you or anyone else ever again."

I nodded, but my thoughts returned to the baby. The baby I saw in flashes of my dreams. The baby who didn't look right. The baby who wasn't moving or crying. Would I learn the truth soon? If I did, would I be able to cope with whatever I learned?

24

MARTINA

IN THE CONFERENCE room at Drakos Monroe, I sat with a pile of notes as well as my laptop in front of me. I skimmed through the most credible reports from the tip line. Jane Doe's photo had been distributed on social media and traditional news outlets, including television news and online blogs. Selena had even made a Facebook page titled, "Do You Know This Woman?" The post had also been shared on the Alameda County Sheriff's Department website and across Drakos Monroe's social media pages.

Thankfully, we had young people like Selena and Vincent who understood the importance of technology in today's world. They had pushed for an online presence a few years back, which had proven to be quite valuable.

In cases involving a missing person or those needing help from the public, social media had become indispensable. It was the way the world communicated now, especially young people. As time changed, so did we. We couldn't afford to go the way of the dinosaurs, becoming extinct simply because we failed to adapt.

Vincent stood at his usual spot at the white board, setting up a grid for the tips received as a result of our media efforts. Some-times I wondered if he'd missed his calling as a schoolteacher—he certainly seemed to thrive when standing in front of a group, teaching, organizing, and sharing ideas.

Selena, Detective Cromwell, and Hirsch were sifting through their piles of notes in preparation for sharing with the team. We had divided up the tips received to sort through which may help and those that were a waste of time. We had antici-pated a flood of tips, but the real challenge was figuring out how many would actually lead us to answers about Jane Doe.

I looked down at my own stack of reports, most of which were from shelters across California. Many of the tips claimed to have seen Jane, but none of the individuals had provided last names—just first names. It was my responsibility to call them back, confirm time frames and the credibility of the tips. The rest of the team had their own sets of to-do lists.

Selena looked up from her pile. "I got through these last night," she said. "Nothing credible as far as I can see, but they all had interesting stories, that's for sure."

Vincent glanced over at her and raised an eyebrow. "Like what?"

"One guy claimed Jane Doe was his mother," Selena said, shaking her head. "He's 35, and as we all know, Jane's most likely in her early-to-mid twenties."

We all nodded in agreement. That kind of nonsense was expected. It was going to be a mountain of work to sift through everything, but it was necessary.

AFTER A FEW HOURS of all of us making calls and sorting tips, I was ready to get this party started. Or maybe I was just impatient because I had finished reaching out to all the shelters in California that had called in tips. It had only been 24 hours since Jane's picture had been circulated, so more tips could still come in, but what we had was a good start. I said, "Let's do this, Vincent."

Vincent stood up and took his place at the board. "What's the first one, Martina?"

I said, "According to the tips, from April through July of last year, she was in a shelter in Siskiyou County, near the Oregon border, and went by the name Karen."

Vincent scribbled on the board, adding a timeline.

I continued, "From August to October, she was at a shelter in Shasta County and went by the name Rachel."

Vincent added the latest details to the board, and I continued, "November to February, she was at a shelter in Sonoma County and went by the name Kathryn." I paused to let Vincent record. "March to June, she was at a shelter in Oakland and went by the name Tina. April to August of this year, she was at the shelter in Hayward, where she went by the name Angie."

"Okay, just give me a few minutes," Vincent said, as he continued to scribble on the board. His hand flew across the surface, sketching timelines, names, and locations. The beginnings of the pattern were starting to emerge. The tipline had done its job—or at the very least had given us an idea of where Jane Doe had been in the sixteen months prior to her attack.

As he drew, I realized what he was doing. "This is good, Martina," he said with enthusiasm. A moment later, Vincent stepped back and gestured toward the board. "Not only do we have a full timeline of Jane Doe's whereabouts under different aliases, but we also have a visual map of the state of California."

On the board, he had drawn the state and marked her journey. He pointed at the top of the map. "She started up north near the Oregon border," he said, tracing his finger downward, "and made her way south—farther and farther south—until she finally ended up at the shelter in Hayward and was found at Quarry Lakes where she'd been attacked."

Selena's mouth dropped open in surprise. "It all fits. It absolutely all fits!" she exclaimed.

We all stared at the board, seeing how the clues we had collected lined up. There was no digital record of her, no medical history, no government-issued ID. She hadn't been reported missing and wasn't in any database. She had homemade tattoos and wore artisan jewelry, the kind that felt personal, like it had a story.

"She must've been living in an isolated community up north," Selena said, her eyes widening as the realization sank in. "A community that stays away from law enforcement and modern technology, keeps to themselves. Like Jolie, the woman from the Hayward shelter, had suggested based on her conversations with Jane. And Jane's latest dreams of fields and barns. Why visiting hospitals seemed foreign. Because it was. Maybe she was living in a religious community that avoided all that stuff. Likely a fundamentalist group who takes the scripture quite literally."

"I agree."

Nods from around the room

"If we don't get an identity soon," Hirsch said. "We could take a road trip up north to question communities in Northern California and Oregon. See if anybody knows her. They may not be watching the news, and they may not be on social media, but they could be looking for her."

"Agreed."

Vincent said, "But she left the community. Why?"

The baby. I said, "Maybe she left the community with the father of her child. Something goes wrong, with the baby or he's abusive, and she runs from him?"

Selena chimed in, her voice somber. "A story as old as time. She trusted her partner, thought he loved her, but really, he just wanted to control her, own her. She did whatever it took to keep him happy, to stay in line. But it wasn't enough and she ran for her life."

I glanced at Selena. My heart broke for her every time she brought up what was clearly from her own painful memories. She was only twenty-two, but she'd been through more in her young life than most people twice her age. Her mother had been murdered, and she'd been abused by her own high school boyfriend, who had nearly killed her, then had a loving and kind boyfriend who had been killed. That kind of past leaves scars, and yet here she was keeping on, headstrong, determined, with sharp instincts. I just hoped that in her pursuit of truth, she wouldn't end up getting hurt again, as sometimes her determination to solve a case didn't include worrying about her own safety.

"You're probably right, Selena," I said softly, acknowledging her insight. "Unfortunately."

She said, "We'll keep sifting through the other tips. If nothing comes up in the next couple of days, and if we've got the time, we should take teams to search Northern California and Oregon. I don't think anyone should go alone though. If we're right, and she's from one of these fringe communities, they won't trust strangers. We need to be careful."

There was a murmur of agreement from everyone in the room. I couldn't help but think of my daughter, who was in veterinary school up in Oregon. If we ended up heading north, maybe I could pay her a visit. A two-for-one trip.

With a final nod, we all put our heads back down and returned to work, more determined than ever to find out the truth about Jane Doe.

25

SELENA

I WATCHED Jane's eyes grow wide as I showed her the countless social media postings with her photo, all asking for help. The realization that she was the focus of such widespread attention seemed to hit her hard. I could see her shoulders tense, her breath quicken as she processed it all. I did my best to scroll past the nastier comments—there were plenty of them, and no one should have to see that garbage.

Here we were, trying our best to identify a young woman who had been beaten, bruised, and left with no memory, yet the trolls of the Internet still found a way to spew their venom. They didn't care about her pain or her story. Instead, they focused on her appearance, objectifying her with vile remarks, even making disgusting suggestions about what they'd like to do to her. I blocked each one as it popped up, but it was like playing whack-a-mole at an arcade—a never-ending task. For every one I silenced, another would appear just as quickly.

There were so many creeps out there. Sometimes it felt overwhelming, and I found myself wishing for the impossible— that we could just rid the world of people like them. But that was a big job. Quite frankly, there were too many.

At least I could protect Jane from the ones I could find or the ones who tried to find her.

"How do people even know to go and look on social media—the Internet?" she asked, as if she were confused.

"You don't remember the Internet?" I asked, more in confirmation considering our current theories about her past.

She shook her head slowly. "No. I mean... Instagram? Facebook? I've never heard of any of it."

Considering what we knew, it fit. Still for someone so young, it seemed almost unthinkable to not know about social media. I couldn't imagine growing up in a world without it. These days, it was where half our investigations took place. Everyone recorded their lives online, from the mundane to the monumental—what they ate, where they went, who they were with. And that footprint could be dangerous if you weren't careful.

"I can't imagine not knowing about this stuff," I said, more to myself than to Jane. "I mean, we do so much online. Like almost everything."

It was ironic, in a way. I had an account just to search other people's accounts. I rarely posted anything myself—my presence online was never personal. Most of my time was spent managing Drakos Monroe's social media sites and working with Vincent on web design and the blog. It wasn't glamorous, but it was necessary.

"Really?" Jane asked innocently.

"Yeah, there's like a billion users on the Internet. We do our banking, socializing, get groceries, watch movies... the list is endless," I explained to her, hoping to give her some sense of the scope. "And mostly, a billion people across the globe look on the Internet every day to see whatever everybody else is doing."

She stared at me, her eyes wide with disbelief. "That's incredible."

I could see the wheels turning in her head. The sheer scale of it—one billion people all connected, all sharing, all watching. For someone who had been so removed from that, I could only imagine how overwhelming it must feel. "It is," I agreed and looked at her more closely. Jane seemed to be doing better, at least outwardly. Her posture wasn't as stiff, and the dark circles under her eyes had faded a little, though I knew the nightmares still plagued her. Maybe they were filled with fragments of the life she couldn't remember, scattered memories of where she came from, haunting her as she tried to rest.

"How are you doing?" I asked, my voice soft. "It's been almost three weeks since the attack and you lost your memory."

She sighed, looking down at her hands. "Well, the therapist has been really helpful. She's helping me navigate this world." She hesitated, glancing at me. "But I'm eager to find out where I'm from and what happened to me."

Her voice carried a strength I hadn't heard before. Despite everything, she wanted answers. "That's great. It's progress."

She gave a small smirk. "You're starting to sound like my therapist."

"I'm so sorry, I didn't mean—" I stammered.

"No, don't be. It's okay," she said. "I guess I'm just prepared for whatever I learn. I figure it won't be happy news, you know? I know I had a relationship with someone, since I had a child and... the injuries the doctor said are typically from abuse..." She trailed off. I could see the pain etched on her face. "It's just horrible, you know? The people you love aren't supposed to hurt you, they're supposed to love you."

Her words hit closer to home than I cared to admit. "Do you want to know all the details of what happened to you?" I took a deep breath, steadying myself. "When I was attacked, held captive, almost killed... I'm not sure I'd want to know everything if I didn't already know. Like I told you before, I still have nightmares. Not every night, of course, and I'm doing a lot better than I used to. But sometimes I wish I didn't remember."

Jane's face softened. "I understand what you're saying. And I guess... just because I don't know anything else, I really want to know everything, even if it's painful. I'm assuming, according to the psychiatrist, that's why I can't remember. But once I do, the therapist can help me through it. So, I think I'll be all right."

There was something about the way she spoke, the determination behind her words. Jane's outlook was certainly positive. The therapist must've been doing something right. And maybe, just maybe, after running for almost a year and a half, changing cities and names, Jane was finally starting to feel safe and stronger.

As we continued to scroll through social media, Jane seemed amazed. Her eyes lit up with curiosity as she clicked through posts and photos. Sometimes she laughed when she came across a meme on someone else's profile, a brief moment of lightness. It was nice to see her smile, to hear that soft, genuine laughter.

My phone buzzed in her hands, and she glanced down at the screen.

"Oh, looks like you're getting a call from Martina," she said, handing it to me.

I took the phone. "Hey, Martina, what's up?"

"We have a credible lead." Her voice was low and serious. "Is she with you in a safe location?"

"Yes, we're at her apartment," I said, glancing at Jane. She looked back at me, curiosity in her eyes.

"Good," Martina said. "Can you come down here to the office?"

"Of course, I'll be right there," I said quickly, a surge of adrenaline running through me.

"Tell Jane to lock up and not let anyone in. I'll see you soon."

I hung up, my mind racing. A credible lead—this was good news. I turned to Jane, explaining the situation quickly before pulling her into a brief hug. I could feel her grip tighten around me. After another promise that we'd find answers, I hurried out of her apartment.

26

MARTINA

Sitting in front of the young woman named Keisha, I said, "Selena will be here shortly. Can I get you anything?"

She shook her head. She was in her twenties, with dark hair, dressed modestly in what looked like a homemade cotton dress, and wore no makeup. She had mentioned she had information about the Jane Doe, but she would only talk to Selena. Apparently, they had messaged on Facebook. She didn't seem to trust me and certainly didn't like the look of me. I wasn't sure what that was about, but I tried to be as accommodating as I could.

"Okay, well if you need anything, I will be right outside the room. I have a few things I need to take care of."

"Thank you," she said softly.

There was a sadness in her eyes. It made me believe she knew Jane personally, but like many others, she had assumed Jane was dead. We couldn't let on that this wasn't true until we were sure the person who knew her wished her no harm. I stepped a few feet away from the door, turning to Hirsch who had just arrived.

"What do you think?" he asked.

"I think she knows Jane. She even has similar features—

between the hair, hairline, the shape of her nose, and eye color. Maybe a relative."

"How about her demeanor?" Hirsch asked.

"She's very demure, quiet, doesn't make a lot of eye contact."

"Perhaps from the same community as Jane. This could be how we learn Jane's identity."

"Let's hope so," I said, glancing back at the door.

Selena arrived a few minutes later, her long, wavy hair looking wild, as if she had literally run here. She burst in with her usual energy. "Martina, Hirsch, what's going on?"

"A woman named Keisha came in about an hour ago. Says she knows Jane, but she'll only talk to you. She mentioned she saw the posts on social media, and that you messaged back and forth."

Selena looked puzzled. "I message a lot of people. Most of them just shared condolences and said they hoped we'd find her."

"She's in the conference room," I explained. "I will join you even though she really only wants to talk to you."

Selena raised an eyebrow. "What's your assessment of her?"

"By the looks of her, I wouldn't be surprised if she's a relative of Jane's."

Selena nodded.

I said, "She must be very particular about people. Somehow, she's fine with you, though. You must've said something on social media that resonated with her."

"I guess it's one of my gifts." Selena shrugged, a small smile tugging at the corner of her mouth.

I told Hirsch we'd fill him in after we spoke with the woman. I opened the door, and Selena walked in first. I followed her and sat down across from Keisha.

"Hi, Keisha, this is Selena," I said gently. "Is it all right if I sit in while you speak with her?"

Keisha looked at Selena nervously. Selena smiled reassuringly. "It's okay," she said. "Not only does she work here, but she's also my stepmother. It's fine, I promise."

"Okay," Keisha said, her voice a little shaky.

Selena settled into her chair. "So, how can I help you?"

Keisha fumbled with her hands, glancing down before speaking. "The photograph... I messaged you on Facebook."

Selena paused, her eyes narrowing as she thought back. "Keisha... yes, I remember now. You said you hoped we'd find her identity and that she looked like someone you used to know."

Keisha's gaze was fixed on her lap. "It's not just someone I used to know," she said. "She's my sister."

Selena and I exchanged glances, the weight of her words hanging in the air.

"Your sister?" I asked, trying to keep my voice steady and not reveal my genuine surprise.

"Yes," Keisha continued. "I'm sorry I didn't call. It's delicate... where we're from, we don't—we're not supposed to talk to outsiders. My friend, Marilyn, has family in our community. They're not as strict as mine. She lives in town now and has the internet. She saw the Facebook post and let me use their computer to message you. I had to see for myself."

Selena leaned in gently. "And where are you from?"

"Oregon," Keisha said. "Right outside Ashland."

Ashland. That matched some of what we thought—Jane, or the woman we were calling Jane Doe, had likely made her way down south starting near the Oregon border until she reached the Bay Area.

"When was the last time you saw your sister?"

Keisha bit her lip. "It's been about three and a half years. She met a boy, and she got pregnant. That's not acceptable where we're from. It's not acceptable in our family. They weren't married, and it wasn't approved. She knew that. So, they ran away together. My papa deemed her leaving the community as a betrayal and said she was never to return. The whole community agreed and turned their backs on her, and we never saw her again."

Ouch. "Do you know who this boy was that your sister ran off with?"

Keisha nodded. "His name is Jacob Stoddard. She met him through a friend. He was new to the area. He wasn't from our community."

Selena exchanged a glance with me. "Was your sister happy when she left with him?" she asked.

Keisha nodded again, a sad smile on her lips. "She was so excited about the baby. She was only sad because she knew how Papa would react... the whole community. It's just... it's not like the outside world."

"Did you ever meet the baby?"

"No, I never saw her after she left the community."

"We tried to find out who she was based on dental records, driver's license, and medical records, but we couldn't find anything," I said, hoping she could explain.

"No, my papa is strongly anti-government. He wouldn't even let us go to school. Our mother homeschooled us instead. But Mama's not like Papa. Anyhow, no driver's license, no birth certificate. Papa said that's how 'they' keep track of you." She paused, her eyes flicking between me and Selena. "I guess you'd call him a prepper. He spends most of his time working in the fields to make money on our farm, but he's always saving food. The apocalypse is coming, and only the righteous will survive. When Hanna left, he was worried she had gone to the devil."

"Her name is Hanna?" I asked.

Keisha looked at me somewhat suspiciously, but considering she had just shared everything right in front of me I wasn't sure why. Maybe she was warming up to me, or perhaps knowing I was Selena's stepmother helped. "Yes, her name is Hanna Wren."

"How old is she?"

"She's twenty-four. She was my big sister. We were only a year apart... we were really, really close." Her voice broke as she spoke, and she dropped her forehead into her hands, tears streaming down her cheeks.

I pushed the Kleenex box toward her, and she grabbed one. "Thank you so much," she said, dabbing her eyes. "We thought... I thought I'd see her again."

Keisha's grief felt genuine, but I remained cautious. "We'd like to confirm that you're really her sister."

Keisha looked up at me. "How?"

"We could test your DNA," I explained.

"How do I do that?"

After a brief explanation of the collection procedure, she said, "That would be fine."

"Great."

"How did she die?" she asked quietly.

Before I could respond, Selena quickly jumped in. "She's alive. But we can't let anyone know that yet. Somebody tried to hurt her very badly, and she doesn't remember anything."

I wished Selena hadn't shared that. Why had she done that? While Keisha seemed sincere, it didn't necessarily mean she wasn't dangerous or wouldn't accidentally reveal that Hanna was still alive to someone who may want to hurt her. But Selena's words had already been said, and there was no taking them back.

"Can I see her? How's the baby? She must be getting so big.

Must be two, almost three by now," Keisha said, her voice filled with sudden hope.

"We've been keeping Hanna safe. We need to confirm that you are who you say you are and that you didn't have anything to do with what happened to her. And we can't have you tell anyone she's still alive until we figure out who tried to hurt her."

Keisha said, "I understand, but... I may not be able to come back. My friend Marilyn drove me here. I don't have my own car, and we drove hours and hours to be here. I have to go back today before anyone worries about where I am. Papa wouldn't approve."

Selena said, "Give us a minute." She ushered me out of the room, and said, eyes pleading. "We could bring Hanna here. She'll be safe."

"What if she's not really her sister?"

"But if she is, maybe it will help Hanna get her memory back? Plus she'll be safe here."

Selena had a point. Hirsch hurried over and I explained the situation. He said, "It's a risk but may be worth it."

Both had valid points.

With a nod, I agreed. But I couldn't help but wonder, if we had found Hanna, where was Jacob and the baby?

27

SELENA

My heart raced as the realization sank in—we had identified Jane, or rather, Hanna. Would she be happy to be reunited with her sister? I thought so, but I knew Martina had some doubt, knowing it could all be a scam and Keisha wasn't related to Jane. But I could see the family resemblance. Keisha's story was believable and fit with what we did know about Jane.

This type of case was one of the reasons why I did this job. I'd seen what a reunification could do for a family. It was near magical.

Martina had been working on these types of investigations for years and had experienced reuniting long-lost family members, some presumed dead but brought back together because of her and the team. She'd told me the stories, and I had listened in awe. It didn't happen often, but when it did, it was akin to a miracle.

I remembered the first time I helped reunite a family. There was a little girl abducted by terrible people, and we managed to find her and bring her home. That case had stayed with me all these years. I had never forgotten the girl, Emily, and her love of birds or the look on her face when she saw her father. I smiled at the memory. And now, I had the chance to reunify two sisters.

My task was to pick up Jane, or should I call her Hanna? I'd have to ask her if she wanted to use her real name since we knew who she was. I'd bring her back to the cheerful conference room with the photographs on the walls and the wide windows that was usually reserved for family members of our clients, or victims.

As I walked through the lobby, I waved at Mrs. Pearson at the reception desk. In one of the visitor chairs, I spotted a woman absorbed in her cell phone. I glanced at her and walked over to Mrs. Pearson and whispered, "Who's that woman?"

Mrs. Pearson quietly said, "She came in with the woman who knows the Jane Doe."

Looking back over to the woman, I deduced she was probably in her mid-twenties, with sandy hair and a pale complexion. She seemed riveted by her phone, furiously texting as if her life depended on it.

Keisha had told us a friend of hers had notified her about the Facebook page where she first saw Jane's picture. These friends used cell phones and the Internet, unlike Keisha and her family, who seemed to stay away from technology. I wondered why this friend had chosen to stay in the lobby instead of joining Keisha. It struck me as a bit odd.

After a quick thanks and goodbye to Mrs. Pearson, I left to pick up Jane and let her know the truth—that we knew who she was and that she was about to be reunited with her sister. I took a deep breath, hoping this was the beginning of something good for both of them.

AT THE SAFE HOUSE, Jane opened the door with a smile, gesturing for me to come inside. I accepted, stepping into the small, dimly lit room.

"What did you learn? You said you wanted to tell me in person?" she asked eagerly.

Over the last few weeks, we'd gotten to know each other—trauma-bonded, some might say. She had been assaulted, and I, too, had been through some rough experiences. I'd almost been killed once—twice, actually. It's a strange thing, finding camaraderie in shared pain.

I guided her to the sofa and motioned for her to sit. This was big news, and I didn't want her to collapse or something. People responded to this sort of revelation in all kinds of ways. I sat beside her, choosing my words carefully.

"Jane," I began gently, "we think we've learned your identity."

Her eyes widened. "You did? Did you find my child too?"

We hadn't found her child, and according to her sister, there was no reason to believe Jane wouldn't have her child with her. "No, I'm sorry. Not yet."

Her face dropped. "But you know my identity?"

"Yes, we had someone recognize you from the Facebook page I put together. Remember, I showed it to you on my phone? They showed up at Drakos Monroe and asked to talk to me about you. That's why I left earlier." I paused. "She said she knows you."

Jane leaned forward, her expression turning intense. "How?"

"She says she's your sister."

"Sister?" she said. "And you believe her?"

"At this point, we don't really have a reason not to believe her," I said. "And quite frankly, there is a strong physical resemblance. Plus, what she told me about your—her—family all fits with what we've learned so far. Even the little details, like the homemade tattoos and lack of medical records."

She clutched onto the edge of the sofa before she said, "What's my name?"

"Hanna Wren."

"Hanna," she repeated softly. "Hanna," she murmured again, almost to herself.

"Does that sound familiar?"

"Maybe..." She hesitated. "It doesn't sound wrong."

"Well, she's still at Drakos Monroe and would like to see you. I know you don't remember her, but maybe seeing her will help jog some memories."

Jane—Hanna—swallowed hard, then met my gaze with determination. "I'd like to meet her. Is it safe?"

"Yes, it's safe. We'll be right there with you the whole time."

"Good."

"Do you have any questions?"

"No, I guess not. I just want to see this person who claims to be my sister, and maybe—maybe she can help me figure out what happened to me. What did she say about me?"

I explained everything Keisha had told us about her—Hanna's—life. How she had run off with a boy named Jacob, and she'd been pregnant at the time. But after that, Keisha knew very little about what happened to her since they hadn't spoken in more than three years.

Jane said, "But that doesn't explain why I had changed shelters and kept heading south. I must have been running from something—or someone. Could it be this Jacob person?"

"Maybe." *Most likely.*

"Then why wouldn't I just go home if I were in trouble? Do you think I was too afraid of our father? If what she says is true, I was *banished*. Do family's really do that to one another?"

"Maybe. We're not sure yet, but we promise we'll try to figure it out."

She scrunched up her face as if she were straining to remember something.

I leaned in slightly and asked, "Are you okay?"

"I don't know," she said. "I do want to meet her. I just... something doesn't feel right. I mean, why didn't she look for me if she hasn't seen me for the last three years?"

Another great question. I hoped she asked Keisha when they met. "I'm not sure," I said, apologetically. "Do you want me to start calling you Hanna?"

She hesitated, looking down at her hands. "Can we just stick with Jane for now? I still don't know if it's real."

"Of course. No problem."

She stood up abruptly, determination flashing in her eyes. I got to my feet as well, watching her closely. She was clearly ready to go and meet this woman claiming to be her sister. But there was hesitation too. Instinctively, I picked up on the unease —it was the same wariness I'd seen when she'd recoiled at the sight of the knife I'd found at the park. It was as if Jane was fearful but didn't know why.

Maybe Jane had been running from her family all along? I didn't voice my concern. Instead, I smiled gently. "Ready?"

"Ready," she echoed softly.

As we walked out, side by side, I couldn't help but wonder: What kind of family reunion were we about to walk into?

28

MARTINA

I GLANCED at the watch on my wrist. Selena should be back with Jane any minute now. In the meantime, I had settled Keisha and her friend into one of the nicer conference rooms—the ones we reserved for good news. The walls were adorned with pictures of the Bay Bridge and serene ocean scenes. Large windows let in a soft, glowing light that cast a warm atmosphere of hope.

Standing next to me in the lobby was Hirsch. He said, "Another reunification for Martina on the books."

I chuckled softly. "You've had a few of your own, haven't you?"

"I have, I have," he said with a small nod.

"You don't seem exactly thrilled, though. What's going on?" I asked, studying him.

"I still think there are a lot of questions we need answers to. Something doesn't feel quite right."

"Are you worried about Jacob?"

"Yeah, that—and if something went wrong between Hanna and Jacob, why did she choose shelters over just going home?"

"If what Keisha says is true, she may not have been

welcome, and maybe she knew that," I said. "All three of us should be in the room when she meets Keisha. You're good at picking up on people's cues, and Selena's got a knack for it, too. Let's watch their reactions and take note. We'll compare observations at the end of the meeting."

"Good thinking."

Through the glass door, I saw Selena walking toward us beside Jane. Both of them were smiling, engaged in conversation. It was great to have Selena on our team—not just for her investigative skills but for her empathy and warmth. She had a natural gift for connecting with people, and sometimes, that was exactly what our clients needed—a friend when they had no one else in the world. I could tell that she and Jane had gotten close during the short time they'd known each other.

I stepped forward and opened the door as the two women entered. Selena looked around, glancing at the chairs lined up against the wall before turning her attention back to us.

"Hey, guys," Selena said.

"Hi. Jane, how are you holding up?" I asked.

"I'm okay," she said with a hint of anxiety in her voice. "Just... looking forward to getting this over with."

Getting this over with?

"Keisha and her friend are in a conference room. Do you need anything before I bring you in?" I asked, trying to keep my voice calm and reassuring. "Maybe a drink? A restroom break? A snack? It's okay if you're nervous; we can give you more time."

"Maybe just a quick stop to the restroom," Jane said.

She seemed tense, so we escorted her quietly through the halls of Drakos Monroe. When we reached the restroom, she hesitated before heading inside.

Standing outside, Selena leaned closer and spoke in a low voice. "She's a little apprehensive about meeting her sister. She doesn't want to be called Hanna—not yet."

"Did she say why?" I asked.

Selena shook her head. "No, but it reminded me of when we found that knife at the park. She didn't remember the knife itself, but the look of terror in her eyes... It's like something deep in her subconscious is holding her back, making her reserved about meeting her sister."

As we suspected, maybe things weren't right at home before she left with Jacob. It was not uncommon for someone to be abused at home and then fall into the trap of another abusive relationship, thinking they'd escaped only to find they hadn't. I said, "Understood. We'll proceed cautiously."

Jane emerged from the restroom a moment later. "Okay, I'm ready."

We exchanged glances and led her down the hall to the conference room where Keisha and her friend, Marilyn, were waiting. As we opened the door, Keisha and Marilyn both stood up, their eyes widening in surprise.

Keisha's jaw dropped, and a sob escaped her lips. "Hanna... it's you!" Tears streamed down her cheeks, and she took a step forward as if unsure whether to rush over or hold herself back.

I kept my eyes on Marilyn, the friend. She watched Keisha intently, studying every move. Her expression was harder to read—more controlled, less emotional.

"Hi," I said, breaking the tension. "Why don't we all sit down?"

There were murmurs of agreement as everyone settled into their seats. Keisha and Marilyn sat across from us, and I took a spot next to Jane. Selena positioned herself on Jane's other side, while Hirsch sat toward the end of the table, keeping a good vantage point to observe everyone's reactions.

I cleared my throat gently. "We've explained to Jane that you believe she's your sister, Hanna," I began, choosing my words carefully. "And as I mentioned to you earlier, Keisha,

Jane has lost her memory. She doesn't remember her life, where she's from, or what her real name is. That's still the case, and she'd like to be called Jane for now."

Keisha said, "I understand. And thank you for finding her."

I glanced at Jane, who was sitting stiffly beside me, her eyes locked on Keisha and Marilyn. She wasn't smiling, but she wasn't frowning either. Finally, she spoke, her voice soft. "Who are you?" she asked, looking directly at Marilyn.

"This is Marilyn," Keisha said quickly. "She's a friend of mine. Where we come from, we don't use the Internet or go on social media, but Marilyn does. She lives in town. She's the one who told me she saw your picture, and she drove me here to see if it was really you."

Jane swallowed hard. I could see her discomfort—her shoulders were tense, her hands gripping the edges of her chair as if she were bracing herself.

Jane glanced at Marilyn and then back at Keisha. "They told me you haven't seen me in over three years?"

"No, not since you left with Jacob," Keisha said, her voice trembling.

There it was again—that name, Jacob. I watched Jane closely, but her face remained neutral.

Jane looked down at her hands, then back up at Keisha. "And you're sure I'm Hanna?"

"Yes. You even have the necklace Mama made you and the rest of the sisters," Keisha pulled hers from underneath her top. It was the exact same as Jane's.

Jane touched the charm that she now knew was from her mother. Her mother must have been nurturing and protective. Jane composed herself, taking a deep breath before speaking. "Can you tell me about our family? And the last time we saw each other?"

"Sure," Keisha said "Well, we live in a small community

outside of Ashland, Oregon—that's up north. We have a big property, a farm. We have a mama and a papa. They're still together, and we have four siblings—three brothers and another sister. They all live in little houses on our property. We're all very, very close. We believe in the good Lord, and we don't have things like smartphones and the Internet. We don't believe in modern medicine. We take care of ourselves. It's a simple life. It's good."

Jane's breathing seemed to quicken. I noticed the slight rise and fall of her chest as if she were trying to keep her emotions in check. Something in what Keisha was saying wasn't sitting right with her.

"Then why did I leave?" Jane asked.

Keisha frowned, glancing down before she spoke again. "You met a boy, Jacob. He lived in town, and you started seeing him. You didn't tell Mama and Papa—and certainly not our brothers. Then... you got pregnant. You were really scared because, to be honest, that's a pretty big sin in our community. Papa would've been very upset, maybe even cast you out. So, I understood why you left, but they didn't know why you ran. I told them you'd likely run off with Jacob. But they didn't know about the baby. I never told them."

Jane's gaze sharpened. "But I told you I was pregnant?"

"Yes, you did. We were very close. You loved Jacob, and you really wanted your baby. You thought leaving was the only way to make things work. I remember telling you that you could just get married and then the baby would come, and everything would be okay. But you insisted Papa would never approve. You were probably right," she added sadly.

Jane said, "Nobody ever came looking for me. The detectives and investigators said no one reported me missing."

Keisha and Marilyn exchanged looks, a shared understanding passing between them. Keisha cleared her throat before answering. "Where we come from, that's not something we do. We don't talk to law enforcement or government agencies. We have our own rules, our own way of life. Our community is self-contained—we don't need anybody else to take care of us."

"But did you look for me?" Jane's voice was sharper now, an edge creeping into her tone as if something in her subconscious was shouting that this wasn't right.

"We didn't look," Keisha admitted, her voice dropping. "We assumed you were happy with Jacob. We thought you ran away to get married. We didn't know you were missing."

The room fell into a heavy silence.

Beside her, Selena and I exchanged a look, both of us studying the people around the table, trying to decipher anything that might give us more insight.

"Do you have any more questions for Keisha or Marilyn?" I asked gently, my gaze flicking to Jane.

"No."

She looked down.

I said, "Keisha, thank you so much for coming in. Now that you know she's safe, we'll have a talk with Jane and see how she wants to move forward."

Marilyn shifted uneasily in her seat. "So, we can't just bring her back with us?" she asked, her voice laced with surprise.

I glanced at Jane, noticing how she reached under the table to grab Selena's hand. The gesture was small, but it spoke volumes. I took that as a hard *no*.

"No," I said, turning back to Marilyn and Keisha. "Not if she doesn't want to, and you have to understand—she doesn't remember who you are. To her, it would be like going with strangers. I think it's best she stays here with us, unless—" I paused and looked directly at Jane. "Jane, would you like to go with them?" I asked, realizing that I was speaking for her.

Jane shook her head vigorously. "No."

Keisha's face fell, and Marilyn's eyes widened slightly in shock.

I said, "Not to worry. We're going to help her reclaim her life and get her memories back. We're taking good care of her."

Keisha said, "That's good."

Locking eyes with the two women, I said, "Have you seen or heard from Jacob since your sister left your family's property?"

Keisha shook her head immediately, but Marilyn's expression flickered with something—something quick, almost hidden.

"And you, Marilyn? Did you know Jacob?" I pressed, not letting her off so easily.

"Just from around town," she answered vaguely, avoiding my gaze.

"And you haven't seen him recently?"

She shook her head. "No, I haven't seen him since they left."

"Did you know any of Jacob's family? Or friends he keeps in contact with?"

Marilyn said, "I didn't know his family. He was friends with my brother, but I don't think anyone has seen him since he left with Hanna."

I would be sure to get all the information they had about Jacob before they left. We needed to find him. "Would you mind sharing your brother's information so we can contact him?"

"I can share the information."

"Great. Thank you both for coming in. Learning her identity is really going to help us—and her. We'll keep in touch."

Hirsch said, "I can take you out to reception and get your information and your brother's before I escort you out."

They nodded.

We all stood. Keisha said, "Bye, Hanna. I hope to see you soon."

Jane waved.

With that, Hirsch stepped forward, leading them out. I stayed behind with Jane and Selena. As the door clicked shut behind Keisha and Marilyn, Jane spoke up, her voice shaking. "Don't let them take me back there."

29

JANE

After Martina and Selena assured me I wouldn't have to leave with Keisha and Marilyn, I felt a huge sense of relief and was glad to be going back home. Inside Selena's car, she looked at me and said, "How are you doing?"

I hesitated, turning the question over in my mind. How was I doing? My fingers drifted to the pendant on my necklace, rubbing it as if it held the answers I needed. An image of Keisha's face flashed in my mind—my sister. At least, that's what she claimed to be. I didn't have any memories of her, but something in my gut told me she was telling the truth. She looked like me. She even wore the same necklace.

But something else, something I couldn't quite put into words, told me that I needed to stay away. "Just processing everything, I think."

Selena started the car and began to drive out of the parking garage. "That's understandable. I mean, you seemed like something was off. Do you not think she's really your sister?"

"I do... I just—" I faltered, struggling to articulate my feelings. "I think maybe I have trust issues. Like she said, I ran away because I was afraid of how they would treat me... because I was pregnant. Maybe it wasn't such a happy home."

Selena's gaze stayed fixed on the road, her expression thoughtful. "That's a possibility."

"You seem to know a lot about crimes against women, you and Martina. Is that normal? I mean, when someone leaves an unhappy home, is it common for them to end up with someone who would hurt them?"

"Unfortunately, it's very common," she said. "Predators, they know the signs. They see you're from a broken or unhappy home, and they know exactly what to say and do to make you believe they're different. But once they get you alone, they show their true colors."

Maybe she was right, but nobody had addressed what I was most concerned about: my child. The doctors confirmed I had a child. Keisha confirmed that I had told her I was pregnant and planning to marry a man named Jacob. But where was my child now? Where was Jacob?

"Have they looked for my baby?"

Selena's hands tightened around the steering wheel. "The team has been combing through various databases, trying to match your DNA to any missing children. But there hasn't been a match, which means either the child wasn't reported missing, or they haven't been found... or both."

"Or maybe she's just... just off the grid, like I was."

"That's very possible," Selena agreed. "If the child wasn't born in a hospital and this Jacob person was also an 'off the grid' type, it would make tracking them a lot harder."

My chest tightened, the air in the car feeling heavy. "What does that mean for finding my baby?"

"It'll be difficult," she said. "But trust me, Martina doesn't give up, and neither do I. We'll learn the truth, even if it takes us some time."

Her words should have comforted me, but they didn't. The thought of my child—somewhere out there, alone, just like I'd been—gnawed at me, filling me with a sense of dread I couldn't shake.

The truth was supposed to make me feel better, right? I had a name. I had a family—or mostly, anyway. But what about Jacob? What about my child? Where were they?

As we drove, Selena slowed at a stoplight near the safe house. I watched her carefully. She checked her rearview mirror, glanced at her side mirrors, and then turned to look over her shoulder.

"Is everything okay?" I asked.

"Yeah, everything's fine," she said, but her tone was unconvincing.

Selena turned down a street that wasn't in the direction of the safe house. Was she afraid someone was following us? Who —Keisha? I opened my mouth to ask, but before I could, Selena spoke.

"Just making a quick stop. Want some coffee?" she asked, with what I thought was a fake smile.

"Sure..."

Her smile remained strained, and unease settled in my stomach. She was hiding something from me. But what? She pulled into a parking space in front of a small coffee shop. I reached for the door handle, ready to get out, when Selena's hand shot out, stopping me.

"Wait," she said firmly, turning to look at me. "I might be acting overly cautious, but I thought I saw a car following us earlier. It's possible it's just a coincidence and they're going the same direction as us. But I didn't want to risk it."

"What if—what if they know who I am?" I said, the panic rising in my chest. "What if they're after me?"

"They could be," she said. "That's why we have a safe

house. We always knew it was a possibility that someone would find out you're still alive. If they know that, they could try to... try to make sure you're dead."

"Why?" I demanded. "Why would they want me dead? That's what I don't understand, Selena."

She glanced around the parking lot, her eyes scanning the area with a hawk-like intensity before she met my gaze again. "Some people are just wired differently—psychopaths. They need to control people. It has nothing to do with you and everything to do with them and their problems."

"I just don't see how I could be a threat to anyone," I said, shaking my head in confusion.

"There's more to your story and we're going to figure out what it is."

I bit my lip, my thoughts a jumble of fear. Almost subconsciously, I reached up and touched the pendant on my necklace again, closing my eyes. Suddenly, a flash of a memory surfaced— a baby lying in a crib, quiet... too quiet. Panic gripped my chest as I tried to move toward her, but a man's hands stopped me, holding me back. I could see his shadowy figure in the corner of the room. I was sobbing, begging to hold her, but he kept whispering that I shouldn't look.

My eyes snapped open, breath coming in short gasps. Selena leaned closer, concern on her face.

"What is it?" she asked urgently.

"My child..." I choked out, my voice shaking. "A girl... my daughter. It feels like a memory."

"What's happening in the memory?"

"She's lying in a crib," I said, the images flashing through my mind. "She's not making any noise... there's a man there, and I'm crying. I'm trying to get to her, but he's holding me back. He keeps telling me not to look."

"Who is the man?"

"I... I don't know." Tears stung my eyes as I struggled to grasp the details slipping through my mind. "He—he feels familiar. He has brown hair. He wouldn't let me hold her."

A terrible sense of dread wrapped around my heart. What had happened to my daughter? Why couldn't I remember more? And who was the man keeping me away from her?

"We'll figure it out," Selena promised quietly. "One piece at a time."

But I wasn't so sure. Because the memory, blurry and incomplete as it was, filled me with a terror that told me things could be far worse than anything I had imagined.

30

MARTINA

THE UPDATE from Selena was troubling. Jane had recovered her first memory while fully conscious, and that could mean that more memories would begin flooding in soon. Until that point, her dreams had been fragmented—brief snippets that didn't always make sense. But having a waking memory, albeit a grim one, was a significant step forward.

Based on what Jane described—the baby lying so still in a crib and a man holding her back—it seemed likely that the child might have died. It wasn't unusual for a grieving mother to refuse to believe her baby was gone, her mind creating barriers to shield her from such an unbearable truth.

If Jane's daughter had died—there was no record of it. At least, none that we had found so far. Using Jane's DNA, we also searched for unknown remains or a missing person's report that could be the match for an offspring of Jane's. But since we had a name—Jacob Stoddard, the man who had fathered Jane's child, we could search for a child related to him.

The first thing I'd done after learning about Jacob was run to Vincent, asking him to pull up any records of deceased infants with that surname. Alongside this, I requested a search for every person named Jacob Stoddard in California and Oregon. He'd told us he'd come up with a few leads and called a meeting.

Hirsch, Vincent, and I met in the dimly lit conference room. Vincent stood in front of the white board with all the information on Jane's case. It had taken him all afternoon, and it was already late—almost dinnertime. We all had people to go home to, families waiting.

But Selena, as always, had insisted on staying with Jane at her apartment. Jane was upset, and Selena didn't want to leave her alone, especially since she had a gut feeling that they'd been followed earlier. I didn't like that one bit.

Vincent turned away from the whiteboard. "First off, I didn't find any death records for a child with the last name of Stoddard in the past three years."

Thank goodness. It could mean the baby hadn't died. But considering where Jane came from—a community that didn't use hospitals and therefore no official birth or death records—it was entirely possible that her child's existence had never been documented. "Let's hope that's because it's still alive."

Nods from Hirsch and Vincent.

Vincent continued, "And now moving on to the man in question. I've narrowed it down to three Jacob Stoddards in the right age range. One in Oregon, two in California."

My eyes narrowed. "How did you obtain the information? What records came up?"

"Great question," Vincent said.

If Jacob was new to Jane's community, it could mean that he hadn't always been anti-government like the rest of them. Maybe there was a time when he was more "on the grid" than off. That would mean records—driver's licenses, employment history, maybe even relatives—people we could track down and ask questions if needed.

"Jacob Stoddard has a driver's license. All three of them do," Vincent reported.

"Well, then we should have photos," I said.

Hirsch said, "We could show them to Marilyn or Marilyn's brother, Caleb, since they both use technology... if he'd ever call us back... and he could tell us which Jacob Stoddard is the right one." His brow furrowed as he glanced over at me. "I've called him a few times. He hasn't answered. Makes me wonder if Marilyn gave us the right number in the first place."

"Are you suspicious of her?" I asked, a little surprised. Marilyn had seemed quiet and a bit skittish, although from a less strict family than Keisha's, maybe she didn't trust outsiders too. Or she was just shy or scared. Intimidated, even.

"I don't know." Hirsch rubbed his jaw. "She seemed cagey when I took her information, like she was trying to remember it. Almost like she was reciting it from memory. And when I asked for her brother's phone number, she didn't pull out her phone to check—just rattled it off like she knew it by heart."

Vincent perked up. "Red flag."

"How so?"

Hirsch snorted. "Young people don't memorize phone numbers anymore, Martina. Everyone relies on their phones. Only older folks or people with something to hide keep that kind of information in their heads."

Vincent said, "It's true. Think about it—when was the last time you memorized a phone number?"

I hesitated, considering it. They had a point. Most people didn't even know their own family's numbers by heart these days. Was Marilyn hiding something? Or just overly prepared?

"So, what do we do?" I asked, scanning the profiles again.

Vincent said, "We've got two options: we either track down

all three of these Jacob Stoddards ourselves, or we call Marilyn and her brother, again, and get them to confirm which one is the right guy. But that assumes we trust them."

"Good point. We may not be able to."

Hirsch said, "I'll call Marilyn to see if she'll help identify him."

We quieted as he pulled out his phone and reviewed his notes before dialing. With the phone up to his ear, we waited. A few moments later, he shook his head before saying, "Hi Marilyn, this is August Hirsch, I'm working with Drakos Monroe. We met earlier today. Can you please call me back? I have a question for you about Jacob." He gave his contact information and ended the call. He eyed me and said, "I'm not going to hold my breath."

Vincent leaned back against the wall. "Well, there's three of us and three of them. If we're going to investigate all of these guys, we're going to need more help."

"Agreed. Hirsch, do you think Cromwell and Alameda County would pitch in?"

Hirsch grimaced. "He says he's swamped with a full case load. He's glad we found Jane's identity, but he doesn't think it helps much with the investigation itself. Said he'd do what he could on his end, but as for tracking down friends, brothers, or any loose ends... he just doesn't have the time."

Frustration simmered beneath my skin. It was beginning to feel like Cromwell hadn't done much investigating at all. We'd only been on the case for a week, and already we'd identified Jane and discovered she had a history with a man named Jacob Stoddard—along with possible family connections in Oregon. "But in most investigations, Jacob would be the number one person of interest and Cromwell doesn't have time to look for him?"

Hirsch shrugged. "Says he'll do what he can, but he's working a new murder and is tied up."

Fine. "Where exactly are the two in California located?" I asked.

Vincent said, "One's up north in Red Rose County, a few hours away. The other is in Oakland—not too far, less than an hour from here, give or take."

"And the one in Oregon?" I asked.

"Portland area," Vincent said. "All three of them are in reachable locations, but we'd need to coordinate if we want to check them out properly."

My mind whirled with possibilities. If we split up, we could cover all three locations within a day or two. But the risks were high—Jane's safety was paramount, and if any of these men were dangerous, we'd need backup.

"We'll need to proceed carefully," I said. "If one of these Jacob Stoddards is our guy, then we're not just dealing with a potential father and boyfriend of Jane. We're dealing with someone who could be desperate to keep his secrets buried. And if he thinks we're getting too close—"

"He might lash out," Hirsch finished grimly.

"Exactly," I agreed. "Let's keep trying to reach Marilyn and her brother. Maybe they're avoiding us on purpose, but we need to get them to talk. If they can ID the right Jacob, that'll save us a lot of legwork."

Hirsch said, "Will do."

Vincent said, "I'll stay on the electronic trail. Learn everything I can about each of the Jacob Stoddards."

Hirsch glanced up at the clock on the wall. Yes, it was late. "Let's break for tonight. We all have families to get to. Jane is safe, and waiting on background for a night won't impact the case. Agreed?" I asked.

Hirsch said, "Agreed."

"You got it, boss."

With that, we wrapped up our meeting. In the old days, I'm not sure I would have taken the break to be home by six. But some might say I'm older and wiser these days. If this job has taught me anything, it's that you never know how many minutes, hours, weeks, or years you have left with your loved ones. *Family first.*

31

SELENA

Looking into Jane's sad brown eyes, I asked, "Are you sure I can't stay?" Jane had been rattled by the events of the day, and I'd offered to spend the night on the couch, but she'd been insisting she was fine.

"I'll be fine, I promise."

"All right then. I'll talk to you tomorrow."

"Okay. Drive safe."

She walked me to the door where I gave her a warm hug before stepping outside. The cool midnight air hit me, sending a slight shiver down my spine. I lingered for a moment, waiting until I heard the heavy sound of the deadbolt sliding into place and the sound of the chain lock in place. Only then did I turn and head down the narrow path outside of the apartment unit to my car in the dark parking lot.

I was exhausted, ready for some sleep myself. Reaching my car, I opened the driver's door but paused, glancing around the dimly lit parking lot. My pulse quickened as I noticed a man sitting in a four-door sedan, staring straight at me.

I glanced up at the security cameras and made a mental note to review the tapes later if needed. My hand instinctively patted the baton in my pocket as I started walking toward the man's car. The vehicle's headlights suddenly blazed to life, and the engine roared as it sped out of the lot.

"Dang it!" I muttered, sprinting back to my car. I jumped into the driver's seat, fired up the engine, and tore out of the parking lot in pursuit.

My heart pounded like a jackhammer against my chest. Nobody should be sitting in a dark parking lot at midnight outside these apartments. This was supposed to be a safe house —well-vetted, with monitored security cameras everywhere. Could this guy be after Jane? Or was he after me? Either way, I had to find out.

The sedan weaved through the empty streets, and I pushed my car harder to keep up. I edged closer, squinting to memorize the license plate number. The driver tried to shake me with a quick right turn, but I skidded behind him, tires screeching, refusing to let him out of my sight.

I repeated the plate number silently in my head, determined not to forget it. I should call someone—maybe Martina. But she was probably asleep. Besides, what could she possibly do right now? No, I told myself, I could handle this on my own.

We barreled down a residential street lined with darkened homes, the only light coming from the occasional porch lamps casting light across the road. He veered left, and I followed suit, my grip tight on the steering wheel. There was no need to pretend I wasn't following him—he knew. And when I got him to stop, he would tell me who he was and why he was lurking outside Jane's place.

I was so laser-focused on the chase that I almost missed the flashing lights of a police car speeding behind me. Sirens blared, and my heart rate skyrocketed.

32

SELENA

THE MAN PULLED OVER, and I reluctantly did the same. The police car screeched to a stop behind us, and two officers rushed out, one heading toward the man's car in front of me, and the other stalking toward me.

"Great," I mumbled under my breath as he rapped sharply on my window.

I turned off the engine and lifted my hands in a show of compliance.

"Get out of the car!" he barked, his hand hovering dangerously close to his holstered weapon.

He saw me as a threat.

I took that as a compliment.

I slowly got out of the car, my hands raised in surrender. The officer glared at me. "Do you have any idea how fast you were going?" he asked sternly.

"About ninety," I said, forcing myself to keep my tone even despite my rattling nerves.

"Can you explain to me why you were going ninety and chasing the other car?"

I glanced over at the man I had been chasing, who was

now being questioned by another officer outside his car, so I could get a better look at him. Before I could answer, a second patrol car pulled up, lights flashing in the otherwise silent street.

Great, backup.

The first officer motioned for me to walk to the rear of my car, out of earshot from the man I'd pursued.

"What's going on here?" he asked.

Taking a deep breath, I steadied myself. "My name is Selena Bailey. I'm a private investigator. I work for Drakos Monroe Security & Investigations. I was at a safe house for one of our clients, and when I came out to the parking lot, this guy was just sitting there, like he was stalking or watching someone. So, I tried to approach him to find out what he was doing, but he took off. So, I followed him."

I shrugged nonchalantly, as if pursuing strange men at high speeds was a completely normal thing to do.

"What you did was very dangerous," he said flatly.

Before I could respond, another officer—one who looked young enough to still be attending academy classes—approached. He eyed me skeptically.

"Everything okay here?" he asked, glancing between us.

The first officer nodded. "Got an interesting story." He explained why I was pulled over and what I'd told him. The younger officer looked at me with curiosity. "Interesting."

The older officer said to the younger one, "You stay here with Ms. Bailey while I go see what's with the other guy."

The first officer turned and walked back to where the man stood, his posture still stiff and tense. I tried to make out what they were saying, but the distance made it difficult to hear.

"You know it's not legal for a PI to speed and chase after people, right?" He folded his arms and looked me up and down. "Are you even old enough to have a PI license?"

"Yes, I am," I replied coolly. "As a matter of fact, I work for Drakos Monroe. Ever heard of it?"

His eyes widened slightly. "Yeah, I've heard of it."

"Well, my stepmother is Martina Monroe, and if you have any questions about it, you can talk to her. Or to her pal, retired Sergeant Hirsch, who I was with earlier today."

The officer's gaze lingered on me for a moment longer before he sighed. "What did you say your name was?"

"Selena Bailey."

"Give me a second." He took a few steps back, his eyes still on me as he pulled out his phone. I didn't know who he was calling—maybe someone who could confirm my story. I hoped so because a reckless driving ticket wasn't exactly on my agenda for the evening.

The older officer—the uniform said Johnson—returned. "You have ID, Miss Bailey?"

"Yes, I do. My purse is in the front seat of my car," I replied, jerking my thumb toward the passenger side window.

"Do you have any weapons on you?"

"Just my baton, taser, and pepper spray. Oh...and a firearm in the glove box. And yes, I have a concealed carry permit," I said, shrugging nonchalantly. "Oh, and these." I wiggled my fingers with a playful smirk.

He shook his head, looking at me like I was either amusing or a complete lunatic—maybe a mix of both. "Do you mind walking over to the passenger side so I can get your driver's license?"

"Sure, no problem." I walked slowly, careful to keep my movements calm. No need to spook the officer. Getting shot was also *not* on my agenda for the evening. "So, who's the guy? Why was he in the parking lot? Did you ask?" I probed, glancing back at the sedan.

"He's a private citizen who says he was visiting a friend."

The younger officer walked over. "I've got someone on the phone who wants to talk to you," he said, his expression unreadable.

My heart leaped. I hoped it was Martina. She loved a good lecture, and I'd been long overdue for one.

I took the phone. "This is Selena."

"It's Hirsch."

Oops. "Hey, Hirsch," I said immediately.

"Officer Keller told me you were following at high speed. Who were you following?" His deep voice rumbled through the phone.

"That's the thing, Hirsch—I don't know who it is. When I left Jane's, I spotted a guy sitting in his car in the parking lot—at midnight. So, obviously, I wanted to know who he was. I ran up to him but then he sped off. I followed."

"Selena, that's incredibly dangerous. You shouldn't have done that." His voice was sharp, cutting through my bravado.

I sighed. He was just like Martina—overprotective to a fault. But I could take care of myself. *Most* of the time.

"I'm fine," I assured him, glancing at the officers beside me. "These lovely officers have been assisting me, and they know who the guy is, so maybe ask your pals to share the info. It could help the case."

I could practically hear him grumbling through the phone. "I'm going to request that you go home, not follow any other mysterious vehicles, and we'll talk in the morning. Do you think you can do that?"

"I can do that." I swallowed my irritation. It was sensible advice, but still frustrating.

"Please, Selena, be safe," he added, softer this time.

"Okay, okay." I handed the phone back to the young officer, who exchanged a few more words before hanging up.

Officer Johnson said, "What was that about?"

Officer Keller, the younger one, said, "That was Sergeant Hirsch. He confirmed she works for Drakos Monroe."

"Like I said before, I'm on a case," I said, my voice dropping low. "Can you tell me who the guy is?"

"I can't tell you that," he replied firmly. "He's a private citizen."

"But I've already memorized his license plate, and I'll just run it when I go back to the office," I shot back, crossing my arms.

Johnson sighed and shook his head. "Have a nice night, Ms. Bailey, and drive safe," he murmured, his tone dismissive.

I didn't move.

"We'll stay here with that gentleman until you go home."

"Fine," I grumbled. "Let's do it the hard way."

Grudgingly, I turned and made my way back to my car, every nerve in my body buzzing. I'd get answers. I didn't know who this man was—tall, brown hair, brown eyes, probably mid-to-late twenties, and with a face that looked like it was carved from stone. He had a mean look about him. Something in his eyes suggested he wasn't just some random guy passing by. We'd meet again, I was sure of it.

Sliding back into my car, I watched in the rearview mirror as the officers walked back to him. The man I'd been chasing glanced in my direction, his gaze lingering. He'd remember me too.

33

MARTINA

My jaw dropped as I listened to Hirsch explain the late-night phone call he'd received from local law enforcement. He described how Selena had been pulled over by a police car for excessive speeding and chasing some unknown person all on her own. He ended with, "She's lucky she didn't get a ticket—or worse, get thrown in jail or seriously hurt for as fast as she was going."

"Selena…" I said, shaking my head. What else could I say? "She hasn't always put her own safety as a priority."

"I know she's gotten herself into some pretty tough scrapes before. Like almost getting herself killed. Don't you worry about her?"

"Yes. All the time, Hirsch," I said. "Sometimes she doesn't have the most sound judgment. I'll be the first to admit that. But she's got good instincts, and I try not to be too hard on her… considering I might have done the same thing if I was in her shoes. It is concerning there was someone sitting in the parking lot of the safe house."

"Are those apartment safe houses just for Drakos Monroe?" he asked.

"No, we own a few of the units, not all of them. But we did install the cameras, and they're monitored 24 hours a day."

"So, the man could have been there for anyone. Not necessarily a threat against Jane."

"True. Between Selena and the surveillance, we should be able to find out who he was. Your friends didn't tell you who he was?"

"I didn't want to put them in that position."

Hirsch, the Boy Scout.

Before we could continue, I spotted Vincent and Selena hurrying toward us, their eyes bright and faces flushed with excitement. Whatever they'd found, it was big.

"We got him!" Vincent exclaimed breathlessly.

"Got him?" I asked.

Selena stepped forward, a fierce light in her eyes. "Jacob Stoddard. It was him—the guy from last night. He knows where she is. We need to move Jane right now."

Suddenly, my worry for Jane escalated to full-blown panic. I glanced at Hirsch, my heart thumping against my ribs. To Selena, I said, "Have you talked to Jane? Is she all right?"

"She's fine," she reassured me quickly. "She says everything's been quiet."

At least she was safe. *For now.*

Selena continued, "But I think we should go over there, pack her up, and move her somewhere else. We can't take any chances, Martina."

"You're right. Jacob was sitting outside her apartment—who knows what else he might do." I took a steadying breath.

Hirsch said, "I'll call Detective Cromwell and let him know we've spotted Jacob Stoddard. Alameda County will want to talk to him."

"Agreed."

Hirsch turned to Vincent. "Did you get an address for him?"

Vincent said, "I did. Based on the plates Selena memorized when she was following him, I tracked it down. Got his last known address and his driver's license. He's the one in Oakland."

Hirsch said, "I'll call Cromwell and arrange to have him picked up for questioning. You let me know if you need help with Jane. Otherwise, I'll work with Cromwell."

I said, "Go."

With a nod, Hirsch hurried off.

"I can take Jane to my place. It's secure enough. I'll call Charlie and let him know, but for now, she can stay with us."

Selena suddenly bounced on her toes. "Or she could stay with me."

It was a reasonable suggestion. Selena's place was just as fortified as mine—her apartment was practically a fortress, with reinforced locks, security cameras, and all the bells and whistles a paranoid investigator could want. But that thought worried me too. If Stoddard had seen Selena chasing him, he might already know who she was and track her down.

"Are you sure that's a good idea? He may know who you are."

"Even if he does know who I am, I can handle it. He shows up at my place, I'll be ready."

"Or you could both stay with your dad and me," I said, worried about both of them.

She hesitated. "Okay," she said. "Now, what about Stoddard? Are we just going to let Alameda County have him?"

I said, "Cromwell will bring him in for questioning. While he's at the Alameda County Sheriff's station, I'm sure Hirsch will arrange for us to interview him."

Vincent said, "Sounds like you two and Hirsch will be busy. While you're off taking care of Jane and Jacob, I'll pull everything I can find on him—background, associates, family, anything electronic going back as far as possible."

"That's appreciated, Vincent. Thank you."

"No problem, boss."

To Selena, I said, "Let's go."

With that, we turned and moved quickly out of the room, adrenaline propelling us forward. There was no time to waste.

34

JANE

THEY HAD FOUND HIM—PRESUMABLY my boyfriend or my husband, the father of my child. They found him because he found me, and now they were coming over to pick me up, pack up all my things, and move me to another location to make sure I was safe. They had assured me I'd be safe before he showed up —most likely the man in my dreams, the man I feared, the man who tried to hurt me.

A sharp knock on the door interrupted my thoughts. I hurried over, peeking through the peephole as I'd been instructed to do on more than one occasion by Selena. I knew she was just looking out for me. She was pretty much my only friend, so I heeded her advice. Martina was nice too—but she was more like a mother, as opposed to the girlfriend-like figure Selena was.

I opened the door, and Selena and Martina stood there, both with fake smiles on their faces, as if nothing was wrong, but I could tell something was off.

"Hey," I said cheerfully, trying to mask my anxiety.

They hurried inside, and I closed the door behind them.

Selena said, "Hi."

Martina looked at me with concern. "How are you holding up?"

"I guess I'm a little nervous... unsettled," I admitted, fidgeting with the hem of my sweater. "You said you found him —the man who was the father of my baby..."

"Yes," Selena said. "The Alameda County Sheriff is going to pick him up and bring him in for questioning."

"You're pretty sure he's the one who attacked me?" I asked, the knot in my stomach tightening.

Selena glanced at Martina before looking back at me. "Like we talked about, he's the most likely suspect, but it doesn't mean he was the one who did it. It could've been random. It could've been anyone. We're still trying to figure it out."

I nodded, trying to process everything. They were here to protect me, but it didn't change the fact that I no longer felt safe.

"Have you started packing?" Selena asked, glancing around the small apartment.

"Yeah, I don't have a lot of things, so that makes it pretty easy." The only possessions I had were what had been given to me by the hospital and a few items I'd picked up during shopping trips with Selena and Martina. Both of them were so kind. I wasn't sure what I had done to deserve their kindness. "I'm ready to go," I said, standing awkwardly in the middle of the small living room.

Martina glanced at Selena and then back at me. "Why don't we sit on the couch and just talk for a minute?" she suggested, patting the cushion beside her.

"Okay," I said sinking down onto the sofa.

Martina leaned forward slightly, her expression serious. "I was thinking maybe you could stay at my house—with Charlie, my husband, and of course, Barney, our dog. Selena's going to stay with us too. I'm a little concerned that until we know for sure that Jacob Stoddard is going to be locked up, or at least isn't a threat to you or Selena, you should stay with us."

I hesitated. "Okay... but for how long?"

"I'm not sure," Martina admitted. "But hopefully not very long. I'm sure you'd like to start your life at some point without having to look over your shoulder."

"I would." Then another thought pushed its way forward, and I looked up, my voice strained. "Do you think he knows where my baby is? Or at least what happened to her?" I could feel the tension tightening in my chest. "I have a bad feeling about the whole thing."

Martina's expression softened, sympathy in every line of her face. "We're definitely going to ask him about that. We're going to ask him everything—about you, where he's been, and if he tried to hurt you."

"So... this could all be over soon?"

Selena leaned in, her voice gentle. "We hope so. We'll do everything we can to wrap it up."

If this was over soon... What did that even mean for me? What would happen in the future? I had no job history, no money, and a terrible feeling about my family. Something deep inside me knew that I couldn't go back home. But what then? How could I move on from here? Selena and Martina couldn't keep supporting me forever.

I stood up abruptly, shaking off the spiral of thoughts. "I suppose we should get going."

Martina looked startled but quickly recovered. "Yes, unless there's anything else you want to talk about?"

"No, I think I'll feel better if we just get going."

"Okay."

I went to pick up the single cardboard box by the door—my whole life reduced to this one small box. I supposed it was more than I had a month ago. As I bent down to lift it, a sudden flash of memory surged through me.

In my mind's eye, I saw another box—something was inside. Before I could open it in the memory, a hand shot out, grabbing my arm and yanking me backward. The force knocked me to the ground. The face was clear now—his face. The man stood over me, blocking my path back to the box.

More memories flooded back in rapid succession. He kicked me, hard, and then hauled me up by my wrist, throwing me against a chair. "Sit down," he ordered, his voice cold and terrifying. "You're not going anywhere."

I gasped, snapping back to the present. My heart was racing, my pulse pounding in my ears. I stood up and turned to Martina and Selena, trembling. "Do you have a photo of Jacob Stoddard?"

Martina's eyes widened slightly. "We have his driver's license photo. Would you like to see it?"

I nodded frantically.

She pulled out her phone and swiped through the screen for a moment before handing it over to me. I stared down at the image, my breath catching in my throat.

As my body shook, I said, "It's him... It's definitely him."

Selena said, "Did you remember something else too?"

"Yes," I said, my eyes still fixed on the photo. I could feel more memories bubbling up, dark and suffocating. "And he's not a good man."

35

MARTINA

At home, I was greeted by both Charlie and Barney. Charlie, with his easy smile and warm presence, wrapped me in a comforting hug, making me relax instantly. Barney, our little ball of fluff, was more exuberant. Despite his age and the slight stiffness in his legs, he bounded toward me, his tail wagging furiously as if I'd been gone for weeks. Even though Barney was getting older, his spirit hadn't dimmed one bit.

I stepped back and said, "Thank you for always letting me bring home people who need a place to stay."

Charlie smiled, a slight crinkle forming at the corners of his eyes. "It's never a problem. This isn't the first time, and it likely won't be the last."

That was one of the reasons I loved him so much. He had an openness, a generosity that extended to anyone who needed it. Charlie wasn't just a husband; he was a steady rock in a world that sometimes felt too turbulent. I smiled back, grateful for the support he gave.

A few steps behind us, Selena and Jane entered quietly. Selena, with her auburn hair tucked neatly behind her ears, gave a small, tentative smile. Jane, by contrast, looked a little uncertain, glancing around with wide eyes. I turned, opening the door to Zoey's room and ushering the two girls inside.

I hesitated briefly in the doorway, my gaze lingering on the room. Should I still keep it preserved just as Zoey left it? With its pale pink walls and the collage of photos pinned above her desk, it looked exactly as it had before she went off to college. But with her getting married soon and spending more time with her fiancé's family, she likely would stop coming home as often as she used to. The thought hit me with a pang of bittersweet realization. She was growing up, and this room—her room—felt like a time capsule of the girl she used to be. Part of me wanted to hold onto it, to the memories it held, but another part told me it might be time to let go, to let it change as she did.

Inside Zoey's room, I led Jane over to the dresser. The drawers were mostly empty, except for the bottom one where Zoey kept a few emergency clothes—a spare pair of jeans, some comfy sweaters—things she didn't take to college but might need if she ever stayed the night unexpectedly.

"Feel free to use the first two drawers," I said, gesturing to them. "And there are hangers in the closet if you need them."

Jane's shoulders seemed to relax slightly as she ran her fingers over the polished wood. "Thank you again for letting me stay here. It's really kind."

"Think nothing of it," I said. "And Selena, do you need to go by your house to pick up anything, or do you have enough in your room?" I asked, turning to her.

Selena, who had been standing quietly to the side, shook her head. "I'm probably fine until tomorrow. I might swing by later to pick up a few things."

"All right," I said. It wasn't just about giving them a place to stay—it was about making them feel safe, wanted, and as close to 'home' as I could offer. No matter what.

Charlie stood in the doorway of Zoey's room, watching us while

Barney circled around Selena before padding over to greet Jane. Selena walked over to Charlie and wrapped her arms around him.

"Hey, Dad."

"Hi, honey," he said, hugging her back.

Jane shifted a little awkwardly. "Mr. Bailey, thank you for letting me stay here."

"Please call me Charlie," he corrected gently, waving off the formality. "The more, the merrier! I get to see my daughter and have more people to try my new recipes on."

I glanced over, curious. "What is it this time?"

"I've been experimenting with a new Dijon mustard sauce. I think you'll like it."

I smiled. It was a real blessing to be married to someone who loved to cook. I wasn't much of a cook myself, but I certainly loved to eat—especially Charlie's recipes.

"How's the book coming, Dad?" Selena asked, tilting her head.

"It's going well. Barney's been helping," Charlie said, giving the dog a playful look.

I chuckled. "And by helping, do you mean he sits on your laptop when you're not paying attention to him?"

"Yep."

"I'll let you get settled, and we'll just be in the living room if you need anything," I said, starting to back out of the room.

Charlie said, "If you're hungry, I can make sandwiches, or we have some lasagna and garlic bread in the fridge leftover from last night."

"I could eat," Selena said.

Jane smiled too. "Yeah, if you're making stuff anyway."

It was almost lunchtime. "Great, then! Coming right up," Charlie said as he hurried out. I gave Jane a quick hug before leaving her and Selena in Zoey's room. I made my way to the kitchen, where Charlie was already busying himself at the counter.

"You are the best," I said warmly.

"Oh, stop," he said with a playful grin, glancing over his shoulder. "Do you really think they're both in danger?"

"Well, until I hear that this guy is in custody and no longer a threat to Selena or Jane, I want to make sure they're somewhere nobody can get to them."

"Hirsch working on it?"

"Yeah, he's coordinating with Alameda County. They should be picking up the guy any moment now."

"Good."

Just then, my phone buzzed. Glancing at the screen, I saw Hirsch's name flash. "It's Hirsch," I said, excusing myself from the kitchen and stepping into the hallway. I swiped to answer. "What's up?"

"I think you should come down here pretty quick, Martina," Hirsch said, his voice tense.

"What? Why?"

"We picked up Jacob Stoddard. He's down at the Alameda County Sheriff's Station. They brought him in for questioning, but... he's asked for a lawyer. I think they're gonna let him go soon. You might want to get down here as soon as possible to ask him questions before he leaves."

"Thanks, Hirsch. I'll be right there." Ending the call, I hurried back to the kitchen, planting a quick kiss on Charlie's cheek. "Rain check on lunch?"

"Oh?" he asked, eyebrows raised.

"Jacob Stoddard is at the station, but he might be released soon. I need to be there before that happens."

Charlie's expression shifted from confusion to understanding. "Be careful."

"I will." I walked back to Zoey's room and found Jane and Selena sitting on the bed, deep in conversation.

"Ladies," I began, "I'm going to have to head out to question Jacob Stoddard. He's at the Alameda Sheriff's Station."

"Already?" Jane asked, sitting up straighter.

"Since he was pulled over recently, they were able to confirm his last known address pretty quickly, and we already had information on where he worked. It was a quick pickup."

"Then why the rush?" Selena asked.

"They think they might have to let him go soon."

Jane stood up abruptly. "Can I go?"

"You want to go?" I asked, thrown by the request. "Why?"

"I'd like to see him. Ask him questions. Maybe it'll help bring back more memories."

"I'm not sure it's a good idea, Jane," I said hesitantly, weighing the risk.

Selena jumped in. "Maybe I can stay with her inside the station while you question him. And once you're done, maybe we can arrange for Jane to see him—just briefly. Nothing official, but I think she deserves that, don't you?"

I glanced at Selena, wishing she'd asked me privately and not in front of Jane. I didn't like the idea, not at all. But... she had a point. He would be in a sheriff's station, unarmed, surrounded by law enforcement. If he tried anything, we'd be there to protect her.

"Okay," I said reluctantly. "Let's go. We need to hurry."

36

MARTINA

THE AIR in the car was thick with nervous energy on the way to the Alameda County Sheriff's Station. There were long stretches of silence interrupted by occasional questions about safety and what I planned to ask him. I knew Selena wanted to be in the interrogation room with me, but her priority was to protect Jane, to be a friend and a source of comfort. Jane was about to see the man who had hurt her and might have tried to kill her. She needed Selena with her.

As I pulled into the parking lot of the station, I glanced back at the two women sitting quietly in the back seat. Jane's hands were clenched tightly, and Selena sat close to her, their shoulders almost touching.

"Hirsch said he'll meet us at the entrance," I said. "Selena, you'll wait with Jane until I've had a chance to question Jacob."

"Does he actually have to talk to you?" Selena asked.

"No, he doesn't. And he's already asked for a lawyer, so technically no one from law enforcement can ask any questions," I said. "But I can—and so can Hirsch, because he's not law enforcement either."

Selena nodded slowly.

"All right. Let's go."

We all exited the car, and I watched as they walked slightly ahead of me, their steps in sync.

As we approached the entrance, I spotted Hirsch standing by the door. He waved when he saw us, and I lifted a hand in return.

"Hey, how are you doing?" he asked as we came closer.

"We're okay," Selena said.

Jane remained silent, her gaze downcast.

"Good," Hirsch said. "I talked to Cromwell. He's right inside. He'll take the two of you to a room while Martina and I try to talk to Jacob."

With quiet nods of agreement, we followed Hirsch into the station. Detective Cromwell was waiting for us, his expression serious.

"Good to see you, Martina," Cromwell said, extending a hand.

"You too."

Cromwell said, "And you're looking well, Jane. Good to see you. Selena, good to see you too. Is there anything I can get you before we head into the room?"

"I'm fine," Selena said.

"And you?" Cromwell asked, looking at Jane. "Anything you need?"

"Nothing, thanks," Jane murmured, her voice barely audible.

I could see the tension in her shoulders, the way her gaze flitted around the room, searching for exits. Understandably, she was nervous. She was about to face her abuser, the man who might very well have ended her life if given the chance.

Cromwell led us to a small conference room, gesturing for Jane and Selena to enter. Before closing the door, he looked back at us. "If you need anything, I'll be right outside."

"Thank you," Selena said, placing a reassuring hand on Jane's arm.

The door clicked shut, leaving Hirsch and me standing in the hallway. This was it. Time to confront the man. As we continued down the hallway, Cromwell leaned in slightly and said, "She looks nervous."

"I think she is," I said, glancing back at the closed door where Jane and Selena waited.

"Has she remembered anything?"

"The memories are coming back bit by bit. She's recalled a few things while she's been awake, but most of it has surfaced through nightmares," I explained. "She's fairly certain Jacob has abused her."

"That doesn't surprise me," Cromwell said, shaking his head. "But at the same time, this doesn't feel like a straightforward case of attempted murder."

"Agreed," Hirsch said. "There's no solid evidence yet, but if he abused her in the past, it's not far-fetched to think she was running from him, and he finally caught up to her. That's my theory, anyway."

Cromwell said, "But he's been in the Bay Area for quite a while, at least during the last year."

I said, "Yeah, that doesn't mean he hasn't been looking for her."

"True," he said. "Just so you know, his lawyer hasn't shown up yet."

"Thanks, Cromwell," I said

"Sure thing."

Cromwell paused outside a heavy, steel-reinforced door, took a deep breath, and then swung it open. "You have a couple of visitors, Jacob," he announced.

The man inside the interrogation room, sitting alone at a metal table, turned his head. His dark brown eyes were sharp, scanning us with curiosity, but it was fleeting—more an appraisal than actual interest. He leaned back slightly, crossing his arms in a casual defiance.

"I invoked my right to an attorney. I'm not talking to you," Jacob said flatly, his tone clipped.

"These are visitors, not law enforcement," Cromwell clarified with a hint of a smirk. "Just visitors. Friends."

Jacob's gaze narrowed, clearly not pleased, but he didn't protest. I stepped inside, with Hirsch trailing behind me.

We both took seats across from him, keeping our posture relaxed, almost friendly. "Hi, Jacob," I began, my voice even. "My name is Martina Monroe, and this my associate, August Hirsch."

"Why are you here?"

"I'm a private investigator, and Hirsch is helping me out with the case," I explained. "We were told there was a woman who couldn't remember her identity, so I've been trying to find out who she is. We're not law enforcement."

"I see," he said, tilting forward slightly, eyes narrowing.

"Do you know who we found?" I asked.

His lips twitched, almost a sneer. "From what I understand, you found Hanna."

"Yes, we found Hanna. And so did you," I said softly. "I'd like to understand how you found her."

He cocked his head, considering me for a moment before giving a nonchalant shrug. "A friend told me."

Perhaps Marilyn or her brother? Both of whom had never bothered to call us back. "And what exactly were you doing sitting in the parking lot outside her apartment last night?" I asked.

"I just wanted to know that she was okay. How is she?"

I didn't believe he cared about her well-being for one second. His body language was too controlled, too precise. He was lying through his teeth, and we both knew it. If I were a betting woman, I'd say he'd been outside that apartment for far more sinister reasons.

"She's fine," I said, my smile thin. "That's really kind of you to ask, though."

"Yeah, well, I care a lot for her. I was so worried when she ran away," Jacob said, his voice dropping into a faux-sincere tone.

"Not worried enough to report her missing, though," Hirsch pointed out.

"That's not how things are done where we're from. Well, where *she's* from."

"Do you mind telling us about where she's from? She doesn't remember much—very little, actually," I said, hoping to keep him talking.

He snorted softly. "Well, I heard you talked to her sister, so you probably know she's from Oregon. She grew up in a... let's just say, in a unique family. Anti-government types. Heck, Hanna doesn't even have a birth certificate." He leaned back, shaking his head as if the absurdity of it still amazed him. "I was floored. We were going to get married, but we had to go through the process of getting her a birth certificate—a delayed birth certificate. Do you have any idea how hard that is to get?"

"No, actually," I said.

"It's a nightmare." He sighed. "You have to get sworn statements from relatives, verifying when she was born. It's a whole mess. So, anyway, we didn't get married because of that."

"And how long were you and Hanna together?" I asked, shifting the focus back to Hanna.

"We were together for about two years before she took off on me. I mean, I understand why," he said, letting out a long exhale.

I raised an eyebrow. "Why did she run off?"

"As you probably know by now, she was pregnant, and she had the baby. We were so happy."

"Was it a boy or a girl?" I asked.

"A little baby girl. Beautiful. Looked just like Hanna," he said, a shadow crossing his face.

Like in Hanna's memory. "So then, what happened?"

"We were devastated. The baby, Abigail—she died. She was only eight months old. It was SIDS, Sudden Infant Death Syndrome. There's nothing we could've done. We had no idea it was even possible," he said with little emotion.

"Did Hanna go to the hospital to have Abigail?" I asked.

He shook his head vehemently. "No, no. Her family had turned her against doctors and medicine. They didn't ever want her to go to a hospital. I'm telling you, those people are kind of nuts."

"Where did she have the baby?"

"At home," he said. "I helped her through the delivery. I looked up things online—had to, to know how to do it right. I wanted them to be safe." He paused. "But I failed at that."

"If you never went to a hospital, how did you know Abigail had died because of SIDS?"

Jacob hesitated for a few beats. "I looked it up online."

A Google search was hardly a substitute for an autopsy. I looked over at Hirsch and he raised his eyebrows.

"So, what happened with Hanna?" I asked.

"She... she just freaked out on me," he said. "I understood. I was grieving too, devastated. Our baby girl—gone, just like that. We were so happy, young and in love, and then we had this beautiful baby, and it was all taken away so fast. I just don't think she could handle it."

"So... she ran away?" I asked, skeptically.

"Yeah," he said. "She ran away, and I tried to stop her. You know, told her we could get through it together. We loved each other. We could get through anything if we were together."

I studied his face, his eyes slightly too wide, his voice too practiced. I wondered if he thought he was a better actor than he actually was. I'd seen Jane's X-rays. I'd heard her fractured memories. He didn't want her to stay out of love—he wanted her to stay because he thought he owned her.

"Right," I said. "And when exactly did you stop trying to help her, Jacob?"

He glanced away, jaw tightening, and I knew I'd hit a nerve.

"Did you look for her?"

"I did. I tried finding her. I wanted to get her help," Jacob insisted, his eyes widening as if pleading for understanding. "But it was like, every time I got an idea of where she might be, she'd disappear again. You know? I swear, I was so happy to hear that she was found, and she's... she's alive and healthy." He paused, taking a deep breath. "I just want to talk to her."

"Then why didn't you go to her when you knew where she was?" I challenged.

Jacob shifted uncomfortably. "Honestly, I didn't go and talk to her because I was scared she didn't want to talk to me considering she ran away the last time I saw her."

I exchanged a quick glance with Hirsch, who gave me a knowing look. I turned back to Jacob, leaning in slightly. "When was the last time you saw Hanna?"

"It's been... probably about a year and a half. That's when she ran away."

"And what happened to the baby after she died?" I asked softly, watching his reaction.

"We buried her," he said quietly, his gaze dropping to the table.

"Where did you bury her?"

"Back up in Oregon, near where she used to live. We

didn't go to her actual home, though, because, well, like I said, her family's... different. And her father, my gosh—violent, awful man. If he'd known she had a baby and wasn't married..." He trailed off, shaking his head. "I don't know what he would've done. But he sure as heck wouldn't have let her stick around. She would've been cast out by the rest of them."

I nodded slowly, piecing together his narrative.

"Do you remember exactly where the grave is?" I asked. "If we had a crew go out there, could they find the baby?"

Jacob's face twisted with sudden anger. "I'm not gonna let you dig up my baby girl. Are you crazy?"

I raised my hands in a calming gesture. "I'm not saying that's what we're going to do. I'm just asking."

He glared at me for a long moment, then leaned back, shaking his head again.

"Where were you living at the time?"

"We were living in Northern California, right on the border," he muttered, crossing his arms defensively.

"So, you drove back up to Oregon to bury the baby," I repeated slowly, "and then, when you came back, that's when she ran off and went missing?"

His expression darkened. "Yeah, I wished she would've stayed with me. I just wanted her to be safe," he said, his voice dripping with false sincerity.

"Safe from what?"

"From herself. Her family."

"And you've settled here in the Bay Area for the past year, from what we understand?"

"Yeah." He sighed. "I gotta work, you know? I wanted to spend all my time looking for her, but I just couldn't. I gotta pay the rent." He paused. "But I wish she'd come home with me. Is there any way I can talk to her?"

"Yes, actually," I said, leaning back slightly. "We brought her to the station."

Jacob's eyes widened. "Oh, great!" he exclaimed, a smile breaking across his face. The sudden eagerness was unsettling.

"But I'm a little concerned about that," I said.

"Why?" he asked, his smile fading. "I just want what's best for Hanna. I really love her."

"I think she remembers it differently."

"I thought she didn't have any memories?" he snapped, his tone suddenly sharp.

I leaned forward. "She's had nightmares, Jacob. And a few flashes of memories. She still doesn't remember everything, but from what she does remember... Well, I've been doing this for a long time. And you see, my friend here used to work homicide. We're both really concerned about the safety of people we're meant to protect."

"She's got nothing to worry about with me. I swear."

I studied him for a long moment, weighing my next question carefully. "Where were you on August 23, Jacob?"

He stiffened, his eyes narrowing. "That sounds a little bit like a law-enforcement question," he said slowly. "Are you interrogating me now?"

"No," I said, not breaking eye contact. "I'm just trying to understand what happened to Hanna."

He leaned back, arms crossing defensively over his chest. "You said you weren't law enforcement."

"I'm not," I assured him. "But like I said, I'm very concerned about Hanna's safety."

"Yeah, well," he said. "Like I said, she's got nothing to worry about with me. I love her."

I glanced at Hirsch, who gave a slight nod. We both knew what Jacob's kind of "love" looked like. And it was far from harmless.

"If that's true, why wouldn't you talk to the police?" I asked, keeping my gaze steady on him.

"I just don't like talking to cops, you know," Jacob said, shifting in his seat. "I swear, I never would hurt her. I have an alibi, if that's what you're asking. August 23—I remember it clearly. I was in Vegas for a buddy's bachelor party."

"An alibi?" I raised an eyebrow. "Did you tell Detective Cromwell about this?"

"I told you, I'm not talking to him without a lawyer."

"Would you be willing to give us some details about your trip?" I pressed. "Did you fly? Did you drive?"

"Look," he snapped. "I'm not interested in any kind of interrogation. I just want to see Hanna. I want to bring her home, let her know I love her. I want to protect her."

I leaned in slightly. "Well, I'd like to know for sure, as someone who's been protecting Hanna, that you weren't the one who almost killed her and left her for dead on August 23."

Jacob's eyes flashed angrily, but he forced a calm expression. "I already told you, I was in Vegas with my buddies. It's all under my name—you have my information, from what I understand. Check the flight records. Check the hotels. They've got security cameras everywhere in Vegas. I wasn't even in the Bay Area when she got attacked."

I studied him, weighing the truth of his words. He seemed too eager to prove his innocence, but that didn't mean he was lying. If he was in Vegas, it couldn't have been him who attacked Hanna that night. So, who did?

"Okay," I said slowly, leaning back. "I appreciate your cooperation. We'll check your alibi. And we will let you see Hanna, but only for a few minutes. As you can imagine, she's been through quite an ordeal."

Jacob's face softened, and for a moment, I almost believed the concern in his eyes. "I just want what's best for her."

37

JANE

SELENA WAS TELLING me a story about the first time she'd been in a police station. She made light of it, but I could sense the weight of the memory; it was a traumatic experience for her. I think she used humor to help her cope. That first time had been right after her mother was killed—a terrible memory for sure— but she didn't focus on the loss. Instead, she talked about what it felt like to be inside a police station and how she met a great police officer who would eventually change her life.

She said that was when she decided she wanted to dedicate her life to helping people, whether through law enforcement or private investigations. That experience, she told me, had given her a clear direction on what she wanted to do with her life.

Suddenly, the door swung open, and Martina and Hirsch walked in. Their faces were grim, lacking any trace of a smile.

"How did it go?" I asked.

"He talked to us. He says he has an alibi and that he wasn't the one who attacked you," Martina said. "I've already called Vincent to start verifying his alibi to see if it's solid."

Selena said, "Did he tell you anything else?"

Martina and Hirsch exchanged glances before settling down

into the chairs opposite us. Martina cleared her throat. "He did. He confirmed Keisha's story about where you're from and how the two of you ran away... and had a baby."

My heart nearly pounded out of my chest. The words hit me like a tidal wave. What happened to my baby girl?

"He said that you ran away from him," Martina added quietly.

"That's what I remember," I said. "I assumed I tried to leave again and was successful. Did he say what happened to our baby?"

Martina swallowed hard. "He said your daughter, Abigail, died when she was eight months old... of sudden infant death syndrome. I'm so sorry."

The room spun around me. A memory, not just a nightmare —a living nightmare—surfaced. The baby in the crib, so still. Someone was telling me not to look, but I had. The sight of her tiny form, eyes closed, unmoving.

"Where is she buried?" I asked.

"He said the two of you buried her up in Oregon, near your family's land but not on it," Martina explained. "He said that's where you wanted her to be... Home."

I processed the information slowly. My baby had died. Abigail had died. Martina continued, "He said that's why you ran away. You couldn't cope. It had nothing to do with him. He said he tried to find you. He says he loves you and wants to keep you safe."

Selena's face tightened. "You don't believe that, do you?" she asked.

Martina shifted uncomfortably. "I'm cautious of him, especially given the fragmented memories you've recovered so far."

I shook my head. Something didn't feel right. The story felt hollow. But I had seen the baby in the crib—eyes closed, still... not crying, not wiggling.

"Do you believe him?" I asked. "Do you trust him?"

Martina looked directly at me. "No," she said firmly. "I don't. Jacob said he tried looking for you, but something about him doesn't sit right with me. I don't think he's being 100% honest. It's just a hunch, not fact-based. But if you still want to see him, we'll go with you. Otherwise, we can just leave him be for now."

I took a deep breath, trying to piece together the memories in my mind.

"Why was Jacob outside the apartment at midnight?" Selena asked.

"He says he didn't want to upset you," Martina said. "The last time you left him, you were really upset. He just wanted to make sure you were okay."

Her words washed over me, but they didn't trigger anything. There were no memories that matched up. My nightmares were filled with worry and fear, not safety. None of this felt right. My instincts screamed at me not to trust him. Selena was watching me closely; her own intuition seemed to align with mine.

"Did he say anything else about my family?"

"He did. He said they likely wouldn't have accepted you back into the community since... well, since you'd had a baby out of wedlock."

"How did he find me?"

"He didn't say that exactly. But somebody told him—maybe Marilyn, or maybe Marilyn's brother—I'm not sure."

My resolve hardened. "I want to see him. I want to see his face. I need to confront him."

Martina studied me, then said, "All right. If you want to do this, we'll be with you. You don't have to face him alone."

A sense of determination pulsed through me. There was something about this encounter that felt critical, like I needed to unlock something buried deep inside.

I followed Martina down the hallway, Selena trailing just behind me. We moved quietly, tension thickening the air as we approached the conference room. Martina knocked on the door, then opened it slowly and stepped inside. She spoke to Jacob softly, informing him that I was coming in.

"Oh, good," Jacob responded, and something about his voice sent a shiver down my spine. The hair on the back of my neck stood up. Martina motioned for me to enter, but I hesitated at the threshold.

I turned to Selena and said, "Can we keep the door open?"

"Absolutely."

Steeling myself, I stepped through the doorway. The moment my eyes locked onto his, a cold certainty settled over me. He was why I ran. He was the monster in my nightmares. He stood up slowly, his gaze fixed on me.

"Hanna, it's so good to see you," he said with a grin. "I've missed you so much."

I didn't move closer. My body tensed, my heart hammering in my chest. Without thinking, I reached for Selena's hand, clinging to it for support. She stepped forward slightly, her voice firm. "Just stay right there, Mr. Stoddard."

"My name is Jane now," I said quietly.

"Jane," he repeated softly. "I'm just so happy... happy you're safe."

"Why?"

"Because I love you."

The words felt like ice against my skin. I'd heard them before, the same way, in a different place. A memory flashed through my mind—my face swollen, my hands clutching at my head, his voice dripping false sweetness. "I love you. I'm sorry," he had said.

I stared at the floor, fighting to keep myself grounded. But then the memory sharpened—me, broken and bruised, cowering under him. I glanced up sharply, my gaze locking onto his.

"No," I said. "I remember now. You don't love me. You hurt me. You... you hurt our baby."

"That's not true!" His voice rose, panic flashing in his eyes. He turned desperately to Martina and Hirsch. "I don't know where she's getting this from."

"I never want to see you again," I spat.

I turned sharply and bolted for the door, Selena chasing after me. Martina and Hirsch tried to calm me, their voices a blur as I stumbled down the hallway. Everything was spinning out of control. Selena caught up, her arm wrapping around my shoulders, pulling me close.

"Are you okay?" she asked softly, her breath warm against my ear.

"He's responsible," I choked out. "Whatever happened to my baby... it was him. He hurt me. I remember now. All I have are memories of him hurting me. It was him... standing over the crib. I think... I think he killed her."

Tears streamed down my face, my body shaking with sobs. Selena tightened her grip, her own body tense.

"We'll find out what happened," she promised fiercely. "We'll find her, Jane. And he's going to pay for what he did."

I said, "If he hurt her, he has to pay. *He has to pay.*"

"He will," Selena said. "He'll pay for everything."

38

MARTINA

Selena and I entered through the heavy glass doors of Drakos Monroe. It was a Saturday, so we had to let ourselves in. Vincent was presumably already inside. He'd agreed to work over the weekend to dig deeper into Jacob Stoddard's life. The reception area was empty except for the soft hum of the air conditioning, and the scent of freshly brewed coffee drifted toward us.

Inside the cubicle area, I spotted Vincent standing by the coffee maker, his tall frame leaning casually against the counter. We made our way over to him.

"Morning, Vincent."

"Morning, Martina, Selena. How's Jane doing?" Vincent said, glancing up from his cup.

"She's hanging in there, but... she's devastated," I said.

"I can't even imagine. It's like she's had to learn her baby died all over again. That's rough," Vincent said.

He was a parent, too, and I could see the empathy on his face. There was nothing more devastating than losing a child, but having to experience that knowledge twice? It was doubly cruel.

I said, "Well, thank you for coming in. I'm hoping we can get to the bottom of this as soon as possible."

"Do we know if Alameda County is doing anything to confirm Jacob's alibi?" Selena asked.

"I talked to Hirsch. He said they're pulling warrants for the flight manifest and hotel reservations," Vincent said, setting his mug down with a soft clink.

"Sounds like that's gonna take a while," I commented, crossing my arms.

"Yeah, we want his cell phone records, but that could take a while too. Hopefully, they'll rush it," Vincent said. "But considering there's not really an active threat against the community, they'll probably take their time—a few days to a few weeks."

Vincent would know. He used to work for the CoCo County Sheriff's Department in their research division. He was intimately familiar with the red tape that came with gathering evidence and waiting on warrants for information.

Selena said, "So, what do we do? We aren't just going to sit around and wait on Alameda County for warrants, right?"

I understood Selena's concerns. Jacob could be trying to find Jane as we spoke.

Vincent said, "I've been working with some of our best tech guys to see if we can get through the back door to check on Jacob's alibi."

Selena's eyes lit up. "You mean breaking into systems? That's so cool."

Cool? It was illegal, for starters, but I bit back the comment. We operated in a gray area at times, often sharing what we found with law enforcement agencies. They rarely asked where we got certain information, choosing not to know, as long as they could acquire it legally later to make an arrest or build a solid case.

"Any luck so far?" I asked.

"He says we should learn something new soon, but there's a lot of data to sift through. That's where I think it might be helpful if you guys could step in. Or... we could just call Jacob and ask him directly—what flight he was on, what time, and what hotel."

"Then you'd pull security footage from the hotel to confirm he was actually there, right? Make sure he didn't just board a plane, turn around, and board another one back to set up a perfect alibi," Selena suggested.

"If we find out what hotel he stayed at, we'll definitely want the surveillance footage," Vincent agreed. "Most hotels will oblige if we ask in the right way."

I said, "Fingers crossed."

I spotted Lewis, our top computer genius at Drakos Monroe, walking toward us. His disheveled hair and slightly wrinkled shirt were telltale signs of someone who spent more time behind screens than under the sun. He moved with an easy confidence, his gaze sharp behind his glasses.

"Hey, Lewis. Thanks for coming in," I said.

"No problem. I got some information for you," he said casually, reaching up to grab a mug from the cupboard and setting it under the coffee machine.

"What did you find?" I asked.

"Finding the flight wasn't as tricky as I thought it would be," Lewis said. "Since he said he left on Friday and lives in Oakland, I made a few assumptions like he flew out of Oakland International Airport and into Las Vegas. There were quite a few flights that day, but I managed to narrow it down. I pulled the manifests, and—*bingo*—Jacob Stoddard was on a plane to Las Vegas from Oakland International Airport on August 22, the day before Jane was attacked. He returned late on Sunday, August 24, back into Oakland."

His alibi checked out? The timelines matched, but that

wasn't enough confirmation for me. "How about his hotel stay?" I pressed.

Lewis said, "He checked into the Horseshoe Hotel in Las Vegas, under his name."

"Can we get surveillance footage from the hotel to verify that it was really him? Not someone else pretending to be him, or him checking in and then driving back to the Bay Area to attack Jane and return when he finished?"

Lewis scratched the back of his head, considering. "I haven't pulled the footage from the hotel yet, but I'll see what I can do. Driving from Vegas to the Bay Area is a ten-hour drive, though. He would've literally had to check into the hotel, drive back to the Bay Area, attack her, then drive back to Vegas. It's not very probable, but I'll get you that surveillance footage. Computer security's not super tight at places like the Horseshoe—it's no government agency," he added with a smirk.

"It's so cool that you're able to get information almost like the flick of a wrist," Selena said admiringly, leaning against the counter.

Lewis said, "It definitely can come in handy in situations like these."

I exchanged a glance with Selena. Much as I appreciated her enthusiasm, I worried about her impulsive nature and draw toward the illegal. The part of her brain responsible for caution hadn't fully developed yet, and it showed. I didn't like the idea of her skating so close to the line between legal and illegal. But then again, that was the business we were in.

"All right, Lewis. Do what you can," I said with a nod.

"Sure. I'll grab the surveillance footage and do some recon for you. I'll get back to you. You'll be here a while?" he asked, taking a long sip of his coffee.

"We're here until you're done," I said. "And we're going to

work with Vincent, look into more of this guy's background as well."

"Good luck," he said, raising his mug in a mock salute before heading off to his workspace—affectionately dubbed "the Cave"—where he worked his tech magic.

As he disappeared around the corner, I turned back to Selena. "Let's see if we can piece together more of Jacob's movements. If there's a hole in his story, we'll find it."

"Do you need some coffee first?" Vincent said with a grin. "It's been a long time since I've seen you in the morning without a coffee cup in your hand, Martina."

"Dad made it for us this morning," Selena explained.

"That makes sense," he said, giving a knowing nod. "Let's head to the conference room."

We moved down the hall and entered the familiar space. As I stepped inside, I looked up at the whiteboard already filled with scribbled notes and pinned documents. It was covered in background information on Jacob Stoddard, all neatly categorized. Vincent gestured to the board, his expression serious.

"This is everything I found," Vincent said. "Jacob, who has no criminal history, is a Bay Area native, born and raised. The only gap in his Bay Area residency was for about a year, presumably when he was in Oregon ruining Jane's life." Pausing, he pointed to the board. "He's held somewhat steady work. Mostly retail and customer service positions. No college degree."

"What about his family?" I asked.

"He's got some family in the Bay Area—his mom and an uncle, but that's about it."

"What about known associates?" Selena asked.

Vincent shook his head. "No criminal record, so no known associates in the system."

Selena crossed her arms, a look of frustration flashing across her face. "It all seems a little too perfect, doesn't it? He just happens to have an alibi for the weekend when Jane was attacked—right after she's been on the run from him for over a year and a half. And then, as soon as she shows up in the Bay Area, something happens. She must've known that's where he was from. Something—or someone—lured her back."

But what? "Maybe Jane's attacker was someone connected to Jacob. He may have had somebody else do his dirty work for him. It seems unlikely, but abusers will go to great lengths to exhibit control. Maybe Jacob had been looking for her to kill her and realized he'd be the number one suspect, so he had a friend help him out." What kind of friend would do that? "What about financials, Vincent?"

"We haven't gotten them. I wanted to confirm his alibi first. But I'll tell Lewis to look once he's done with the surveillance. If there were large amounts of cash moved around, it could point to a hired hit."

Based on Jacob's work history, I'd be surprised if he could afford a hired hit. But then again, I've heard of killers-for-hire who would do the deed for five hundred dollars. It was entirely possible. I said, "In the meantime, regardless of his alibi and financials, I think we should follow him, find out who he's meeting with, and see where he goes. I'd also like to interview his mother and uncle. See what they can tell us. I want to learn everything there is to know about Jacob Stoddard."

Vincent said, "Good thinking, boss."

"Let's put together a plan."

My instincts screamed that Jacob Stoddard had everything to do with what happened to Jane, and we wouldn't stop until we uncovered the whole truth and ensured Jane's attacker, and her child's killer, was brought to justice.

39

JANE

I waved goodbye to Charlie as he left to go to the grocery store. Before leaving, he had asked if I had any special requests. He was always so nice. So were Martina and Selena. They were too good to me, and in some ways, I felt bad that I was about to deceive them.

After they told me Jacob hadn't been the one to attack me—that his alibi checked out—I still couldn't believe it. It didn't ring true. With the knowledge my baby died, I had been a wreck, staying isolated in the room all by myself, only coming out to eat.

But then it happened. I startled awake in the middle of the night with memories flashing vividly through my mind. I remembered. *Everything.* My memories were restored. I couldn't believe it. It had been revolutionary. Startling. As my mind cleared, and I remembered exactly what they did—I knew exactly what I *needed* to do.

At first, I thought I should tell Martina and Selena, have them help me. But they already knew Martina and Selena were investigating along with the detectives. They were likely being careful, not revealing what they had done to me. When I had first learned the truth, I'd screamed and cried. He told me I was crazy and had to accept reality.

He'd underestimated me.

The last time I confronted him, he'd beaten me until I complied, until I accepted his story. But I knew better. I knew where to look and how to get my life back.

Some of the details were still fuzzy, but in my heart, I was certain of the truth. That truth was clear in my mind, but I couldn't tell just anyone about it. I would be met with skepticism, and nobody would believe me. And by the time Martina and the detectives could prove it, it would be too late. I had to do this on my own.

Gathering my things—a small bag with a phone, Selena's extra baton, and cash they had given me "just in case"—I readied myself for what was to come.

Peeking through the kitchen window, I watched as Charlie drove off. I knelt down to scratch Barney, the little pup, and slipped out the front door.

I didn't know how long it would take me, but I would get what I had come for.

What I'd almost died for.

And nobody was going to stop me this time.

40

MARTINA

"Do you think she'll talk to us?" Hirsch asked as we pulled up in front of Jacob Stoddard's mother's house. She was his closest relative in the Bay Area, and we hoped she could answer some questions about Jacob and Hanna's relationship.

"I sure hope so," I said. "I don't like how little we know about this whole situation. I don't believe that Jacob is innocent. I just don't know how he did this—how he managed to hurt Hanna. He had to have had someone else attack her. And if we go with the physical evidence, it was likely a man and a woman. But how and why would he get two people to try to kill her?"

"It's a great question," Hirsch said.

We exited the car and walked down the path to Mrs. Stoddard's house. It was a well-maintained Victorian—white with a trimmed lawn and a white picket fence around it. The neighborhood was charming, full of similar homes likely built in the late 1800s.

I knocked on the door and took a step back. It only took a few moments for a woman to answer. She looked at us with curiosity and then asked, "May I help you?"

I immediately noticed her resemblance to Jacob. "Hi, my

name is Martina Monroe. I'm a private investigator and this is my partner August Hirsch," I said, gesturing toward him. "We have a few questions for you."

"Oh? What is this about?"

"We'd like to ask you some questions about your son, Jacob, and his former girlfriend, Hanna. Would you mind if we come in?"

She hesitated for a moment, then stepped aside. "Please, come in." Mrs. Stoddard led us into the living room. "May I offer you some tea? Or perhaps coffee?" she asked politely.

"Yes, I'd love some tea," I said, hoping to ease her nerves and give us some time to look around.

Hirsch said, "None for me, thanks."

She nodded and hurried into the kitchen. Hirsch and I studied the home. The house was immaculate—the furniture looked to be from the '80s or '90s but was in impeccable condition. There were framed photographs on the walls, capturing various moments of Mrs. Stoddard's life with her family. I studied a few of them, seeing Jacob's face in several.

She returned with a tray, setting down cups of tea on the dining table. "Please, have a seat," she said, motioning to the chairs. We sat down, and she joined us, her expression wary. "What is this all about?"

"We'd like to know a bit more about Jacob and his former girlfriend, Hanna," I began, choosing my words carefully. "We recently found Hanna. She'd been attacked. We just wanted to know more about Jake and Hanna's relationship. What can you tell us about them?"

"She was attacked? He didn't mention it," Mrs. Stoddard said, her eyes widening.

"Well, before we get to Hanna... is Jacob an only child?" I asked.

"Yes, I was blessed with just the one child."

"Jacob's father—is he still around?" I asked.

"Oh, no, he passed a few years ago."

I picked up the china tea cup and took a sip.

Hirsch said, "Do you live here alone?"

"I do now. Jacob was staying here for a little while before he got his own apartment."

Setting the cup down, I said, "How long ago was this?"

"He moved back home about a year and a half ago, and he stayed for about a year," she said.

"And where was he before that?" I asked.

"Well, he did a brief stint up in Oregon for about a year. One of the chefs he had worked for in the Bay Area recruited him to work at his new restaurant—the pay was good, and the cost of living was lower there, so he tried it out. I guess it wasn't for him though, because he came back."

"And the two of you are close?" I asked.

"We are. I don't have a lot of family left—just my brother in town. But you said this is about Hanna? Jake said she stayed in Oregon. But you said she was attacked here in the Bay Area?"

"Yes, about a month ago."

"Do you think Jake had something to do with it?" she asked.

Did she know her son could be violent? "No, we don't think Jacob did it, but we're just trying to understand more about their relationship. Did you ever meet Abigail?"

"Who is Abigail?"

"Hanna and Jacob's daughter. You never met her?"

"No, I think I would've known about a grandchild. Are you sure? Jake wouldn't have kept that from me," she said, clearly taken aback.

"Do you remember him talking about Hanna?"

"Oh yes, she was his girlfriend. They broke up when he wanted to move back to California, and she didn't want to come.

She's got a family—they live a bit differently than we do. He said she didn't want to come to California."

It was clear that Jacob had lied to his mother and never told her about the child he had with Hanna. Why?

"When was the last time you saw Jacob?" Hirsch asked.

"He was over for dinner last night," she said. "I just can't believe... You must be mistaken. He had a child... a baby?"

"Jacob told us that she died when she was eight months old," I said softly.

Mrs. Stoddard shook her head, trying to process the information. "Are you sure you have the right Jacob Stoddard?"

Hirsch said, "Yes, ma'am. I see the photos of him on your wall."

"I don't know why he wouldn't tell me," she said, her voice trailing off.

"Did he mention anything about being questioned by the police on Saturday?" Hirsch asked.

"No."

"Was he acting normal when you saw him yesterday?"

"He seemed a little stressed. He said work has been busy. He works in the restaurant industry—sometimes they have busy times, and he works so much."

"Does Jacob have any close friends—someone he really trusts? Maybe somebody he grew up with?" I asked.

"He has lots of friends. He always has, and he likes his coworkers. I don't know all of their names off the top of my head. When he was growing up, his closest friends were Mike and Tim. I'm not sure if they're still in touch."

"Do you have their contact information?"

"No. I'm afraid not," she said. "I still can't believe what you're saying. I just can't believe Jacob would hide a child from me... a grandchild," she said, putting her hand on her chest.

She looked away, clearly overwhelmed. Something told me

she was truly surprised—not one of those mothers who would hide her child's crimes to protect them. She was genuinely concerned, and rightfully so, because I had a feeling Jacob was very guilty in ways that would shock her even more.

"Was Jacob ever violent growing up? Get in fights at school or have a bad temper?"

She met my gaze. "A temper, yes. He got that from his father. But he didn't get in many fights in school. Nothing unusual," she said. "Do you think he hurt Hanna? Is that why you questioned him about her attack?"

"We're not sure."

She exhaled sharply. Something told me Mrs. Stoddard knew what her son was capable of. Quietly, she said, "I don't know about a child or that Hanna was in the Bay Area."

"I believe you."

"Is she all right?" she asked.

"She is now."

With a slight nod, she said, "I'm glad."

She definitely knew what Jacob was capable of. We asked a few more questions and thanked her for her time. With more questions than answers, I believed a second conversation with Jacob was in order.

41

SELENA

Outside the restaurant in downtown Oakland, I snapped photos of the front using my cell phone. I wanted to get pictures of everyone Jacob worked with, just in case they gave me fake names when I interviewed them. The outdoor dining area had umbrellas, small tables, and a smattering of patrons. One of the servers was tall, with a tattoo of a snake on his forearm.

I walked up to the host stand at the entrance of the restaurant.

"Can I help you?" the hostess asked.

"A table for one, please."

"Sure, would you like inside or outside?"

Since I didn't see Jacob outside, I figured it would be better to sit outdoors. I didn't really want him to be my server, so I needed to talk to the guy with the tattoo instead. "Outside is fine," I said.

"Sure, come this way." She grabbed a menu and led me to the patio. She seated me and handed over the menu. It had a modern farm-to-table concept, and it looked good. One of the perks of being a PI was that I could expense my meals when I was on surveillance.

The waiter with the snake tattoo approached. "How are you doing today?" he asked.

"I'm doing great, thanks."

"Can I get you some water or something to drink?"

"Water, please."

"Sparkling or tap?"

"Tap is fine."

As he poured the water, I glanced at his tattoo.

"Nice ink," I said, nodding toward his arm.

"Thanks, had it for a little while," he said with a grin.

I admired it briefly, knowing this was my way in to get him talking.

"Have you worked here long?"

"Two years."

"Pretty good gig?"

"Yeah, it's great."

"Cool. So, what's good here?" I kept my questions light, mixing in some covert ones.

"What do you like?"

"Something healthy would be good."

"We have a few salads. You can add different types of protein. We also have a great turkey burger," he said with a flirty smile.

"I'll go with the turkey burger," I said, handing back the menu.

As he walked away, I noticed the wedding ring on his left finger. Maybe the friendly, flirty smile was just part of the job to get a bigger tip.

Suddenly, I spotted Jacob heading out to the patio. Quickly, I tipped the brim of my baseball cap and turned to the side, pretending to dig through my bag. We didn't want Jacob to know we were following him, and I was hoping he wouldn't recognize me. Our encounters had been brief, but I didn't want him to get a good look and put two-and-two together. I had a gut feeling there was something really rotten about him, beyond the fact that he was abusive toward Jane.

I hadn't bought his act at the police station, and neither had anyone else. Jane had been a mess—crying, terrified. She said Jacob had hurt her and their baby. She desperately wanted to know where her child was buried. And I was going to find out, one way or another.

When I saw Jacob pouring water at a table, I instinctively turned away, covering my face as I pushed out of my chair and crept toward the door to head inside the restaurant.

As I approached the hostess inside, I asked, "Where's the restroom?" She pointed toward the back of the restaurant, and I casually made my way there, covertly snapping photos with my phone.

The restaurant wasn't large, and there didn't seem to be many staff or patrons. Most of the customers were sitting outside. It was late for lunch, which might have explained the low turnout. I spotted an older man in a black button-down shirt wiping down the bar. Perhaps the manager.

I decided to strike up a conversation. Waving slightly to get his attention, I called out, "Hey, how's it going?"

The man stopped what he was doing, looked up at me, and said, "Doing all right. Can I get you something?"

"Yes, are you the manager?"

"Yes. I'm Jeff."

We shook hands across the bar. "Tonja. How long have you worked here?"

"Five years," he said. "Why?"

"I was wondering if you were hiring," I lied smoothly.

"Do you have any experience?"

"I was a server once," I said, though that wasn't true at all.

He shrugged. "We don't have any openings right now, but you never know when we might need help. You could give me your résumé and I can put it on file."

"Maybe I'll drop by another day with my résumé," I said casually. "I'm having lunch today."

"Sure," he said.

"What's the environment like here?" I asked. "Everyone pretty friendly? Do people hang out after work and that sort of thing?"

He gave me a puzzled look before replying, "Some of the guys are friendly. A few of our servers know each other outside of work, but we don't really have many gatherings except around the holidays."

"Sounds nice. Well, thanks."

"Enjoy your lunch."

"Thanks." I glanced around before heading to the restroom. The lighting inside was dim and modern. After quickly washing my hands, I left the bathroom and made my way back to my table.

When I returned, I noticed my water glass had been filled. The waiter with the tattoo approached again.

"I was wondering what happened to you," he said, in a cheerful tone.

"I just went inside to use the restroom," I said. "I talked to your manager about a job. He said you're not hiring but I might drop off my résumé. We might be coworkers one day. What's your name, by the way?"

"Ben Milton."

"Nice to meet you, Ben. I'm Tonja. What's it like working here? Jeff was telling me that some people here hang out after work. Do you?"

The waiter shrugged. "Not too much."

"How did you get your job here?"

"A friend."

"How about the other server—how long has he been here?" I asked, trying to keep my voice casual.

The waiter cocked his head slightly before answering, "About a year and a half."

"Did he just walk in off the street like me? Like, do I have a shot at getting hired here?"

"Nah, not Jacob. He's a friend of mine. I got him the job," he said.

Ah ha. "Oh, so I need to be friends with you?" I teased with a wink.

"I don't know if I'd be too much of a help, but yeah, like the manager said, drop off your résumé. We get busy sometimes, especially closer to the holidays, and could use the extra help."

"Sure, yeah." He was friends with Jacob. *Now we were getting somewhere.*

"So Jacob..." I said casually. "Does he have a girlfriend?"

The waiter raised an eyebrow. "You interested?"

I forced a light laugh. "He's cute." *In an icky, man-monster kind of way.*

"He's unattached, as far as I know," Ben said. "You want me to introduce him to you?"

I shook my head. "No, I'm just curious. I like to know about people before I go out with them, you know?"

"So... what do you wanna know about Jacob?"

Perfect. Time to dig deeper. "Well, does he have a past? Does he go through girlfriends? Is he single now? Is there something wrong with him?"

"Nah, nothing like that. He dates now and then, but nothing serious."

"You've known him a long time?" I asked, keeping my tone light.

"Yeah, my little brother went to high school with him," he said.

"Oh, so you stayed in touch? That's nice. And you got him this job here—pretty cool," I added, trying to seem interested but not too pushy.

He seemed to step back slightly, as if realizing I was asking a few too many questions.

"Well then, maybe I'll bump into him later," I said, trying to wrap up the conversation without arousing suspicion.

"Are you sure? I could introduce you," he said.

"No, that's all right. I can be shy," I lied with a small smile.

He smirked. "You don't seem very shy to me."

"It's different with a romantic interest," I said, waving it off.

"All right, well, your turkey burger should be out pretty soon."

"Thanks," I said, as he walked away.

A few moments later, Ben returned with what looked like a perfectly cooked turkey burger with fries on the side. "Bon appétit," he said before heading back inside the restaurant.

I grabbed a fry, took a bite, and then went after the burger. It was juicy, topped with avocado, mayo, and tomato—exactly what I needed. I was halfway through when Ben returned to check in.

"How's the turkey burger?" he asked.

"It's great," I said between bites.

"Good to hear. I'm off soon, so Jacob will take care of you when I'm gone," he said with a wink.

With a smile, I thought, *I'd better hurry up then, because if Jacob remembers me, he might not be too happy to see me.* The cap I was wearing wasn't the best disguise out there, but I was hoping it would be enough. Before I returned my attention to my burger, I glanced up and caught sight of someone standing in the doorway. My stomach dropped—it was Jacob. He was looking directly at me.

I quickly bent down to grab my wallet, ready for a quick exit, but it was too late. Jacob stormed over, eyes locked on me.

"Hey! Don't I know you?" he demanded, his voice tight with anger.

Uh-oh. Looks like the jig is up.

42

SELENA

"I don't think so."

"Yes, I do. You... you were with that private investigator who thinks I'm a criminal."

"I'm just having lunch."

"Are you, *really*? I can't believe you came here. You can't just come in here and harass me at my place of work," Jacob spat, his eyes narrowing with anger.

"I'm not harassing anyone," I said. "I'm simply having lunch. Is this how you treat all your customers?"

Before Jacob could respond, Ben approached. My heart sank—this was going to blow my cover.

"Is there a problem here?" Ben asked, looking between us.

"Yeah," Jacob said. "She's with the firm that's been investigating me. The reason the police picked me up for questioning."

Ben's expression shifted. "So, all those questions you asked earlier... you weren't thinking about dating him?" he asked, raising an eyebrow.

Jacob cut in. "What?"

"You were grilling me for information? Is that even legal?"

Of course it's legal. I was just asking questions. "Yes, it is. I was just trying to get some info. And no, I'm certainly not trying to date him. I work at the firm trying to help a young woman. A young woman Jacob used to date who ended up nearly dead in a park."

Jacob's face tightened. "I told you, I had nothing to do with that. They checked my alibi. I'm innocent."

Hardly. "Look, I believe you," I lied. "But the problem is, Jane really wants to know where her baby is buried. So, I'd like to know where she is, so Jane can pay her respects. That's all we care about at this point." Another fib, but I needed to push him.

Jacob's jaw clenched. "I told you, we drove up to Oregon. We buried her near her family's property, and that's it."

"Did you see anybody while you were there? Anyone to verify that's where she's buried?"

Jacob's gaze hardened. "Sure. I met up with Caleb, maybe a few other people when we went up. That was over a year and a half ago."

"Anything else you can tell me? Is there a marker at the grave?"

"We put a small rock under a tree. Flowers at the time. Obviously, it's not legal to bury a child like that, but that's how Hanna's family does it. That's what she told me," Jacob snapped. "Now, I'd appreciate it if you finish your lunch and leave."

With that, he turned on his heel and walked away, leaving me sitting there.

Ben lingered for a moment, his eyes full of disdain. "He's a good guy. You shouldn't be harassing him."

"Maybe he's not such a good guy. Maybe there are things you don't know."

"I know enough."

I exhaled slowly, pulling some cash from my wallet. "Will this cover it?" I asked, not really caring how much the meal cost.

"I'll get your check," Ben said curtly, heading back inside. A moment later, he returned with the bill. "Here you go, ma'am," he said, his tone cold. He was clearly siding with Jacob, and if Jacob was innocent, I could understand their anger. But I knew, deep down, Jacob wasn't innocent. He was a creep with a capital C.

I paid in cash, leaving a decent tip, even though I didn't want to. Just as I was about to get up and leave, my phone rang. I glanced at the screen—it was Dad.

"Hey. What's up?"

"Is Jane with you?"

"No, why?"

"I haven't seen her in a few hours," Dad said, the worry in his voice intensifying. "I went to the grocery store. She was here when I left. But when I came back, I thought maybe she was taking a nap. She's been so down. But when I made lunch, I went to check on her, see if she was hungry, and... she's not here. She's not in the house, Selena."

My heart skipped a beat. "Have you talked to Martina?"

"No."

Maybe she was with her? "I'll call Martina. Thanks, Dad." Panic rose in my chest as I called Martina.

43

MARTINA

INSIDE OUR CONFERENCE ROOM, Vincent said, "Any word from Selena yet?"

"Not yet."

"Do you think she'll get much out of the restaurant workers?"

"I don't know. We know he's working, but we're not sure if he'll recognize her or not. I was a little concerned about Selena going alone, but she convinced me it would be fine." Considering it was a public place in daylight, I had to concede.

"Couldn't she have just waited until he wasn't on shift and then questioned all his coworkers?" Hirsch asked.

"It was Selena's idea to go undercover, to learn what she could. It's kind of her way." Selena had always been resourceful. It usually yielded good results, but it sometimes led her into dangerous situations too.

Hirsch said, "Fingers crossed she gets something useful. But once he's off his shift, I think we should go talk to him. Ask him why he never told his mother that he had a child. I find that pretty strange."

"I do too."

Vincent said, "Isn't it all a little strange, though? Like, he had this totally normal life in the Bay Area—probably not the right word, but you know—like, traditional. Went to school, had a job, and then suddenly gets mixed up with a girl who lived unconventionally, abuses her, and their baby dies. I'm just thinking... It's weird, right?"

"It's certainly unusual," I said. "Have you found anything on the home surveillance cameras that were sent in from the neighborhood around the park?"

Vincent cocked his head. "Not unless you're interested in folks walking dogs and cats stalking around at night. We have two more to review. Maybe we should do a second canvas, see if anyone else with a camera may want to help. People who weren't home when the two of you did door-to-doors."

It had crossed my mind. "Maybe if nothing comes in the last two." We hadn't had a lot of cooperation, and I had a feeling we wouldn't.

I was about to discuss logistics when my phone buzzed on the table. I glanced down, eyebrows raised. "Oh, here's a call from Selena now. Hi, Selena. How did it go at the restaurant?"

"I'll tell you later. Is Jane with you?"

"No. Why?"

"I just got a call from Dad. He said she's not at the house."

Feeling a cold knot of concern forming in my chest, I said, "Did he check the cameras?"

"No, I don't think so."

Charlie didn't usually fiddle with the surveillance system. That was my domain. "She's not with us," I continued. "We can access the security cameras from my computer here at the office. I'm here with Hirsch and Vincent. We'll check the security footage, see if we can figure out what happened. Are you coming back to the office?"

"I'm going to head home and look around. See if there are any signs of a struggle."

"All right, let us know what you find. We'll check the security cameras now."

"Let me know how it goes," Selena said before hanging up.

I turned to Vincent and Hirsch, explaining the situation.

With a quick motion, I flipped open the lid of my laptop and logged into our home security system. I needed to know the last time Jane had been seen by Charlie. I dialed his number. "Hey, honey," I said.

"Hey."

"When was the last time you saw Jane?" I asked, my fingers hovering over the keyboard.

"When I left to go to the grocery store. It was about 10 o'clock this morning."

"And when did you realize she wasn't home?"

"Around 2 o'clock when I went in to see if she was hungry."

"Did you notice any signs of a struggle?"

"No, I didn't see anything out of place."

"What time did you get home from the grocery store?"

"Ten forty-five at the latest."

"Okay, thanks, honey. I'm going to check our surveillance footage online."

"All right. Let me know if you need my help for anything."

"Thanks. Selena is on her way to the house. She wants to check things out, see if there are any clues to what happened."

"I'll be here."

"Thanks. I love you."

"I love you too."

After a quick explanation to Hirsch and Vincent, I started playing the surveillance video starting at 10 o'clock that morning.

"There's Charlie," I said, pointing at the screen as Charlie walked out of the house toward his car parked in the driveway. We watched as he drove off, the footage clear and steady.

Switching to the outdoor camera focused on the front door, my attention shifted. The door opened, and there she was—Jane. She walked right out, closing the door behind her, and walked down the street until she was out of view.

I sat back in my chair, turning to Hirsch and Vincent, who had been watching the screen with me, their faces tense.

"She left. She just left," I said, confused.

"Why?" Hirsch asked.

"I don't know. But based on the timing, I think she did it as soon as she knew Charlie wasn't there. She didn't want to be stopped."

We sat in silence for a moment. I said, "She has a cell phone we gave her."

Vincent turned his attention to his laptop and said, "What's her number?"

I quickly rattled off Jane's number while glancing over at Hirsch. He said, "We'll find her, Martina."

A thought gnawed at me—what if she didn't want us to find her? Why had she left? Why hadn't she told us she was leaving? "I don't understand why she would do this."

Hirsch said, "Maybe she remembered something."

"But what? Why wouldn't she tell us?"

Was she not as innocent as we thought?

After a few minutes of typing and searching, Vincent lowered the lid of his laptop and said grimly, "She turned off her phone."

A sinking feeling settled in my chest.

Her phone was off.

She had left of her own accord, and despite my concern, we had no legal right to go after her. But still—where could she have gone? And why? Despite the questions in my mind, everything inside of me was screaming that we had to find her, and fast.

44

JANE

ON THE TRAIN, I had a lot of time to think about what I would say, what I would do—my plan of attack. It all became so very clear now: why I ended up at the park, how it happened, the faces I'd seen. I remembered everything. The relationship we had, going to one of Jacob's friend's house after our baby was born to get the three interlocking hearts tattoo to represent the three of us—our little family.

Because I didn't have a birth certificate, we couldn't get married. Even though I tried, but soon learned I couldn't get a birth certificate without their testimony—that I was who I said I was, that I was born when I thought I was born. Truthfully, they may not even remember. But I had always celebrated my birthday on the same day, year after year, assuming it was the right one. I learned, though, when I went to the courthouse to try to get the birth certificate to marry him, that it wasn't going to be that easy. I needed a witness, and I couldn't go back to my family.

We decided to get matching tattoos to prove our commitment instead. But when he pointed out the hearts were a little girly, only I got the tattoo. Jacob said he'd wear a ring instead so that women would know he was taken. I thought that was sweet. What an idiot I was.

As I touched the necklace my mother had made, I thought about her. I wondered if she worried about me. When my sister had come to the offices to claim me, she wore the same necklace. I remembered my sister, of course, because I remembered everything.

My sister was like the others in my family—not forgiving. She was probably the person who told Jacob where I was. Or maybe it was Marilyn's brother, Caleb. He and Jacob had been close when he lived in Oregon. Marilyn and Caleb had introduced me to Jacob. At the time I'd thanked them, my sentiment was different now.

When I learned I was pregnant, I knew my family wouldn't approve of me having a baby out of wedlock. Papa would say it was against God, and that it was a sign I was with the devil. That's why Jacob and I left.

Although Mama was different—growing up, she protected us when she could. She homeschooled us, teaching us to read and to do arithmetic, but not much else. Papa wasn't for it. He wanted us working on the farm. It was our livelihood, our purpose, our calling. But every once in a while, Mama would do something special for me. She'd set me aside, read me a story, tell me about what life was like before she met Papa. She'd secretly take me to town to show me the shops.

Mama hadn't always lived in a community like ours. She used to be part of society, she said, and there were things she still missed. But I could never tell anyone she missed them. Yet, I knew. I knew Mama was different, but I also knew she wouldn't stand up to Papa either. Papa's words were the law in our house. Mama swore he hadn't been like that when they first married, but over time he had gotten more paranoid and more religious. Jacob was different before we'd run away together too. Had I made the same mistake as my mother?

I stepped off the train and wandered over to the bus schedule, trying to find the right bus to take me back to the park. I didn't exactly know where the house was, but I remembered it was within walking distance from the park—where they had found me after the struggle. After scanning the schedule, I spotted the bus I needed and walked over to the stand, waiting for it to come.

As I stood there, memories of my life kept flooding my mind, like a tsunami. It wouldn't stop. Ever since I woke up in the middle of the night, it had been like this—every painful memory rushing back, but the good ones too. I remembered when my baby was born. Jacob had delivered her since I refused to go to the hospital. Papa had always taught us that medicine was just a trick, the government's way of trying to control us.

But now, I saw things differently.

I'd been in a hospital for almost two weeks after the attack, and they helped me heal. Maybe medicine wasn't so bad after all. And law enforcement—they'd tried to help me too. Martina, Selena, Hirsch, and Vincent—each of them had dedicated their time to keep me safe, to help me uncover my past. Papa was wrong. I wasn't evil for having a baby and neither were people on the outside.

I thought back to the day Abigail was born. I was so scared when I went into labor, but Jacob had said he would take me to the hospital if I needed to go. I didn't want to. Mama had told us about childbirth. All Jacob had to do was make sure the baby came out, pull her gently, clamp the umbilical cord, and clean her up. Everything would be fine.

And it was. The first time I held her in my arms, it was instant, overwhelming joy. I burst into tears, feeling love like I'd never felt before. But then, Jacob had taken her from me.

He'd taken *everything* from me. *My baby. My sense of safety. My freedom.*

The bus pulled up, breaking my chain of thought. I inserted my ticket into the machine—it beeped—and I climbed up. The driver smiled at me, and I found a seat near the front.

Jacob was going to pay for what he did.

For taking her from me, for hitting me, for trying to kill me. He and his friends—they were all going to pay. As I sat on the bus, I couldn't help but think about what was worse: Jacob or his friends.

As soon as we left Oregon, that's when I saw Jacob's true colors. Once he got me away from my family, in California, that was the first time he hit me.

I had asked him too many questions, he said. He smacked me across the face and told me, "I'll tell you when I want to talk about that." All I had asked was about his family—whether he'd had girlfriends before. He didn't want to talk about that. Later, he apologized, crying, saying he couldn't believe he'd hit me.

But that was just how it started. It soon became our routine.

Even when I begged him to stop, fearing for the health of our unborn child, it didn't faze him. He still hit me. He was a monster. He had to be held accountable for what he did—to me, to her. I would never forgive him. *Never.*

As much as I appreciated what Martina and her team had done for me, I couldn't let this go. I didn't care what the consequences were.

The bus stopped in front of the park, and I stepped off, waving a quick thanks to the driver. My feet hit the pavement, and I started walking down the familiar street. I knew the house was near the park, so I continued along the sidewalk, trying to remember how far it was.

The memories came back in sharp, painful flashes. At first, I thought it was just her, so I grabbed the knife to defend myself. I thought I could stop her. But then he was there. So much bigger, so much stronger. I knew I was outmatched. I had run so fast and what seemed like so far that night. He chased and hunted me. I hurried down one of the side trails, near the water. I thought I'd been hidden well enough. But I hadn't. He had over-powered me and then it all went black.

But he had made a mistake that day.

He didn't kill me.

45

MARTINA

I STILL COULDN'T BELIEVE Jane would do this to us. The security cameras clearly showed she'd left on her own and had waited for Charlie to leave first. She didn't want us to know where she was going, but why?

Vincent said, "So, what do we do now, Martina?"

"We can't track her by phone. We could question Jacob, but we know he's at work—or at least we suspect he's at work. Selena will confirm; she was just at the restaurant and is now headed to the house to check for any clues as to where Jane may have gone."

Vincent said, "Well, we could check traffic cameras in your neighborhood. The only thing she could have done is taken a bus—maybe BART or a taxi. Unless someone picked her up. She could have called someone to come and get her."

Who would she have called? Why hadn't she called Selena or me? "Can we look at her call logs from before she turned off the phone?"

Vincent said, "On it." He turned his attention to his laptop.

To Hirsch, I said, "There aren't traffic cams in my neighborhood, but I have neighbors with surveillance cameras. I could go door-to-door, asking my neighbors for surveillance footage to see where she's gone—or at least to find out what direction she went. There are only so many ways out of my neighborhood."

Racking my brain, I tried to figure out why she'd left and how I hadn't seen it coming.

Hirsch said, "I could talk to some friends at CoCo County and see if they can be on the lookout for her."

That was a good idea. I lived in CoCo County, so it made sense to have them look for her too. "Will they really help us with that? A woman who left on her own?"

"If they know she could be in danger. Which she likely is."

Good point. "True."

Hirsch said, "I'll call now." He stood up to leave the conference room to make the call.

I nodded and continued to think about the situation. It was unusual to be so blindsided by a client. A client we'd been working around the clock to keep safe. I scooted closer to Vincent, trying to look at the screen.

Vincent eyed me and said, "She hasn't called anyone. The only numbers in and out are to Selena and you."

"So, she can't be meeting up with anyone. Where could she have gone?"

"Maybe she was so distraught after learning about the baby that she decided she needed to be alone. Kind of like after the baby died the first time. Jacob had said she had a mental break and left him. That's why she bounced from shelter to shelter. Maybe she remembered it and it was too much and she's fleeing again. We should check local shelters to see if that's where she went."

"Good idea," I agreed. "We can divide up the phone numbers to the closest shelters and each make calls. Starting with the last one she resided at. The one in Hayward." Everything inside me was saying we *needed* to find her.

Vincent said, "Good idea. Even on public transportation, she could've made it to Hayward by now."

Bay Area public transportation was slow *at best*. To get somewhere in the Bay Area that would take twenty minutes to drive by car could easily take over an hour using the bus and BART, the *Bay Area Rapid Transit* system. Rapid. Ha.

"All right, I'll take Hayward. Which one do you want to take?" I asked.

"I'll comb through the list of nearby shelters and pick a few closest to your house," Vincent said. "We'll call all of them and see if anybody has seen her."

"Thanks, Vincent."

I lifted my phone and called the Hayward shelter.

After a few explanations of who I was calling about, I finally got a woman on the line I had talked to before—Jolie.

"Hello, yes, I heard you're calling about one of our residents?" Jolie asked.

"I'm looking for a woman—Jane Doe. She had been at your shelter up until about a month ago. She went by the name Angie. I wanted to know if she's returned."

"What was the name again?"

"She went by the name Angie before, but now she may be going by Jane or a different name." At this point, I had no idea what Jane was thinking or what she was calling herself.

Tapping of keys on the other end sounded. "No, I'm afraid not."

"Could you give me a call if she shows up?"

"Is she in danger?" Jolie asked.

"She might be."

"I'll definitely give you a call if I see her."

"Thank you so much."

Vincent looked over at me, and I shook my head.

"I'm still working on the list. Give me a few minutes and

we'll split them up." He paused, then added, "Any reason why she'd go back to the park where she was attacked?"

"Maybe if she remembered who she was supposed to meet that day. Maybe there's a clue there that we missed."

"Well, let's call around to these shelters, and then we'll head out there to see if we can find her."

"That'll be the quickest way to see if that's where she's at. Good thinking, Vincent."

Hirsch returned to the conference room, looking a little flushed. "You won't believe who I just talked to."

"Who?" I asked.

"That was Marilyn's brother, Caleb. He said he's sorry for not getting back to me sooner, but he's been out of town. I asked him a few questions about Jacob and Hanna. He said that he knew them and that they were *so happy* together."

"Did he say when was the last time he talked to them or saw them?" I asked.

"He told me the last time he saw them was when they left for California two years ago."

"When was the last time Caleb talked to Jacob or Hanna?"

"He said that he got a call from Jacob when Hanna went missing a year and a half ago—he was worried sick about her—but hadn't talked to him again until recently. Marilyn told Caleb they'd found her, so he called Jacob."

Well, that mystery was solved. As we suspected, somebody had told Jacob where Jane was. Marilyn, and maybe even Hanna's sister Keisha, weren't friends to her. And Jane could feel it. Her instincts told her not to go with them. It seemed like she'd been right.

"Did he say if Jacob went up to Oregon to look for Hanna when she went missing?" I asked.

"I asked. He said no. He hasn't seen Jacob for two years. Only the phone call."

"Did anything feel off about the call?"

"Yeah, I got the vibe that he was practically reading from a script."

"Like he was covering for Jacob?"

"Maybe."

Well, that didn't bode well for Jane and her safety. We needed to find her before it was too late. Before Jacob, or whoever had tried to hurt her the first time, tried to do it again.

46

JANE

I CONTINUED DOWN the tree-lined street, the sunlight flickering on the pavement as a cool breeze ruffled the leaves overhead. I passed the entrance to the park, the one with the sprawling parking lot and serene views of the lake. A moment of hesitation crept in—I'd been here. Ran past it. I hadn't gone far enough.

I remembered crossing the street that night, the moment seared into my mind, and I did so again now—more carefully this time, glancing both ways before sprinting across to the opposite sidewalk.

My pulse quickened with every step. I was close—*so close*. It had been dark when I'd run from them, but there were signs—small but unmistakable—that I was on the right path.

I passed the first street, then the next. My heart drummed in my chest as I neared the third on the left. And then, there it was—the house on the corner. Recognition surged through me like a jolt of electricity. It was *the street*.

My heart rate spiked—I was *so very* close.

Heading down the street, I looked in all directions. The neighborhood seemed eerily still, unnaturally quiet. There was no one—no dog walkers, no retirees tending to their lawns, no children playing. Maybe they hadn't gotten home from school yet. I couldn't be sure. This place, these people—they were strangers to me. I had run for my life in these streets—now I was back to reclaim it.

I spotted the house, the two-story structure looming ahead. A Toyota sat parked in the driveway, confirming what I already knew: This was *it*. And *they* were home. My breath quickened as I hurried up the path to the front door, my fist raising before I could think better of it. I pounded on the door, each knock louder than the last, but I was met with silence. *No answer.*

I stepped back, glancing at the windows. Climbing over the shrubs, I peered inside. The living room came into view, the staircase winding up to the second story. The hallway stretched back to where the kitchen should be—the kitchen where I'd found that knife, where I'd fought tooth and nail, desperate to survive. Desperate to claim what was mine.

Nothing stirred inside. No movement. No voices. But someone had to be there. Maybe they were upstairs. He would likely be at work, but she—*she* should be home.

I returned to the front door, knocking harder this time, then pressing the doorbell until I heard it chime through the house. My fingers trembled with frustration, and for a moment, I almost turned to leave.

But then I heard it—footsteps descending the stairs.

The door creaked open, and there she stood, her face flushed with annoyance. She barely got any words out before she stopped, her eyes locking onto mine. Recognition. She tried to shut the door, but I jammed my foot inside, blocking it from closing. From my pocket, I removed Selena's extra baton. I clicked the button, and it extended with a sharp snap. "Let me in!" I demanded.

"Leave us alone! Why are you doing this?" she cried.

She acted so innocent. But she wasn't. I screamed, "Where is she?"

She used all her strength to keep me out, but I had something she didn't. *Nothing to lose*. With conviction, I said, "I'm not leaving without her!" as I forced my way into the house, shoving her aside.

She reached out to grab me, but I swung the baton, hitting her hard on the side of her face. She gasped, stumbling back, her hand flying to her cheek.

"I said, where is she?"

She cowered, not expecting the blow, her defiance faltering.

She and her husband had left me for dead once. They'd tried to kill me, but they failed.

Ignoring her as she crumpled at the bottom of the stairs, I rushed up, two steps at a time. I could hear her coming after me, her footfalls frantic and uneven, but I was already moving. Upstairs, the hallway stretched before me, doors on either side.

I threw open the first door. Inside was a queen-size bed, a dresser, photographs on the walls. A hamper overflowing with clothes. I swung around and lunged for the next door, heart pounding. I pushed it open and saw a crib. Relief surged through me for a split second. As I stepped inside, a strong arm grabbed me from behind.

One hand clamped over my mouth, muffling my scream, while the other arm wrapped around my waist, dragging me out of the room.

I kicked and thrashed, desperate to break free, but his grip was like iron. My eyes locked onto the woman. She had picked up the baton, raising it high in the air.

I hadn't thought he'd be home.

He dragged me into another room, slamming the door behind us. I struggled harder, but it was useless. He was too strong.

Once again, he had overpowered me. Would he finally do it? Would he kill me this time?

His hands wrapped around my throat, squeezing tighter. My vision blurred, the room spinning as I gasped for breath. In the distance, I heard the faint, helpless cries as the world around me was slipping into darkness.

47

MARTINA

An hour later, we had contacted all the shelters in the area. No one had seen Jane. The team at the CoCo County Sheriff's office hadn't spotted her. We had no idea where she was. Selena walked into the office, her face unreadable. I waved to get her attention.

"Did you find anything out of place at the house?" I asked. "Maybe a clue as to where she'd gone?"

She remained stoic as she walked into the conference room and sat down across from me. "I checked everywhere," she said. "No signs of a struggle. But... there is something missing."

I stiffened. Missing? "She took something from us?" I asked, feeling a knot tighten in my chest. "What?"

"My extra baton."

Vincent, who had been pacing near the door, stopped and turned to her. "Are you sure you didn't just lose it?"

"I didn't lose it," Selena snapped. "In fact, I had been showing it to her. I told her I could teach her some self-defense moves once she was ready. I explained that when I first started out, my weapon of choice was a retractable baton because they're easy to conceal but can be deadly when used properly."

A heavy silence filled the room.

"She knew where it was, and she knew what it was used for?" I asked.

"She knew."

I stood there, trying to piece it together, my mind racing through the possibilities. What was Jane thinking? My eyes met Selena's, and she seemed to read the question in them. "I think she's going back to the park or near there," Selena said. "I think she's getting ready for a fight... one that she doesn't want to lose this time."

Vincent said, "But she was outmatched the first time."

"Yes, but maybe she thinks something will be different this time."

I said, "If that's true, she could be in danger. We need to find her."

"I think we should go back to the park," Selena suggested.

"Agreed. But before we do that, did you get anything useful from Jacob's coworkers? Anything that could help?"

She pulled her laptop out of her backpack, opened the lid, and brought up photos she had taken from the cloud. "I basically talked to the manager at the restaurant, as well as one of the other servers and the hostess. That's all who was working today. It was kind of a late lunch, so there weren't many patrons. But this guy right here"—she pointed to the screen—"said he's known Jacob for a while. He might be someone to question."

My mind went in all directions as I continued to listen.

She paused and gave me a grim look. "But anyhow, my cover was blown when Jacob saw me. He recognized me from the Alameda County Sheriff's station when we went down there with Jane."

"Was he upset?" I asked.

"He was, but I did ask him about the baby. I said we wanted to know where she was buried. He said it was marked with flowers, but he didn't know exactly where. He claimed he had met up with Caleb when they went to bury the baby, but they didn't visit anyone else."

Hirsch said, "But I just talked to Caleb. He said he hasn't seen Jacob in two years, since they left for California—before the baby died."

"Why would he lie?" I asked.

"That's a great question," Selena said, her brow furrowed in thought. "Is it possible he didn't remember?"

I scoffed. "Not remember your friend's baby died and he came to bury it near you? I don't think so."

"Do you think Jacob told him to say that? Told Caleb it was fine to talk to us but then he forgot to tell him about the visit when they buried the baby?" Hirsch asked.

"Maybe," Selena said thoughtfully. "Regardless, we can't trust this guy, Caleb. He's probably just covering for Jacob. I think we need to get to the park. Whoever Jane may have been meeting there, she's out to find them, and she's going to try to attack them with that baton. Everything in my gut is screaming that's what's happening." Her voice took on a hard edge. "I think we need to go to Fremont."

I was about to agree when something clicked in my mind. Out of breath, I glanced at the laptop just as Selena was closing the lid.

"Wait a minute," I said, a sudden realization dawning.

"What?" Selena asked, turning to me.

I leaned in, staring at the image on the screen. "That guy. Can you make the image larger? Specifically, the tattoo on his arm."

Selena did.

My mouth dropped open. "Hirsch, does he look familiar to you?"

Hirsch's eyes widened slightly as he recognized the tattoo. "We questioned him. He lives near the park in Union City."

"That can't be a coincidence."

"What's his name?" I asked Selena.

"He told me his name is Ben Milton."

Vincent said, "I'll run the name."

"Is it possible that Jacob hired him to kill Jane?" I asked the room. Turning back to Selena, I said, "What do you think? You talked to him."

"I mean... sure, it's possible. He's a big guy and could easily overpower her."

I straightened, determination settling in. "Let's head over there. Maybe she remembered the attack, and she's going back."

"But why?" Vincent asked.

That was the sixty-four-thousand-dollar question. "We'd always theorized she was meeting someone. Maybe she remembered who and why. And she's gone back."

Vincent said, "You go. I'll call you with whatever I find on Ben Milton."

With a thank you and a plan, we headed back to the scene of the crime.

48

MARTINA

Behind the wheel driving toward Fremont, I continued to mull over all the reasons Jane might have left on her own and hadn't told us. Was she planning to do something illegal?

"I just got off the phone with Cromwell," Hirsch said, breaking the silence. "He'll meet us at Milton's house to question him."

"Good thinking." We could try to question Milton all we wanted, but we weren't law enforcement.

I glanced over at Hirsch, spotting the tension in his jaw. He wasn't saying it, but I knew he was as on edge as I was.

Hirsch said, "The fact that Ben Milton is friends with Jacob, that his home is so close to the park where Jane was attacked... And remember how when we interviewed them, they told us different stories about their home surveillance system? I knew he was acting sketchy and likely hiding something. Did you get that too?"

Shifting in my seat, I said, "I did. It's why I remembered him. I could tell something was off with those two, but I wasn't sure what. We don't have any evidence, but everything inside me is telling me Milton is connected to Jane's attack."

"I tend to agree."

The quiet hum of the engine was the only sound between us for a moment. This was the first case we'd worked since he was no longer a member of law enforcement. The shift from having a badge to not having one felt heavier than I expected. He was retired now, which meant we couldn't just roll up to Ben Milton's house like we used to. If we suspected something was going on inside that wasn't kosher, we couldn't flash a badge or push our way in. We were just citizens. And that meant we could be arrested ourselves for trespassing. We had no authority.

It had been a while since I'd walked into something so blind, and the uncertainty gnawed at me. I glanced down as my dash lit up with an incoming call from Vincent. I answered. "Hey, Vincent. I've got you on speaker. What's up?"

"I just got the background on Ben Milton." Vincent's voice crackled through the line. "No criminal record. I crossmatched his background information with Jacob Stoddard's. They've known each other a long time. Jacob Stoddard is the same age as Milton's younger brother, Timothy. They both went to the same high school and junior college."

"No criminal history? Did we get it wrong?" I asked.

"There's no way, Martina," Vincent insisted. "He's got to be connected somehow. Can you feel it?"

I exhaled slowly, staring out at the highway. "I can."

"Go with your gut, boss."

That was exactly what I'd do. "Will do. I'll talk to you later. I'll update Selena and let her know what you found." We decided to have her take her own car, in case we needed a second vehicle.

"Let me know if I can help with anything else."

"Thanks, Vincent." I ended the conversation and called

Selena to give her an update and to come up with our plan of attack.

49

JANE

I woke in a darkened room, the only light filtering through the edges of thick curtains. The sun was still out, but I could tell it was fading fast. I tried to move, but my wrists were bound to the bed with what looked like an electrical cord. My legs and ankles were tied too.

A twin-size bed. The kind you'd find in a child's room.

Panic clawed at my chest as my mind raced. What were they going to do with me? I had spent the last year and a half searching for her—searching for them—wondering why they had taken her. Why they had sworn that she was theirs and not mine. *And that woman.* If I didn't know better, I would have believed that Abigail was her baby. Did she believe it?

Jacob had told me I was the crazy one, that I was drowning in grief and couldn't accept that my daughter was gone. He'd said I'd lost my mind, that I was imagining things that weren't real. But I wasn't crazy. And I knew my daughter when I saw her. I knew her better than anyone.

I had spent a year and a half looking for her while evading Jacob, and I had finally found her. And I would fight to the death to get her back.

I struggled against the restraints, but it was no use. My body was weak, still healing from the attack. The doctors had said I was getting stronger, that I was making progress, but right now, I didn't feel strong. I felt helpless. And angry. I had made the same mistake again—assuming he would be at work, thinking she'd be at home alone with my daughter. The first time I showed up at her door, she had acted like she didn't know who I was. For a moment, I had almost believed her.

But how could she not know? How could she look at me and pretend?

It didn't make sense.

I'd been running for so long, chasing any lead I could find, that sometimes I had doubted myself. Sometimes I'd questioned if I really had lost my mind. Was I clinging to the impossible? Trying to see what I wanted to see?

But I hadn't imagined her. I couldn't have imagined that tiny birthmark near her left ear, on her cheek—a soft pink mark, almost in the shape of a heart. I remembered seeing it the first time I held her in my arms, my heart swelling with a love so deep it felt like I could burst. That birthmark was a piece of her, a piece of me. I knew it like I knew my own heartbeat.

They could call me crazy all they wanted. I knew the truth. She was mine. I needed to get out of here. I called out "Hello!" After being met with silence, I yelled, "Help!"

The door creaked open, and I tensed. A figure stood silhouetted in the doorway, blocking what little light remained.

"Be quiet in here," the voice growled. "Or I'll duct tape your mouth shut."

"Why are you doing this? Why did you take her from me?" My voice cracked as I spoke. I hadn't even had the chance to ask them this before. The knot in my stomach twisted tighter, the fear and frustration boiling over.

The man standing by the door sighed, running a hand

through his hair. "Hanna, I hate to do this to you... but we're calling Jacob. We're hoping he can help you."

"Help me? What are you talking about? You tried to *kill* me." My heart raced, confusion mixing with anger. What was he planning?

"No. I didn't want to hurt you. I was trying to protect my wife." His tone softened, as if he were speaking to a child. "Do you remember coming here a month ago? You grabbed a knife from our kitchen and attacked my wife. My innocent wife. Why did you do that?"

I blinked, my mind scrambling to piece together what he was saying. He thought I didn't remember? That I couldn't possibly recall what happened? But I did remember. *I remembered enough to come back here, didn't I?*

"She knew exactly why," I spat. "She stole my baby!"

His expression tightened, and he took a step closer, speaking slowly as if trying to reason with someone unstable. "Jacob warned us about this... the first time you saw her, you thought she was your own. And I'm so sorry, Hanna, truly I am. Losing your baby... I can't imagine what that must've done to you. But I assure you, this little girl is ours. We have a birth certificate, records from the hospital... She's not yours, and she's not Jacob's."

He was almost convincing—*almost*. "If you're so innocent, and I'm the one who needs help, why did you almost kill me?" I snapped, my voice rising. "I remember. I remember both of you —you and your wife—you left me there to die."

His face twitched, the mask slipping just a bit. "I didn't want to do that, Hanna. But you came at my wife with a knife. It was self-defense! I admit, we should've called someone to help you then, but... we panicked. I'm sorry for that."

"Is that what you plan to tell the police?" I asked, my eyes narrowing. "Why won't you let me go now? Why do you have me tied up if you're *so* concerned about my well-being?"

He hesitated, glancing toward the door as if expecting someone to walk in and save him from answering. "Well... if you recall, you came into my house *again* and attacked my wife *again*. I'm just trying to protect my family."

"If that's true, then why don't you call the police? Have them take me away, keep you and your *family* safe from me," I shot back, leaning into the absurdity of his logic.

"Because Jacob asked me to call him if you came by here again. He was shocked when he heard you came here. He cares about you. He loves you. We're trying to handle this civilly, to get you the help you need, not put you in jail. Is that what you want, Hanna? To be in a jail cell?" His voice had shifted to something almost pleading, as though he really believed this would convince me.

I stared at him, my pulse pounding in my ears. "Call Jacob. Have him take me to a mental hospital, like you say. But you know what?" I let out a bitter laugh. "I'd rather you call the police. Maybe I do deserve to be in prison. I keep trying to kill you and your wife, don't I? Doesn't that make sense? I'd go to prison for that, right?"

When I'd come to the house before, I was naïve and didn't understand how the world worked. But I'd learned so much over the past month. And I wasn't so naïve anymore. I didn't believe a word that he was saying to me.

"Hanna, maybe you just need some rest."

I yanked at the restraints on my wrists, my voice cold. "It's a little hard to sleep when I'm tied up. Don't you think?"

He looked away. "I'm sorry... It's the best I can do right now. We weren't expecting you."

"I'm sure you weren't," I muttered under my breath, glaring at him.

Just then, I heard a tiny voice. "Mama..." The sound cut through the tension like a knife.

My breath caught in my throat.

I strained to hear, my heart racing. And then again, clearer this time—"I want a cracker." It sounded like "I wanna quack-uh."

My heart swelled. It was her. *Abigail.* I knew I'd found her. There was no doubt in my mind now. And there was *nothing* these people could do to stop me from being with her.

50

MARTINA

WE ARRIVED at the Milton house just as the sun began to dip down. The Miltons, Ben and Laurel, lived a mile or so from the park where Jane had been attacked. Could Laurel be the woman whose blood was found on Jane's knife and Ben the second person who had overpowered Jane? But the question gnawed at me: Why would they attack Jane? Could the Miltons be a husband-wife murder team?

Parked, I waited for Selena to arrive. Once she had, Hirsch and I got out of my car and met up with her near the trunk. Selena said, "Will all of us go to the door?"

If it were up to me, Selena would stand back, out of harm's way until we were sure it was safe. But if Jane was inside, I knew that Selena would be a source of comfort, if she needed it. I said, "Hirsch and I will take lead in the questioning. Can you be backup? Keep an eye out for Cromwell?"

She nodded.

"Let's do it."

Without another word, we charged down the path to the front door, surveying the area. It was quiet and no neighbors were out.

Hirsch pounded on the door. The house was eerily quiet in response. No footsteps, no voices, no sound of movement from within.

A minute passed. Hirsch knocked again, louder this time, with an impatience that mirrored my own.

We had no time for delays. *Not now.*

Another minute crawled by, and as I was about to walk the perimeter of the house to see if we could see in, the door creaked open.

A woman stood there, holding a toddler in her arms. The toddler clutched a cracker. The woman had a large bruise blooming on the side of her face although it appeared she was trying to shield it from our view.

Adjusting the child on her hip, she said, "Can I help you?"

The child was beautiful. Dark hair and wide, curious eyes. Her small, heart-shaped face was framed by wisps of hair, and she looked every bit as healthy and happy as any child her age should be. But something about the scene felt off. How had the woman received the injury?

"Hi, are you Laurel Milton?"

"Yes."

"I'm a private investigator, Martina Monroe, and these are my partners August Hirsch and Selena Bailey. We spoke a few weeks ago."

She paled.

Hirsch wasted no time. He held up a photo of Jane, his voice sharp. "We'd like to ask you about this woman. She was assaulted around here nearly a month ago. Have you seen her before?"

The woman's eyes flicked to the photo for only a brief second before she shook her head, a little too quickly. "Never seen her," she said with a shaking voice.

Before we could respond, a loud bang and what sounded

like a muffled cry came from somewhere deeper inside the house. It was followed by another, louder this time, like someone —or something—was trying to get our attention. Perhaps upstairs.

Jane was here.

"Is everything all right in there?" I asked, leaning forward just slightly, trying to peer past the woman into the dimly lit hallway beyond.

"Oh, yes," she said. "It's nothing. Just the TV on."

"What happened to your face?" I asked.

"I tumbled. I'm a bit clumsy."

I edged closer. "We'd like to ask you a few questions. Can we come inside?"

Her grip on the child tightened, and she took a small step back, her body language shifting from mildly welcoming to outright defensive. "No," she said, shaking her head again. "I'm sorry. It's not a good time."

Before we could press further, the sound of heavy footsteps echoed down the hallway, and then he appeared. Ben Milton. He was tall, broad-shouldered, with the kind of presence that demanded attention, a snake tattoo on his forearm.

His face was calm, but his eyes flickered with something I couldn't quite place.

I glanced down at his hands. There, on the side of his right hand, was a smear of red. It looked like dried blood, a small, faint splatter, but unmistakable.

"Can I help you?" he asked, his voice smooth and controlled.

The woman said to him, "They're asking about a crime that happened in the neighborhood. To a woman."

Hirsch held up the photo of Jane once again.

"Never seen her."

Now I knew he was lying. And I worried the loud thump

was from Jane. I wished I had authority to enter. But alas, none of us were law enforcement. "We have reason to believe you do know her," I said, nodding toward the photo of Jane that Hirsch was still holding up. "She was Jacob's girlfriend, the mother of his child."

Another bang sounded from within the house. This time, it was louder, clearer. My instincts flared. Someone was inside. Someone who wanted to be heard. *Jane.*

"Is someone else inside?" I asked.

"No," the man said, almost too quickly. "It's the TV."

He was lying. I could feel it in my gut. I shot Hirsch and Selena a look, and Hirsch gave a slight nod. We were thinking the same thing.

Before we could press further, the sound of an engine approached from behind us.

Relief flooded me when I turned and saw Cromwell pulling up in his unmarked car, another officer in the passenger seat. They parked a little way down the street and started walking up the path toward us, their presence a welcome backup.

"That's the detective working the case," Hirsch said, taking a step toward the threshold. "He'll want to ask you a few questions."

With a nod, Selena hurried toward Detective Cromwell and the uniformed officer to explain what had happened so far. Selena and Cromwell spoke as they and the other officer hurried up the path to the house. Hirsch and I stepped aside to give Cromwell the floor.

Cromwell said, "Good afternoon, sir. Ma'am. I'm Detective Cromwell, and this is Officer Adler of the Alameda County Sheriff's Office. We have a few questions for you."

"We were just telling these private investigators that we don't know anything about the crime that happened. And we don't know the woman."

"Where were you the evening of August 23?" Cromwell asked.

Both looked like an animal caught in a trap.

"Were you home?" Cromwell asked.

"Yeah, probably. We don't go too many places with the baby."

"I see you have security cameras. Do you have footage from August 23?"

Ben said, "We don't usually keep the footage for more than a week."

Hirsch and I exchanged glances. When we had interviewed him before, he'd told us the security cameras weren't working.

Everything in my soul told me the Miltons were our suspects.

A flicker of something passed over the woman's face. Fear, maybe. Or guilt. It was hard to tell, but it was there, buried beneath her carefully controlled expression.

Just then, another sound came from inside the house. Not a bang this time, but a faint, muffled voice. It was impossible to make out what was being said, but it was enough to catch everyone's attention.

Ben's eyes darted toward the hallway, at the staircase. His jaw clenched, and for a brief moment, his calm exterior cracked.

Cromwell said, "Who else is in the home?"

"No one. It's just the TV."

Another bang echoed from inside the house, louder this time, unmistakable. My heart lurched, and a cold chill ran down my spine. This was no longer just a hunch or a gut feeling—something was happening inside, and I could feel we were running out of time.

Cromwell's entire demeanor changed in an instant. His hand instinctively moved to rest on the grip of his firearm, his body tense, his eyes locked on the man standing in the doorway.

"I don't think so," Cromwell said, his voice now hard as steel. "Sir, I'm going to ask you one more time. Who else is in the home?"

The tension in the air was electric, crackling with the kind of intensity that told me this was about to go south—fast. The man's posture shifted, his eyes darting toward the hallway as if contemplating his next move.

"Like I said," he repeated, his voice shakier now, "it's just the TV."

Another bang. It was followed by the voice. A woman's voice? It was faint, but unmistakable, someone was trying to make themselves heard. The sound sent adrenaline shooting through my veins. There was no more guessing. No more waiting.

Cromwell's voice dropped, dangerously calm. Weapon raised. "Sir, ma'am. You need to step aside."

51

MARTINA

Over his shoulder, Detective Cromwell gave sharp orders. "Adler, keep an eye on the Miltons and call for backup. Hirsch, Martina, stay with Adler and the Miltons. I'll search the house."

"Yes, sir," Hirsch said.

With weapon raised, Cromwell moved with purpose, heading upstairs while Adler led the Miltons into the living room, forcing them to sit down on the couch. The tension in the air was thick, palpable. The toddler, cradled in the woman's arms, began to fuss and cry, her tiny hands fidgeting, unaware of the danger but sensing the unease in the room.

"It's her snack time," the woman said, her voice trembling. "She's hungry."

"Ma'am, please don't move," Adler said, his tone firm.

The woman's hands shook as she tried to soothe the child, but it was clear the baby was scared. Who wouldn't be? Even a child could sense the tension—the raised voices, the guns, the unspoken threat hanging in the air.

Footsteps echoed from upstairs, and a moment later, Cromwell yelled out, "Martina, come up here."

Hirsch glanced at me. "Go."

I wasted no time, jogging toward the staircase and running up. As I reached the top, I saw Cromwell standing just inside an open door. The light flickered on, casting a glow over the hallway. I could hear Cromwell's voice.

I stepped inside a small bedroom, and the sight that greeted me made my stomach tighten. Tied to the bed with electrical cords, was Jane. Her wrists and ankles were bound tightly, and duct tape covered her mouth. Her eyes were wide with fear, though they softened slightly when she saw me.

"Are you okay?" I asked, my voice soft as I approached the bed.

She nodded, her movements slow, as though every inch of her body ached.

Cromwell stepped forward, taking control of the situation. "We need to document this. Let's take some photos before we untie her," he said, his voice calm but urgent.

I pulled out my phone, working as quickly as I could. The small click of the camera felt oddly out of place in the otherwise silent room. My hands were steady as I took the photos, capturing every angle—her tied wrists, the cords, the blood that had dried at the corner of her mouth, the bruises on her forehead. It was clear she'd been through an ordeal. "I got them."

Cromwell worked with his knife to cut through the electrical cords binding her as my heart pounded in my chest.

Jane sat up slowly, rubbing her wrists where the cords had dug deep into her skin. Angry red marks lined her arms, and bruises mottled her once pale skin. Her forehead was swollen, and the dried blood near her mouth stood out starkly against her skin.

I moved closer and gently removed the duct tape from her mouth, careful not to hurt her further. She winced but didn't cry out. As the tape came off, I crouched down to meet her eye level.

"What happened, Jane?" I asked, my voice low.

Her lips trembled as she tried to form words. She took a shaky breath, her body still trembling from the trauma. "I thought I could get her back," she said, her voice hoarse and her eyes filled with tears. "I thought I could make them see that she's mine."

I wasn't following. "What do you mean?"

"It's Hanna. I'm Hanna. I remember everything."

Cromwell and I looked at one another, both of us obviously surprised.

"Hanna, listen to me," I said softly, reaching out to take her hand. "You're safe now. We're going to get you out of here. But we need to know everything. We need to understand what happened."

She said, "I didn't mean for any of this to happen," she said. "But I couldn't let them keep her from me."

Her words trailed off, and I could see she was on the verge of breaking down. Cromwell knelt beside her, his voice gentle. "You're not alone anymore, Hanna. We'll figure this out. But first, we need to get you to safety."

"I won't leave without her."

Her? Who? "What do you mean?"

"I remembered everything. They stole my daughter. That's why I came here the first time, to get her back. We fought. He chased me to the park. Overpowered me. He attacked me." She paused. "I came back to get her, Martina." Hanna's voice trembled, her eyes wide and desperate. "They have my daughter. I remembered everything—him and his wife. They stole my daughter, and they tried to kill me the last time I came for her."

I stood frozen for a moment, trying to process what she was saying. How could that be? Her daughter had died—at least, that was what we had all been led to believe. There had been no body, though. No closure. And Jacob... he had been elusive about the details, especially the burial site up in Oregon. Everything had always felt unfinished, like pieces of a puzzle that didn't quite fit.

"I thought your daughter had died," I said slowly, careful with my words. "And you buried her up in Oregon. Do you remember that?"

Hanna shook her head violently, her eyes filling with tears. "It wasn't Abigail they buried, Martina. I saw it all. I saw him. Ben. I'm telling you, they stole my child. And I finally found her. My Abigail. Jacob did. He gave her to Ben. I don't know why—I don't understand it—but they have her." Her voice cracked with emotion.

She was adamant, but it didn't make sense. It didn't fit with what I thought I knew. "And you're sure you're all right?" I asked, noticing the deep bruise on her forehead. "That's a nasty bruise."

"I've got a bad headache," she admitted, pressing her fingers gently to her temple. Then she looked straight into my eyes, her gaze intense. "But I'm not crazy, Martina. I'm not. They said they called Jacob to see what to do with me. They're acting like they care, like they want to help me. Ben swore up and down that Jacob loves me, and that's why he didn't call the police when I came here looking for her."

My stomach twisted at her words.

Detective Cromwell stepped closer, his expression unreadable. "So, you're saying that Ben and his wife stole your child and you came here to reclaim her? When you did that the first time, they attacked you. Now a second time, and they've tied you up."

Tears spilling down Jane's cheeks, she said, "Yes. It's true, I swear it. They think I can't prove it, but I've learned so much from you, Martina. About DNA—how it can find relatives. You told me about DNA tests—the DNA will prove she's really mine. Test her DNA, Martina. She's my daughter. I *know* she is."

Her voice cracked, raw with emotion, and she wiped at her tears with shaky hands. I wanted to believe her—I wanted to believe that she wasn't losing her grip on reality.

"We can check that," I said softly, hoping to offer her some comfort. But I could feel Cromwell's eyes on me, his skepticism obvious. And maybe he was right. How could any of this make sense? But I had to trust Hanna, at least for now. I had to believe her enough to investigate further. Hopefully Cromwell did too.

I thought back to the child being held by Laurel Milton—the little girl who had been crying moments ago. She did resemble Jane. The heart-shaped face, the same coloring, the dark hair and wide eyes that mirrored Jane's own. It was possible, wasn't it?

The distant sound of sirens broke through the silence, the backup arriving.

"I'll call an ambulance," Cromwell said, his tone shifting to something more practical, more focused. "Why don't you stay with Hanna?" He glanced down at her briefly. "I'll head downstairs and deal with the Miltons."

He had more than enough to arrest them, considering the state Hanna was in. But what about Jacob? He had to have a hand in all of this.

With that, he left the room, heading downstairs to confront the Miltons.

I turned back to Jane, who was sitting up now, her fingers gingerly tracing the bruises on her wrists. I crouched down beside her, gently taking her hand. "We're going to get you checked out." I said softly. "But Jane, I need to know... Why didn't you call us sooner? Why did you come here alone? We would have helped."

She stared at me, her eyes glistening with tears. "I didn't

think anyone would believe me," she said. "Jacob convinced everyone I was crazy after our daughter supposedly died. But she didn't. No one would have believed me if I said she was still alive. So, I had to do it myself. I had to find her."

My throat tightened as I listened to her, the weight of her words sinking in. "I believe you, Hanna," I said, squeezing her hand gently. "We're going to figure this out."

As the sirens grew louder, I couldn't shake the feeling that this was far from over.

52

MARTINA

HANNA and I descended the stairs together. She seemed steady on her feet, stronger than I expected after everything she'd been through. She probably didn't need to go to the hospital, but it was a precaution. If she had a concussion or if adrenaline was masking any physical pain, we couldn't take any chances.

In the living room, Ben and his wife sat handcuffed on the couch, their faces filled with defiance. Hirsch and Selena were standing nearby. Hirsch held the toddler in his arms while Selena handed her crackers. Hirsch had always had a way with babies—calm, gentle, as if they sensed they could trust him.

Selena looked at Hanna and her face fell. She set the crackers down and rushed over to her. They embraced before Selena stepped back and said, "Are you all right?"

Hanna nodded.

Selena glanced over at me.

I said, "Why don't you and Hanna go into the dining room that's right over there."

The dining room was across from the living room where the Miltons were. With a serious expression, Selena said, "Will do."

Laurel Milton's voice broke through the room, strained and

shaky. "What's going to happen to Kelly?" She was staring at her daughter—or Hanna's daughter—with tears welling in her eyes.

As Selena escorted Hanna to the dining room, Hanna screamed, "She's not Kelly!"

Selena took the cue to hurry Hanna along. We didn't need her making the situation worse.

Cromwell approached the Miltons. "We have a few questions about the child."

"She's not Hanna's," Ben snapped, his voice full of righteous indignation. "We have a birth certificate, records from the hospital. Everything. She's crazy—she needs help." He glanced at his wife for support, but her silence hung in the air like a heavy cloud.

I stepped closer, folding my arms. "Where are these records?"

Laurel Milton looked at me, her eyes flicking nervously toward the staircase. "Upstairs. In our file cabinet. Second drawer."

Ben was quick to jump in again, louder this time, almost as if he needed to convince himself as much as us. "She's delusional! She thinks it's her daughter, but it's not! We have proof!"

If they'd stolen Hanna's daughter, how would they have records?

Cromwell said, "Everyone, let's just calm down." The room silenced. "I'll head upstairs and get the papers." A loud knock sounded on the open door. Cromwell said, "That's likely backup. I'll brief them and then head upstairs. Everyone just stay put."

Nods of agreement from all.

Officer Adler stood at attention, keeping an eye out. My focus turned to the toddler in Hirsch's arms. The child resembled Hanna—the heart-shaped face, the dark eyes. Could it be a coincidence?

Nobody spoke.

A few minutes later, Cromwell, along with three officers, came back down the stairs, holding a paper file folder.

He walked right up to me, his expression grim as he handed me the documents. I glanced through them quickly.

A birth certificate for a baby girl, born two years and five months earlier. If she were alive, Hanna's child would be two years and eight months old. Bills from the hospital for Mrs. Milton's stay when she supposedly gave birth. It all looked legitimate.

Cromwell leaned in close, his voice low. "What do you think, Martina?"

"It's a little convenient, don't you think?" I said back, glancing over at the Miltons. They sat rigidly on the couch, their faces tight with anticipation.

Cromwell gave me a look, pulling me farther aside. "Well, if they knew she was going to claim it's her kid, maybe they had it ready. It looks good for them, bad for her."

I couldn't dispute the evidence, not yet anyhow. "I hear what you're saying, but then why not call the police when she got here? Instead of alerting the authorities, they beat her up and tied her to a bed. That's not the act of innocent people."

"No, it's not. The only way we're going to prove this one way or another is DNA. We need to get that kid's DNA."

"I agree," I said. "How do we handle Hanna?" I asked quietly, not wanting anyone to hear. "What if this is some kind of psychosis? She's convinced that child is hers, and until we prove it one way or another, she's not going to stop. She may come after them again."

Cromwell sighed, rubbing his forehead. "That's exactly

what I'm worried about. If she's not in her right mind, this could get dangerous. But if that is her daughter..."

He trailed off, and I knew what he was thinking. If Hanna was right, we had two suspects who'd stolen a child and tried to pass her off as their own. The stakes couldn't be higher.

"We need that DNA," I said firmly. "Can you get it?"

"If the parents consent, yes. As of right now, they're the legal guardians, and they've got the paperwork. We can ask them to provide a sample. If it's really their child, they shouldn't have a problem with that."

He headed toward the Miltons, while I went to check on Hanna and Selena. The two were huddled in the dining room. "How's it going in there?" Selena asked.

"Cromwell is doing some follow-up. His team will collect evidence," I said. "The ambulance should be here soon."

"I don't need the hospital, Martina," Hanna said, her voice strained. "I need my daughter."

"I understand what you're saying. I do. But until we can prove beyond a shadow of a doubt that she's yours, you can't have her. You're going to have to wait a little bit longer."

"You'll test her DNA?"

"We'll get it."

Cromwell appeared and waved me over. I headed toward him. "They won't consent to the DNA test." he said. "We're going to need a warrant."

"How fast can you get one?"

"I know a judge who might sign off on it pretty fast. It's pretty odd they won't agree. Between you and me, I was highly doubtful the kid was Hanna's but now... I'll make a call. Keep an eye on Hanna. We need to make sure she's safe and doesn't go after anyone."

"You got it."

Back in the dining room, I explained to Selena and Hanna the situation.

"What if the judge says no?" Hanna asked, and I could see the panic rising in her eyes.

"We're going to try our best to get that warrant," I said, trying to keep her calm. "But right now, we have to be patient."

Selena said, "We're going to figure this out. Don't worry."

Hanna stared at Selena and then looked at me, her eyes pleading for some kind of certainty, but I couldn't give it to her. Not until the truth was revealed. And now all we could do was wait.

53

JANE/HANNA

I PACED the hallway of Drakos Monroe Security & Investigations, my steps quick and restless. It had been two whole days since I last saw my daughter—two days of agonizing silence, of waiting, of hoping that the truth would finally set things right. After all I had done to find her.

Thankfully the judge had granted the warrant to collect DNA from Abigail. At least the system had listened to me. But now, she was with Child Protective Services, with strangers. The thought of her in a room with unfamiliar faces, without me to protect her, made my heart ache in a way I couldn't even describe.

I stopped for a moment, pressing my hand to my chest, trying to steady my breathing. I could feel it, though. I could feel that I was close, that the truth was almost within my grasp. Abigail was going to come back to me—I knew it in my bones. I just had to wait a little longer. *Patience.* I just needed a little patience.

Martina had insisted that I stay at the office with her, saying it was for my own safety, and that it was better for me to be around people. But I also knew, deep down, that she didn't trust me to stay home. Not after everything. She was afraid I'd run off again, go looking for answers on my own. But that was fine. I felt safe here. At least at Drakos Monroe, I wasn't alone. Here, I could focus on waiting for the DNA results without the crushing silence of an empty house.

Ben and his wife were in jail for holding me against my will, but that didn't matter right now. All that mattered was the test—the DNA that would prove Abigail was mine.

Selena approached, her expression soft, a cup of tea in her hands. "Here," she said gently, offering it to me. "This should help calm your nerves."

"Thank you." I accepted the cup, the warmth of it soothing my nerves. "You've been so nice through all of this. I don't know how I would've managed without you and Martina."

Selena smiled, though it didn't quite reach her eyes. "We should hear soon."

I stopped pacing, the steam from the tea swirling around my face as I blew on it absently. My mind was racing too fast for any real comfort to settle in.

Selena stepped closer, her voice low, compassionate. "Do you want to talk? I can't imagine what you're going through right now."

I hesitated, my thoughts tangling together. "I'm more than a little anxious, if I'm honest. I know she's mine, Selena. But what am I going to do once they prove it?" My voice wavered. "I don't have a job or any real skills. And they—they stole her. They tried to tell me she had died, but it wasn't her. I don't know why I'm only remembering this now..."

"What do you mean?" Selena asked, her brow furrowed in confusion. "It wasn't her?"

I stared down into my cup, the words spilling out before I could even make sense of them. "That's it, Selena. It was a different child. It wasn't my child who died. She was different—smaller." I knew he'd lied. I'd always known.

Selena's confusion deepened. "I don't think I follow…"

I looked up, feeling the pieces click into place, the horrible truth rising from the fog of my memories. "Jacob switched the babies. The baby who died wasn't Abigail. He wouldn't let me go to the crib. He didn't want me to see her, and we fought about it. But I saw her—just for a moment. She was too small. Too fragile. She wasn't Abigail. That's how I know she's mine. I don't know why I didn't realize it before. I had assumed he'd drugged her to keep her quiet. But it wasn't her."

Selena's eyes widened in shock. "So, you think… Jacob swapped the babies? You think the baby who died was someone else's? Why would he do that?"

Why would he give away our child? "I don't know."

The room felt like it was spinning, the ground tilting beneath my feet as the enormity of what Jacob had done hit me all over again. He had made me believe my child was gone, made me question my sanity. I wasn't crazy—I had never been crazy. But Jacob had twisted everything, warped reality, until I couldn't tell what was real anymore.

Just then, I saw Martina rushing toward me, her expression tight, her steps hurried.

"We have the results," Martina said, her voice breathless, her eyes locked on mine.

My heart pounded in my chest loudly, as if it would burst. This was it. This was the moment that would determine everything—whether I had been right all along or whether I was clinging to a fantasy, to a truth that wasn't mine.

54

MARTINA

Hɪʀsᴄʜ ᴀɴᴅ I stood outside the conference room at the Alameda County Sheriff's Station, the tension thick as we waited for Detective Cromwell. He'd been inside, questioning the Miltons separately, trying to break them down. He believed Laurel Milton would be the one to crack—she was the weaker link, and her emotions had already started to show through in her earlier questioning.

The door opened, and Cromwell stepped out, looking serious but hopeful. "I think she's about to talk. Maybe if you lay it all out—our theory of what happened, mother to mother, I think you can get through to her."

I nodded, exchanging a brief glance with Hirsch before stepping into the conference room. Laurel Milton sat at the table, her hands nervously clasped in front of her. Her eyes were red, swollen from crying, but she was holding herself together.

I approached slowly, trying to keep my tone calm and soft. "Hello, Laurel," I said gently, sitting across from her.

She looked up at me briefly before lowering her gaze again. "Hello."

"Do you want to tell me what happened? From the beginning?" I asked, giving her the chance to come clean on her own.

Her lips trembled, and she shook her head. "I don't know what you're talking about."

"No?" I leaned back slightly, giving her space but keeping my voice measured. "Well then, let me tell you what I think happened. Is that okay?"

She nodded, her eyes flicking up to meet mine, just for a second, before darting back down to her hands.

I took a deep breath. I needed to get through to her, to tap into the grief and guilt I knew she was feeling. "I think you had a beautiful baby girl," I began softly. "But I think she tragically passed away."

Her eyes locked with mine.

"I have a daughter and honestly, I can't imagine what that would be like. The pain. The hole in my heart it would leave."

She shut her eyes as tears streamed down her cheeks.

"And I think Jacob gave you another child—Hanna's child—to raise in place of her."

Laurel Milton's eyes grew wide, the color draining from her face. Her lips parted as if she wanted to say something, but the words didn't come.

I pressed on, my voice gentle but firm. "Did you know that Hanna didn't want to give her up? That Jacob told her their baby had died? Did you know he lied to her—that you did that to her?"

Laurel Milton bowed her head. Her body shook. Moments later, she raised her head slowly, her voice breaking. "I didn't know at first. I didn't know, I swear it! I swear," she cried, her tears flowing freely now.

I leaned in a little, my tone still soft but filled with urgency. "Tell me what you didn't know, Laurel."

Her shoulders shook as she tried to collect herself, her words coming out in sobs. "Ben told me—he told me that the baby's mother had died. That the baby was an orphan. He said... he said it was God's will, that I needed to care for her, that she needed me." Her voice trembled. "But he lied. I didn't know the truth."

"What didn't you know?" I asked, pushing gently, giving her the space to reveal it all.

She took a deep, shaky breath, her eyes filled with regret. "I didn't know Hanna was still alive. I didn't know they'd stolen her child. Not until Hanna showed up at my door, screaming for me to give her daughter back. I thought she was crazy. I didn't know who she was. I didn't understand what she was saying. I told her she was wrong. That the baby was mine."

Her voice dropped to a whisper, and the guilt was written all over her face. "She attacked me and got inside. She grabbed a knife from the kitchen. I... I tried to get her to leave. But she wouldn't stop. She kept fighting, screaming that I had her daughter. Ben came in and ran her out, chased her all the way to the lakes, over a mile. That's when he—" She paused, her voice cracking. "He came back and told me she was taken care of."

I stilled, the hairs on the back of my neck standing up. "He told you that?"

"Yes," she said quietly, her voice barely audible. "He said he'd held her until the police came and took her away. He told me he learned who she was, but not to worry—that she wouldn't come back. But... I knew there was more to it."

I clenched my jaw, trying to maintain my composure. "What else did he tell you?"

Laurel wiped her tears with a trembling hand. "That Jacob had given him the baby. That I knew. But he said Hanna wasn't dead, like he had originally told me. He said the truth was that Hanna was an unfit mother, and that she'd been locked up in a mental hospital and couldn't raise a child. He said we were doing the right thing, taking care of the baby." She took a moment to wipe the tears from her cheeks. "But... but then... then he told me the full truth after I pressed him. It wasn't like Ben to lie to me. He then told me he had never met Hanna and didn't know that the woman who was attacking me was her. But I guess when they were at the lakes, he found out who she was and she swore she'd never been in a mental hospital. Before he got back to the house, he called Jacob. Jacob said Hanna was lying and must have escaped from the hospital. Ben wanted to get help for her, but Jacob convinced him we were better off if she were dead... I'm so sorry. I should have insisted he call for help. But... I couldn't lose her."

I felt my heart sink as I listened to her. I knew there had been more to this, but hearing it laid out so clearly made my stomach churn. Ben had been part of it all along, and Jacob— Jacob had orchestrated it. "So, Jacob just gave you the baby?"

Laurel broke down completely then, sobbing uncontrollably. When a bit more calm, she said, "No. Ben has been giving Jacob money every month. Every single month. I didn't understand why... but then I did. It was payment for the baby. I'm so sorry. I'm so, so sorry."

I glanced at the recording equipment in the corner of the room. It was all on tape. We had her confession.

"Laurel," I said quietly, "will you sign a statement detailing what you've just told me?"

Through her tears, she said, "Yes. I'll sign. I'll do whatever you need. I'm so sorry."

I exhaled, the tension in my body finally releasing. It wasn't over, but this was a breakthrough. A confession. Now, we could move forward.

As I stood up to leave, Laurel Milton looked up at me with

tear-filled eyes. "Please... tell Hanna I'm sorry. I didn't know. I swear I didn't."

I gave her a sympathetic look. "You take care."

Laurel Milton was a broken woman. First her child passed, and now the knowledge of stripping another woman of her child had broken her further. With a look to Hirsch, we stepped out of the room, ready to finish what we had started.

MARTINA

IT HAD TAKEN over a week to reunite Hanna with her daughter. A week of navigating legal red tape, setting her up in an apartment, enrolling her in a job training program, and finding daycare and counseling for little Abigail. It wasn't easy, but Hanna had fought for her and her daughter's life every step of the way—she had fought from the very beginning. Against all odds, she found her daughter, endured unimaginable pain, and survived an ordeal that would have broken most people. It was a miracle the two had been reunited.

Upon questioning, Hanna explained that she had learned Abigail was in the Bay Area after overhearing Jacob on his cell phone. This had happened at a time when she believed the baby was gone. When she confronted him, it led to a violent fight that left Hanna bleeding and broken. But she hadn't given up. Instead, she took action. By snooping through Jacob's phone, she not only discovered information about the Miltons but also found the courage she needed to escape.

For the next year and a half, she hid from Jacob while searching for Abigail. Avoiding him meant constantly moving between shelters, switching every few months—but always heading south, inching closer to her baby girl. Hanna admitted there were times she questioned her sanity, but everything changed when she finally found Abigail. She spotted her being pushed in a stroller by Laurel Milton, right in the neighborhood. Hanna said it took only one look at her daughter's face, at the birthmark she remembered so vividly, to know without a doubt that she had found Abigail.

Because of Hanna's strength—and the pivotal confession from Laurel Milton, combined with Hanna's recovered memories—Jacob was finally behind bars. He was facing charges for the illegal sale of a child, a crime that left everyone who heard the details stunned and sickened. Ben, too, was in prison, awaiting trial for kidnapping not only Abigail and Hanna, but also for the attempted murder of Hanna. His actions had nearly cost her life, all in the name of his own twisted idea of love.

Laurel Milton, on the other hand, would likely only receive probation. She really hadn't known the full extent of her husband's actions. It was clear from the moment she broke down in that interrogation room. Her heart had been shattered by grief, and Ben—motivated by a desperate attempt to shield her from that pain—had made a terrible, irreversible decision. After we told him about her confession and laid out the mountain of evidence against them, Ben had finally cracked. He admitted everything.

He confessed that Abigail was never their daughter, that Jacob had handed her over in exchange for money. Ben admitted he had done it because he couldn't stand watching his wife suffer any longer. She had been drowning in her grief after losing their daughter, and nothing seemed to pull her out of that darkness. In his mind, buying someone else's child was the only way to make her happy. His story was corroborated when the remains of his child, Kelly Ann, was recovered in a grave up north. A grave Jacob had told Hanna was Abigail's.

It was tragic and deeply twisted. In some warped, demented way, Ben thought he was acting out of love—believing that by taking Abigail and faking a new life, he could somehow make everything right. But love, when tangled up in grief, could make people do unspeakable things. In the end, he was willing to kill an innocent mother to protect his wife from the reality of their loss. It wasn't something anyone could just run from. There were no quick fixes for that kind of pain.

Grief, as I've come to understand, isn't something you can patch up with a Band-Aid. You can't go around it, you can't avoid it. The only way out is through it. And Ben, in his desperate attempt to spare his wife that journey, had destroyed lives.

Hanna, too, had walked through grief—grief for a child she thought was dead, grief for the life that had been stolen from her. But she survived it. And now, standing on the other side of that darkness, she was determined to build a new life for herself and Abigail.

Hanna had confided in me one night, telling me about her past and the family she had left behind in Oregon. According to Hanna, her father and brothers had been abusive, and she'd never been allowed to go to school or make any decisions of her own. She had no intention of going back. Hanna claimed that chapter of her life was over because she didn't want Abigail to grow up in that kind of environment. An environment where men dictated the lives of women—where women could be beaten and shunned. Where women didn't have a say in their future.

Hanna decided to stay in the Bay Area and start fresh in California. She told me she wanted to show her daughter how to be strong, how to be independent, and how to make her own decisions—something Hanna herself hadn't had the chance to do until she'd nearly been killed.

As I reflected on everything we had been through together, Selena walked over, her expression warm but tired. "She's settled," she said softly.

A sense of relief washed over me. "You did a great job with her, Selena."

Selena smiled. "It wasn't just me. Hanna... she's stronger than most people. Not to mention how the whole team worked together to help her put her life back together. Vincent and Hirsch. What a team. Do you think you've convinced Hirsch to come work at the firm?"

"I think so." After Jacob's arrest, Hirsch and I had discussed him working with us again. He said he was definitely up for the next challenging case whenever it may arise. I took that as a yes. And I couldn't be happier about it.

Selena said, "You know, I think Hanna's going to be fine. Better than fine. I really believe that."

I glanced out the window. The sun was setting and casting a soft glow. It was a symbol, maybe, of a new beginning. Not just for Hanna and Abigail. I couldn't help but think of the future of Drakos Monroe. With a team like Selena, Vincent, *and* Hirsch, we'd be unstoppable.

"I think so too," I agreed, my thoughts lingering on the incredible resilience Hanna had shown. It wasn't going to be easy, but Hanna had survived the worst—and now, she had a chance to live the life she was meant to, with her daughter.

With a thoughtful look in her eyes, Selena said, "It's a reminder, isn't it? How much people can endure. How much they can overcome."

I smiled softly, thinking of not only everything Hanna had gone through, but Selena too. "It is," I said. "And it's a reminder that, no matter how dark things get, there's always a way back to the light."

With Abigail in her arms and a new life ahead of her,

Hanna had found her way out of the darkness. She had lost everything—and yet, she had gotten it all back. Now, she could move forward, not as the broken woman Jacob had tried to make her believe she was, but as someone who had faced the unimaginable and come out the other side, stronger than ever.

As the day faded into night, I allowed myself a moment of quiet satisfaction. It wasn't a perfect ending—there was no such thing—but it was a new beginning... and that could be just as great.

THANK YOU!

Thank you for reading *Her Fearless Pursuit*. I hope you enjoyed reading it as much as I loved writing it. If you did, I would greatly appreciate if you could post a short review.

Reviews are crucial for any author and can make a huge difference in visibility of current and future works. Reviews allow us to continue doing what we love, *writing stories*. Not to mention, I would be forever grateful!

Thank you!

ALSO BY H.K. CHRISTIE

The Martina Monroe Series —a nail-biting crime thriller series starring PI Martina Monroe and her unofficial partner Detective August Hirsch of the Cold Case Squad. If you like high-stakes games, jaw-dropping twists, and suspense that will keep you on the edge of your seat, then you'll love the Martina Monroe crime thriller series.

The Val Costa Series —a gripping crime thriller with heart-pounding suspense. If you love Martina, you'll love Val.

The Neighbor Two Doors Down —a dark and witty psychological thriller. If you like unpredictable twists, page-turning suspense, and unreliable narrators, then you'll love *The Neighbor Two Doors Down*.

The Selena Bailey Series (1 - 5) —a suspenseful series featuring a young Selena Bailey and her turbulent path to becoming a top-notch private investigator as led by her mentor, Martina Monroe.

A Permanent Mark A heartless killer. Weeks without answers. Can she move on when a murderer walks free? If you like riveting suspense and gripping mysteries, then you'll love *A Permanent Mark* - starring a grown up Selena Bailey.

For H.K. Christie's full catalog go to: **www.authorhkchristie.com**

At **www.authorhkchristie.com** you can also sign up for the H.K. Christie reader club where you'll be the first to hear about upcoming novels, new releases, giveaways, promotions, and a **free e-copy of the prequel to the Martina Monroe Thriller Series, *Crashing Down*!**

ABOUT THE AUTHOR

H. K. Christie watched horror films far too early in life. Inspired by the likes of Stephen King, Jodi Picoult, true crime podcasts, and a vivid imagination she now writes suspenseful thrillers.

She found her passion for writing when she embarked on a one-woman habit breaking experiment. Although she didn't break her habit she did discover a love of writing and has been at it ever since.

When not working on her latest novel, H.K. Christie can be found eating & drinking with friends, walking around the lakes, or playing with her favorite furry pal.

She is a native and current resident of the San Francisco Bay Area.

To learn more about H.K. Christie and her books, or simply to say, "hello", go to **www.authorhkchristie.com**.

At **www.authorhkchristie.com** you can also sign up for the H.K. Christie reader club where you'll be the first to hear about upcoming novels, new releases, giveaways, promotions, and a free e-copy of the prequel to the Martina Monroe Thriller Series, *Crashing Down*!

ACKNOWLEDGMENTS

To Alix Sloan, Dwayne Keller, Emily Haynes, Jolie Castilla, Keisha Frazier, and Angela Griffith. Not only did you win the contest to have a character named after you, or to pick a name, in this book, but you're also some of my favorite people! Thank you!

Many thanks to my Advanced Reader Team. These wonderful readers are invaluable in taking the first look at my stories and helping find typos and spreading awareness of my stories through their reviews and kind words.

To my editor, Paula Lester, a huge thanks for your careful edit and helpful comments and proofreader Ryan Mahan for catching those last typos. To my cover designer, Odile, thank you for your guidance and talent.

To my best writing buddy (aka the boss), Charlie, thank you for the looks of encouragement and reminders to take breaks. If it weren't for you, I'd be in my office all day working as opposed to catering to all of your needs and wants such as snuggles, scratches, treats, and long, meandering walks. To the mister, thank you, as always, for being by my side and encouraging me.

Last but not least, I'd like to extend a huge thank you to all of my readers. It's because of you I'm able to live the dream of being a full-time author.